WHAT COMES NEXT

WHAT COMES NEXT

A Novel

Caitlin Forbes

This is a work of fiction. Names, characters, organizations, places, events, and incidents are either products of the author's imagination or are used fictitiously. Otherwise, any resemblance to actual persons, living or dead, is purely coincidental.

Published by Lake Union Publishing, Seattle
www.apub.com

Amazon, the Amazon logo, and Lake Union Publishing are trademarks of Amazon.com, Inc., or its affiliates.

EU product safety contact:
Amazon Media EU S. à r.l.
38, avenue John F. Kennedy, L-1855 Luxembourg
amazonpublishing-gpsr@amazon.com

ISBN-13: 9781662528118 (paperback)
ISBN-13: 9781662528101 (digital)

Cover design by Kathleen Lynch/Black Kat Design
Cover image: © Iga Serba, © whiteisthecolor, © the_burtons, © Funkey Factory / Getty

Printed in the United States of America

For Erin and Brendan.
Always us three.

Chapter 1

When the doorbell rings, I'm standing in front of my bathroom sink, the picture of indecision: boxer briefs paired with a black silk tank top, made-up face, and completely untamed hair.

I'm supposed to meet my roommate, Holly, for drinks. But it was a last-minute invite—with people I don't know, planned days or even weeks earlier—and now I feel uncomfortable. As if I've become the kind of obligation that I never wanted to be. We've been best friends for nearly a decade, but these days, things are different, and I don't know that I want to feel the strain of it tonight. I'm more tempted by Netflix and cold pizza. My favorite pair of slippers.

I check the weather app on my phone and am almost relieved that it calls for rain.

I'm conceding defeat, turning off the curler, when the bell rings and I physically jump. Because who rings the doorbell in Somerville, Massachusetts, other than someone who wants to kill me? Or someone who wants to sell something, which is maybe not all that much better. But then I consider my upstairs neighbor, who has lost her keys more than once, and is so young, still new to the Boston area, and I feel guilty, so I pad down the stairs of our apartment and crack open the building door. And I swear, I get a whiff of cinnamon, a smell so familiar it knocks me back before I can remember why.

And he's standing there. On my doorstep. Tall. Even taller than I remember.

Nathan Browning.

We stare at each other from either side of the doorframe. And I will him to disappear. Or turn into someone else. Or at the very least, to come back when I'm wearing pants.

Nathan. Those first two years of college. Nights spent squeezed onto a twin bed in his dorm room, pretending we weren't uncomfortable just so we could fall asleep together. The summer I'd spent with his family at Lake Winnipesaukee. Campfires and smoky hair. His lips, pillow soft. Water. An excess of water—one oversize tube, our limbs tangled together. Salty tears.

"Alex?"

It's my name that gets my attention. My name in his mouth, as if it belongs there. As if we still mean something to each other.

I almost shut the door right then.

"What are you doing here?" I ask. I'm relieved my voice sounds calm. Disengaged, even. Because it doesn't matter that he is here. Because it doesn't matter what we once were.

"I need your help," he says.

I stare at him blankly, but he's not looking at me. He's looking over his shoulder. He's looking at the car parked behind him and, more accurately, at what is sitting in the front seat.

He turns back to me with those gray-blue eyes. The ones that were always focused, always so certain, but now hold the smallest hesitation. An expression that seems wrong in this face I still somehow know.

"I saw your video," he says. "And I—we need your help."

The video. The one that changed my life right up until it didn't.

I was a part-time dog trainer then, still trying to make that dream real. Holly and I made a video, and she stuck it up on YouTube, and then it went viral. It was a fluky kind of thing, like those things always are: the right content at the right time in front of the right people. The algorithm was alerted, and the amplification went from there. I was twenty-four and poor and bored—working a second job and involved in a fling to pass the time—and then suddenly, I was also something else. A dog whisperer, people typed. Cesar Millan but softer, with a woman's touch.

Silly. Casually sexist.

But something just the same.

After the video, it was Holly's idea to start the training business. DogKind, we called it. I dropped my second job as copywriter to train full-time, and she did everything else—the administration and the management. The promotions. We'd both majored in marketing in college, but Holly was better at it than me. Maybe because she believed in it: the concept of brands that build trust, and colors and fonts that tell a story. It took her only two weeks to launch DogKind's website and get us live on all the social platforms. We were still twenty-four and poor but suddenly not so bored. I remember the day the site launched—us sitting on the floor in our cramped living room, a five-dollar bottle of red between us. Stained teeth. It was summer in an attic apartment in the city, and we didn't have air-conditioning. Holly had chopped her hair off, and we were trying to convince ourselves it was edgy.

We were young in that way you actually notice. When you're afraid of what will happen when you blink.

Four years ago. The length of high school, or of college, but without the predetermined milestones. The signposts that tell you how and why everything is about to change.

Holly quit the business less than two years later, and I followed her lead not long after. Partly because I wasn't making enough money to cover rent, and partly because of what happened with Cliff, one of the dogs I tried to save. But mainly because I hated being called a "dog whisperer." I hated that people thought I could perform miracles, that they insisted on believing I was more than I was.

I work at Kensington Media now. It covers the rent, and it could one day become a real career. And I don't have regrets. Except, there are these moments—when I see a short haircut on a blonde, when Instagram flashes up a memory of a pup—and it's like my whole body freezes over. A little voice in my head, whispering, You can go back if you just stay still.

"How did you find me? I took down my website ages ago."

"An old testimonial from a woman named Lois, I think?" Nathan says. "Her address is publicly listed. So I called her. She pointed me in your direction."

Lois. She was my neighbor as a kid. She moved closer to the city after my mom left, but she always kept a close eye on me and Mere. A bespectacled not-quite grandmother—that careful mix of kind and overbearing. She's a lifelong dog rescuer and was DogKind's first client.

Lois never wanted me to quit.

I sneak a peek at him while he's checking the car, again. He's still handsome. Those eyes, and dark-brown hair with the slightest hint of red—the red was the part that I liked most, that almost made us match. Behind him, I can see a flash of auburn fur. Two half-bent glossy ears pointed forward. A white-tipped tail.

I swallow. "I don't train anymore," I say.

He lifts a shoulder. The gesture looks comfortable on him. Like he's used to half explaining himself, half caring if anyone understands. And I remember that part, too: the easy confidence. The kind I imagine he still takes for granted.

"She thought you might still help."

I resist the urge to roll my eyes. Lois is one of those people who likes to imagine me as bigger and braver than I am.

"Listen, I don't know what you saw in that video, but it's not—she's not me."

"She sure looked like you."

And right then, our eyes meet. And we get stuck there. Three breaths. Blue-gray eyes, like he still knows me. Like we still know each other. And something electric—something more than anger—passes between us. Right here, on my dirty Somerville stoop, wearing the bottom half of my pajamas, everything else recedes. For three breaths, it's just us.

A car drives by with the windows open, the radio blaring through the street. I take a step back.

"I'll give you a referral," I say. "I know a lot better trainers than me out there."

"Alex." I hate the way he says my name. "I know that you and I . . . that our history makes this tough . . ." His voice trails off as my eyes snap to him. He takes in my expression, then lifts his chin. That confidence. Whatever hesitation I saw earlier is long gone.

"I'm sorry," he says firmly. "You know that I am sorry."

I shake my head. I don't want an apology. I'm embarrassed—mortified, really—that I still care. That *he knows* that I still care. That he's still talking, and I'm falling backward into sand and blue water and the particular ache of a wound that is old but was also first.

I pull my shoulders back. I make my voice flat. "This isn't about us. I'm not a trainer anymore. I haven't worked with a dog in almost two years."

"Her name is Remy," he says. "She only has three months."

I pause, already half turned away, my hand pressed against the battered wooden doorframe. The day we moved in, I hit my shoulder against it and ended up with a splinter. I'd been laughing about something with Holly, and then sharp wood pressed deep under my skin.

"Remy bit someone," he says. I can feel his eyes studying my half-turned face. "She's a rescue, and she has a history of bites. I had to go to court, and they mandated that she see a vet behaviorist and trainer. I did the first part, and they have her on anxiety meds, which will maybe help. But I need to do the training. And if we can't document improvement . . ."

His voice trails off, but I don't need him to finish. I already know how this goes. I've seen it before.

Ninety days. He has ninety days to prove that she can be trusted. Or euthanasia. That's what the court told him.

Of course, they have it all wrong. It's not about us trusting her. It's whether she'll choose to trust us again after whatever made her stop.

I glance back over his shoulder. Those ears, cocked forward above the dashboard, they break my heart. She's waiting for him. The Nathan I remember was too busy for dogs. Too focused on everything he planned to achieve. But here he is, with a rescue who has decided he's worth waiting for.

I bite my lower lip. "Your vet must have given you referrals," I say.

"They were booked out for a month. And the other ones I called wouldn't take her. They say she's hopeless." His jaw clenches. "But, Alex . . . I've seen what you can do."

"You saw an edited video. If they're telling you she's a lost cause—"

"We used to say that lost causes were an excuse."

Our first real conversation. The one that once it started, it felt like it would never stop.

My breath stutters on the memory.

It seems possible, in this moment, that he remembers just as much as I do.

"I know I shouldn't be here, okay," he says. "I know that. But Remy is a wonderful dog. And no one else will help her. Whatever you think of me, and honestly, whatever you think of you . . . none of that matters. You need to try. You can do this."

It's all classic Nathan: unapologetic and determined. Nathan's not used to people saying no, especially when it comes to "doing the right thing." He can be an ass—too cocky, with expectations that are too high—but he's a genuinely good guy. And he's never had much patience for people who don't step up.

It was one of the first things I loved about him.

It was also one of the things that I hated.

"Nathan—"

"Please," he cuts in. His voice hitches, and I see it now: the dark circles under his eyes, the tightness of his expression. I used to know him once. There was a time when he let me further in than anyone, and I can tell that he is scared. He's scared for her.

Remorse crowds my stomach because, back then, I could have helped him. But I am not the girl he remembers, and I'm not whoever he thinks he saw online. "I can't," I say. "I'm sorry. I really am."

He looks like he's about to argue. I expect him to argue. But then, it's as if he deflates in front of me. His whole chest sinks inward. It's not a look I've ever seen on him. Or one that I like.

"Yeah, no, I get it," he says.

"I'm not what she needs," I mumble.

"Sure, okay. I'm sorry for showing up like this." It's awkward now. His voice is clipped, and he's running his hands through his hair like he does in those rare moments when he's uncomfortable. I don't have to check to know the back pieces will stick up.

"Listen, leave your number," I say. "I know a lot of trainers. I'll find her someone, okay?"

He nods. "Yeah, okay, sure. Thank you." I can tell he wants to leave. I can tell I am a disappointment. And maybe it's my imagination, but I get the feeling that it hurts him. Being here. Seeing me.

I think it hurts him, too.

I left my phone upstairs, so he pulls a pen from his suit pocket and a piece of paper from his bag and jots down his number. The promised rain starts as he turns to go, water brushing against my cheeks, and I duck inside the entryway, the paper clenched tightly in my fist. As I watch him jog back to his car, I wonder about the suit. I wonder what he does for work, what kind of man he turned into. I find myself hoping that he got the life he'd planned.

He drives away, and I unstick my feet. I drift back upstairs, past the bright-yellow welcome doormat Holly bought, and collapse on our couch. My mind is strangely quiet, and I let my eyes wander our small place. Everything about it is bright and fun and filled with Holly's energy: colorful, mismatched place mats; a half a dozen of those cheesy quote signs scattered across the walls; and an array of weird glass owl figurines that Holly collects. They catch the light, making everything twinkle.

I pull out my phone, scrolling past a missed call from my sister to a text message from Lois.

A lovely sounding boy called about his dog. He seemed a bit desperate but was so polite. Be nice!!

I shake my head. Lois is not the first person to be easily charmed by Nathan.

I am going to connect him to a good trainer. No more referrals, please!

I see the response bubbles pop up from her immediately. And then disappear. She starts again, then deletes whatever she wrote. The gentle thud of rain starts to pound outside the window.

My phone buzzes.

I just want you to be happy, honey.

I stare at the screen lit up against my hand. I ignore the sudden tightness of my jaw. I read the words again.

I just want you to be happy.

It's such a seemingly innocuous statement. A level of genericness that begs an equally generic response. And I want to type back something funny, something simple, but I'm blinking back water that has nothing to do with the rain.

I should be happy. My life is perfectly fine. And wanting more than fine feels like an obnoxious privilege. Too embarrassing to say out loud. Especially when there's stuff that I could do to improve my life. Books I could read. Skills I could learn. I know there's stuff I'm supposed to be doing. Just like I know there's a person I'm supposed to be becoming.

Except, when I think about that person, she's just as alien as she was when I graduated from college. And I'm not sure how to change that. I'm not sure how to explain that between work and all the daily stuff in my life *that is really not that hard*, that I don't know how to become. How the being takes up all the energy that should go toward the becoming.

I didn't think I would end up this way. I used to want to be different. I used to want to be more like the girl Nathan remembers. I look down at my hands—at the piece of paper still threaded between my fingers, with a number and a name—and a splash of longing bubbles up delicately in my chest. I turn on Netflix, and I find an old sitcom filled with people in their thirties. And as the rain picks up speed outside, I take a careful breath around the bubble. I tell myself I still have time.

Chapter 2

I think most people assume dog trainers are dog trainers because they love dogs. Because they want to spend their days with "man's best friend"—fluff and fur, big brown eyes, and dopey grins. They want to help these smart, loyal, and kind creatures live their best fur lives. Achieve four paws of pawfection. And so on.

And while all that's true (albeit, in a bit more serious fashion), it's not the only reason trainers get into training. And sometimes it's not even the biggest reason. At least, it wasn't for me. Because, yes, dog training is about dogs, but it's also about their owners. The pet parents. And they're the part that I've always found more compelling. The people who choose a dog—buy it, rescue it, whatever their story—and then find out that the dog they chose has behavioral issues—maybe the dog keeps peeing in the house or chewing furniture, or attacking the cat, or never stops barking. Maybe the dog bit them or bit their friend. Whatever the reason, these people now have this dog they didn't expect. This dog, who they chose, who is not at all what they bargained for, and now they need to make another choice. About what to do next.

And make no mistake, however much they love their dogs, it is a choice. What they do next is a choice. That's why I always found it incredible when they'd choose to call me. These owners—these smart, loyal, kind creatures—who would choose to call me. They'd choose to spend their time and money and emotional energy helping their dogs live their best lives. Achieve four paws of pawfection. And so on.

They are incredible, these owners, who would write me long emails and text messages explaining every detail of their dog's history, every little thing they imagine might matter, and always, always, the biggest takeaway, the message that most pops off the page, is love. Big and bold. Absolute in a way that, to me, is somehow more beautiful because we are talking about a dog, here. A member of their family they chose and then kept choosing. Someone who they kept choosing to love even when it would be so much easier not to.

I wake up on Saturday to an empty apartment, a text from a trainer who has declined to see Remy, and two more missed calls from my sister, Meredith. I'm stuck on the trainer—on what this might mean for Remy, this dog I've never actually met—so it takes a moment to register the calls, but when I do, something uncomfortable gathers in my stomach.

Two missed calls. Two missed calls when we only ever text. A constant stream of Meredith's love and worry, the two nearly interchangeable.

How's work? Did you read #GIRLBOSS yet? We had dinner with this great friend of Syed's; can I give him your number? The list goes on. Nineteen different ways of asking the one question that she won't: *When are you going to grow up?*

I stare at the phone, the thing in my gut twisting, but before I can call her back, the screen lights up with her name and a text.

Can you come over today?

I lean back in the pillows. Maybe everything is fine. Maybe she just saw another job I should apply to. I'd had half-formed plans of going to a farmers' market today. Pretending I was the kind of person who cooks fresh vegetables.

But my phone starts to ring again. It takes another second before I press it to my ear.

"Hey, Mere."

"Alex? Alex, I've been calling. Why didn't you pick up?"

There's something familiar about the worry in her voice. A bad memory I can't place.

"It doesn't matter," she says before I can answer. "Listen, something's happened."

"Is it Dad?" The question tumbles out of my mouth before I can stop it. I can't picture the last time I talked to him.

"No, no, it's not him . . . It's about—" she stumbles. The hand on my phone feels sweaty. "Can you come here?"

"Meredith, I'm still in bed. Just—just tell me what's going on."

I hear a scraping sound, and I know that she is sitting at her kitchen table. She's sitting at her table, holding her favorite mug, the blue one, more like a bowl than a cup, and she must have me on speaker, because I *know* that scraping noise. She's twisting the cup in both her hands. She's twisting it round and round without realizing it.

Something—something other than me—has made my confident sister nervous.

I listen to the scraping. And inexplicably, I think about a game we played when we were kids. Something about a monkey. I don't remember the specifics, but when Meredith yelled, "Cling, baby monkey!" I'd run as fast as I could, from wherever I was hiding, and I'd grab her and hold on tight. It was silly, no real point to it at all. But I still remember how much I'd loved it. How I'd knock things over in my rush to get to her. How we used to hold on to each other so tightly.

"It's about our mother. Her lawyer called."

Our mother. As in the woman we haven't seen in over a decade. As in the woman I haven't thought about in years.

"You mean Tessa?"

Three seconds.

"Alex, I'm sorry. But she's dead."

I see my mother's face in the cool dark space behind my lids. I'm maybe five years old, looking up as she reads me *Goodnight Moon*, her voice high and clear, like music, one hand holding the book, the other stroking my hair. I wriggle my body in closer, so I'm pressed against her side. Right here, I am safe.

I don't remember getting dressed, but twenty minutes later, I'm running from my apartment to the Uber. And it's raining again, a snarl of water and of wind, the noise louder than I expected. Everything too loud. And then, I'm in the car. The radio turned off. Silent except for the rain, now pattering against the roof. I watch the suburbs merge into the city as Boston passes by my window. There's a woman in a red raincoat biking in the lane next to us. We keep passing one another in this weird uneven race—her zipping along while we're stuck in a line of traffic, then us speeding by her as she pedals furiously up a hill. This happens over and over again. Every time we pass her, I try to get a look at her face, but I never can.

Tessa. Our mother.

She left us when I was fifteen. Walked out while I was sitting at the kitchen table. I remember my dad smashed a glass lighthouse figurine against the door while she walked through it.

Tessa.

That was thirteen years ago. Another lifetime.

I lean back in my seat, trying to ignore the choking scent of pine. A tree-shaped air freshener swings from the rearview.

I don't like to think about how it was after Tessa left—how quickly my family changed. Mere, flipping like a light switch, turning from my sister into someone pretending to be my mom. My father, shriveling into another person entirely. And me, a girl in a bathroom, crying. The last one to let her go.

That girl doesn't exist anymore. I'm smarter now. More realistic about people. And Tessa being dead . . . it doesn't change anything, not really. Except, I think I always counted on her being there. Somewhere else, but at least somewhere.

The rain stops by the time we get to Meredith's condo, sunlight peppering the pretty streets of Beacon Hill. Meredith lives in one of the most photographed neighborhoods in Boston. It's a picture book of narrow cobblestone streets fringed with antique gas lamps. Quaint redbrick town houses stacked together in a way that looks both neat and accidental. When I get out of the Uber, I walk past a couple holding hands underneath a light post, their photographer click-clicking behind them, weather be damned. I catch a glinting giveaway of a diamond on a finger. I wonder what my face will look like if it ends up in their frame.

Syed, Mere's husband, greets me at the door. His familiar face is as kind as ever, but the concern on his features is impossible to ignore, and when I get inside, he gives me a quick, tight hug. Meredith and I aren't big on physical displays of affection, but there's something about Syed's hugs—their genuineness, their strength—that almost makes me wish we were.

"Hey," I say, trying for casual. "Good start to a Saturday."

He gives me a small smile, then gestures at the kitchen. "She's in there."

My sister's where she so often is: sitting at the kitchen table, a stack of papers in front of her. Poking out from underneath one, I can just make out the beginnings of a checklist: groceries, new luggage, Syed's razors, doctor's appointment. I wonder if sex made the list.

We're opposites, she and I. It's not just that she's tall and I am tiny; it's that she is checklists and five-year plans. When people describe Meredith, they use words like *driven* and *determined*. She always knows exactly what to wear to every event. And exactly what to say. I'm more awkward. Worried about the wrong things, and more comfortable watching than jumping in. A "free spirit," an aunt said once; her backhand way of saying I don't have direction, which doesn't even fit. It implies wanderlust and exploration, someone trying to go everywhere at once when, in truth, I seem to just stay still.

"How are you?" Mere asks, sitting up straighter when she sees me. She's the picture of professionalism: shiny brown curls swept back, wearing a beige linen dress, her jean jacket neatly folded over the back of her chair. At five foot eight, she's almost six inches taller than me, and just as thin. Willowy. Everything about her has always been more refined. "Do you want some tea?" she asks. "Or orange juice? I don't think you get enough vitamin C."

I sink into the chair across from her, resting my elbows on the table, ignoring the comments about drinks. I wait.

I don't have to wait long.

"A lawyer called," she says, glancing down at the papers. "He called me earlier in the week, actually, and asked me to come to his office yesterday. He said it was about Tessa, but I didn't ask for specifics. I didn't know; I—I wasn't sure."

But she suspected. She went without me on purpose.

"She was only . . . what?" I ask. "Fifty-seven?"

"Fifty-eight."

Fifty-eight is young. If I die at fifty-eight, I'm already almost halfway there. The enormity of that thought—of what it implies about who I am and what I've done so far . . . I can't finish the sentence. Nathan's disappointed face flashes in my mind.

"There isn't a funeral," says Meredith. "I guess she was cremated, but I think there's going to be arrangements to have something up in Maine—"

"Maine?" I break in.

"It's where she lived."

Maine. Tessa, in Maine. Just a few hours north of us. All this time.

"I don't want to go," I say.

Meredith just shrugs, and I drop my gaze to my fingers. I fiddle with the chipped green nail polish coming off my pinkie.

"So what happened?" I ask again. "I mean, she was young, right? Relatively speaking."

Meredith hesitates. And I make myself look back up and when I do, I wish I hadn't. Because I realize then that she's been hesitating this whole time. Avoiding the main question. She's holding a paper in her left hand, pressing it against the table. It's folded like a letter, our names scrawled across the top. The handwriting still familiar. And I know, in a gut I never thought I had, that I don't want to read that letter. Because I can see it now—in Mere's hesitation, in the handwriting, in the way she holds the letter—I see it: the part I missed before. The part about how Tessa's death is not why I'm here. It's not the news that matters.

My stomach shifts, and a dull weight settles at the bottom.

"There's something else," I say.

"Yes."

"And it's bad?"

"Yes."

When her eyes find mine across the table, the fear there steals my breath. I actually hear it catch. I hear it because it feels like it's happening to someone else, like I'm watching the whole scene from up above, from the only place I might find oxygen.

Meredith.

She hands me the letter.

"The lawyer had this, too."

Later, I'll go in circles about Tessa's choice to write to us together. I'll be angry that she couldn't be bothered to write to each of us. I'll think her lumping us together shows, again, how little she cares. But then I'll consider whether she may have thought this news would be easier to hear together. And then, ultimately, I'll wonder if it wasn't her choice at all. If, by the time she wrote this letter, she was simply too sick to do it twice.

Huntington's disease. I've heard about it, bandied about in medical dramas, or featured in a health-awareness campaign. Somewhere, once, I saw a sign calling it one of the cruelest diseases. I know it kills you, stealing decades from your life. I know there is no cure. I know it is genetic, something you can inherit from your parents.

And now I know our mother had it.

The weight in my stomach is gone now, a cold, creeping emptiness taking its place. And I wonder if this is what it will be like to die. If I will just become more and more empty until I am nothing at all.

I don't know how long we sit in silence. Through the east-facing bay window, morning sunlight fights with the remaining rain clouds. A beam sneaks through and lands on Meredith's medical degree. My sister is a GP. I wonder if everything she already knows makes all of this worse or better.

I pull out my phone then, without thinking. Without preparing. Google's results leap out at me.

Fatal genetic condition.

Deterioration in a person's physical, mental, and emotional abilities.

No treatment, no cure.

Psychiatric symptoms. Cognitive decline. Involuntary movement. Death.

Every child of a parent with HD has a fifty-fifty chance of inheriting the faulty gene.

I zero in on that last one. Fifty percent chance that my own body is going to attack itself. Fifty percent chance that I am going to die what I've heard is a truly awful death. Fifty percent chance . . . My mother had two daughters. Fifty percent chance . . . Odds are, one of us has it. Memories from high school statistics tell me that's not exactly right, my odds don't affect Meredith's, but all I can think is: one in two, one in two.

I stare at my sister. Her straight back, her fingers tapping gently on the table. When I was in middle school, Tessa stopped coming to my soccer games. Meredith told me not to worry—that lots of kids' parents can't make it to all their games—and still, I'd always find myself looking for Tessa. Tessa and that stupid pink sign with my name on it. Sparkly letters.

I'd look without thinking about it. I'd look before I'd remember I wasn't supposed to look for it; I wasn't supposed to care. I kept looking and looking, tripping over my own feet as often as I got anywhere near the ball. And then one time, I looked up, and there she was. Meredith standing on the grassy pitch. No sign, just my sister, smaller and fiercer looking than every adult around her. Standing there, for no other reason than to watch me play.

Sometimes when I think about that game, and all the games that came after it, I wonder how she got there. She was still too young to drive.

Fifty percent chance.

A world without my mother is uncomfortable. A tightness in my chest I cannot shake.

A world without Meredith is unthinkable.

My eyes move from Mere to the papers on her table. I register that some of them are brochures, and I twist my head to read the glossy blue titles. To read anything else but what was on my phone.

Genetic testing. Navigating insurance. Finding your support group.

"We have time."

I lift my gaze. Meredith's features are stretched in a way that seems almost painful. I think she's trying to smile.

"I've been researching. Tessa died at fifty-eight, and that's old for HD—Huntington's disease," she explains. "Depending on exactly how she died, it means she probably didn't start experiencing symptoms until sometime in her forties.

"Even if one of us has it, daughters often have similar ages of onset as their mothers. Which is good," she adds, mistaking my silence for confusion. For interest. For something other than disbelief at how she's gotten so far away from me so quickly.

I still don't say anything, because I can't say anything. My voice is broken. I'm back to looking at my fingers. And I wish Syed would come into the room. I wish someone else would break the tension.

"I don't know if this had anything to do with Tessa leaving," says Meredith abruptly. "In case you were wondering that, too."

"I wasn't."

My response is automatic. A given. A question answered before it starts. Because we'd made a deal a long time ago not to do this. Not to try to figure out Tessa's motives. Not to open that particularly depressing can of worms.

For Mere, the deal was about moving forward. Moving on. For me, it was how free it felt to decide I didn't need it. That I didn't need any of it, an explanation or an answer. My mother still living in our house.

Mere looks like she wants to say something but stops herself. She holds up one of the pamphlets instead: a woman in a yellow T-shirt with a question mark above her head. "We have time, but we should think about getting tested."

The woman on the pamphlet is smiling. I can't stop staring at her teeth.

"I'm not getting tested," I say. It's the second thing I've said since I found out, but the words make me feel lighter. "You should do what you want, but I don't need to know this."

"Alex—"

"No," I cut her off. "I'm twenty-eight. You said she died when she was fifty-eight."

"Yes, but symptoms usually start one to two decades before"—her voice catches, then breaks—"before it gets that far."

It happens quickly: the air around us solidifying. Me losing my voice again.

"What's the point?" I choke out. "I don't have a medical degree, but from what I've just read, there is quite literally nothing you can do with this disease except wait for it to kill you."

Meredith looks pale. Even from here, I can count the freckles across her nose.

"They can treat some symptoms," she says at last.

"Well, if I get those symptoms, I'll get the treatment. I don't need to deal with this right now."

"Don't do this." All of a sudden, she's leaning forward on the table, her elbow crumpling her list, her words rushing together. "For the past twenty-four hours, I've been trying to figure out how to tell you. How to make sure you don't do what you always do."

I stare at the crushed list; I want to tell her to be careful.

"What are you talking about?" I say instead.

"You can't pretend this doesn't exist." Her fingers are pressed to her temples. "If you don't want to get tested, fine, but you still have to deal with this. Even just being at risk changes everything. You can't pretend that if you wait long enough, it will eventually resolve itself."

"I don't—"

"You do. This is exactly what you do. You'd rather get used to a shitty situation than deal with something that scares you." She registers my flinch but barrels forward. "You switched your major three times in college, and I'm not sure you even like the one you chose. You quit soccer your junior year, right after someone mentioned you might get scouted. You haven't had a serious relationship since you and Nathan broke up. You haven't gotten a single promotion since you started at Kensington, and we both know you're more than qualified. And your dog-training business . . ."

My throat constricts. "You were happy when I shut down DogKind," I say. "You told me it was the right move. You talked about how Kensington had good benefits."

"Yes, because after everything that you went through, I thought you needed a fresh start. But that's not what happened. You haven't started anything."

It's an effort to keep looking at her across the table. My face feels hot; my throat is sore. And I can't believe that she is doing this now. That she thinks now is the right time for this conversation, the ideal time to remind me that what was acceptable four years ago is not acceptable anymore. As if I didn't already know that. And I want to tell her that what I do with my life—both with this bombshell and everything else—is my choice. That her worry is a weight I can't handle. And more importantly, that this is happening to her, too. That I am not her only problem.

But I don't say that. I don't say anything. Instead, I turn to the window. The rain is back again, a steady drum beat pounding against the roof. And I think about the red-coated biker, the way she pumped her legs as she climbed that hill. I wonder if she made it home. Or if she's still out there, pedaling alongside cars in a race that's again shifted even more in their favor.

I still wish I could have seen her face.

Chapter 3

The rest of the weekend disappears in a haze of Netflix, Cup Noodles, and Google searches that leave me nauseous. I make the mistake of opening my email, which is full of messages from Meredith. Articles about Huntington's disease—which she now refers to as HD, like the acronym is somehow less invasive. Articles with links to clinical trials, support groups, and awareness events. Articles about scientific breakthroughs and people who have hope for a cure. Link after link about how to get tested. I can feel her worry leaking through my phone screen.

I need her to remember that this is happening to her, too.

I try to avoid my phone, but one trainer after another texts me, each turning Remy away. One generic text after another that says a different version of the same thing: They've reviewed her history, and they don't think she can be saved.

> Alex, you should let this one go. This dog is a recipe for heartbreak.
>
> I'm really sorry, but I am booked full and focusing on dogs that I can help.

I know they're right; I *should* let it go, especially given everything else. Dead mothers and faulty genes and websites with terrifying stories. But I keep remembering Remy's ears. The tops of them. Bobbing in the window of Nathan's Jeep.

She'd been watching for Nathan. She trusted him. I'm almost sure of that. I'm almost sure that means they're wrong. I'm almost sure she can be helped.

But the truth? I thought Cliff could be saved, too.

A dull tightness takes up permanent residence in my chest. I search online for something positive, something to make all of this less fraught, and I end up on an article about reprioritizing your life. I stare at the words on my screen: *Remember what you have, and focus on what matters.* I consider writing to the author. I want to tell them that I don't know what that means.

When Monday arrives, it comes with a vengeance—the heat of mid-August in the city. My hair hangs limply from a plain black hair tie, and my pants stick to my thighs. I join the usual crowd of people waiting for the T. All of them, just waiting for the train like it's any other Monday. And I try to be like them, to pretend it is any other Monday. But as we squeak out of the station, I hear Meredith's voice in my head.

You'd rather get used to a shitty situation than deal with something that scares you.

Surrounded by strangers, trundling in a muggy tunnel under busy Boston streets, it's easier to do it. To let her point land. Because the truth is that I have let my life slip by these last few years. But the other truth is this: I wasn't always this person. I'd started a training business once. I'd fallen in love. I'd had dreams and plans and so on, and I'd been close, I think. To what Lois reminded me of the other day.

To happiness.

I'd always meant to get back there. I'd always meant to get back to being some version of that person. Just a little tougher. A little more practical. A little more able to stand the bumps without getting slapped all the way back to start.

I think if I were that person, all of this might be easier. If I were that person, Meredith would be able to focus on herself instead of me.

At Kensington, I sink into my cubicle next to four other women, all younger than me, and start my usual routine: clicking and dragging one PowerPoint slide after another across my screen. I'm trying to ignore the noise around me. We landed a big account on Friday, and the rest of the floor is still buzzing with energy. Everyone's leaning over their cubicles, laughing and congratulating one another, as if we're all one big team. People who don't even know my name slap my desk when they walk by.

When Deena from Strategic Accounts emails me about lunch, I grab at the chance to escape this building. To find a space to breathe.

Deena's more than just my colleague; she's the closest thing I've made to a real friend since college. She's less than two years older than me, but miles ahead already. We were copywriters together at my first job, our bond formed under fluorescent office lights and snarky break-room gossip. She stuck with it after I quit, then jumped to Kensington for a massive promotion. She's the one who got me my job now. She's tough and ambitious, with a dry, scratchy humor that matches her voice. She's also Boston born and raised. And not new Boston, of the yuppies, but Charlestown before it got gentrified. Her dad's a cop; her mom's a nurse. She's told me more than once that people who don't swear are wasting words.

If I told her about Huntington's, she'd tell me it fucking sucks.

She swings by my desk at one minute past noon, and then we're out the door, grabbing sushi from the place she loves, and finding our usual bench by the water. I lean back and let the sun brush my face while Deena runs through our usual list of complaints about Kensington. Usually, I love these conversations—I love Deena's razor-sharp humor, her biting social commentary—but today, I'm struggling to keep up while keeping everything else out: The pamphlets in my desk drawer in my apartment. My sister's preoccupation with me instead of herself. Remy and her ears and the list of trainers who have said no. Nathan and his memory of the person I used to be.

"I'm starting to think I might like to meet someone," says Deena.

I open my eyes and look at my food. I try to follow what she's saying. Something about a girl she met over the weekend.

"As opposed to just having fun?" I ask.

"I don't know . . ." She shrugs. "I heard they're coming out with a new dating app. Remember that creepy one that connected you with people you saw on the street?"

I force a laugh. I know the one she means. I'm on all the requisite apps. I'm mainly going through the motions, but I find their presence comforting. The colorful squares on my phone. The random notifications. The potential for romance, supposedly just a swipe away.

"You need to get out there more," says Deena. "When was the last time you updated your profile? They have all those little sentence prompts now. You can really make yours interesting."

One thing you might find surprising about me is . . . I have a fifty percent chance of dying young.

I shrug and spear a piece of sushi, trying to direct my brain to something else. And then, I'm back to Nathan. Nineteen years old and telling me he loves me. Asking me to believe him, as if that's ever easy. And then nine years later, him standing on my doorstep in Somerville, asking me for something else. Asking again. As if no time has passed.

I blink the image away. "Didn't you tell me you'd date around until you died?"

"I know, I know. But I guess . . . I'm getting bored. It's all starting to feel predictable. Like a game, I guess."

"In fairness, I think dating is a game for everyone. Don't want to go all in too fast."

"Sure, but . . ." Deena sighs. She stretches her hands above her head and grins. "Don't you ever want to just dive in? Fuck the consequences."

Blue-gray eyes. His long fingers tangled in my hair.

"No," I say softly. "No, I really don't."

Deena raises an eyebrow. "You have to live a little, Alex."

That bubble of longing again. Rising in my throat. Everything I'm keeping out slams back in.

Over the weekend, I found a funeral announcement for a woman with Huntington's. She was diagnosed at seventeen. She was diagnosed when she was still a child, and she died eight years later.

Juvenile Huntington's disease. Starts earlier; progresses faster.

There was a picture of her in a wheelchair. It looked like she couldn't raise her head.

She was seventeen when diagnosed. Just a kid.

Live a little.

When I don't answer, Deena leans back on the bench and closes her eyes. We stay there for another ten minutes. Deena listening to the lapping of the waves against the docks, me listening to her words run circles in my head. Such a simple phrase, but it's like a song I can't get out of my head. Sticky.

Live a little.

It can't be that easy to be happy. But it's not just Deena acting like it is. It's the internet, reminding me to focus on what matters. It's Holly's equally generic, happy signs scattered all over our apartment. *Break the mold. Good vibes only. Dare to begin.*

Does that work for her? Does it work for anyone?

I think about my sister, worrying about all the wrong things. I picture Remy's ears, and how I just know . . . I *know* she can be helped. I picture myself, four years ago, almost exactly where I am right now.

And I think, again, of the person Nathan remembers, and the person who I'd planned to be. And it seems suddenly essential that I figure out how to get there. Not only for me—not only for a faulty gene, or for this pressure in my chest, or this blind, desperate grasping for *happiness, happiness,* that most nebulous of words—but for them. For Remy and for Mere.

The sun shifts behind a cloud, and all the pieces slide together in my brain.

I exhale through my mouth. I exhale everything.

I think I know what to do. I think I have a plan.

◆ ◆ ◆

Meredith agrees to meet me at a bar in Fenway after work. I'm surprised by the one she suggests among all the other Fenway spots. This place is divey—a holdout among the new, more flashy sports bars that have sprouted up around Kenmore in the last few years. The walls are lined with Red Sox jerseys behind yellowed glass panes, and the air feels musty, a little too solid when I walk through it.

Meredith's sitting at a bulky wooden table, carved up by age and clearly someone's knife. ALLY AND ANDY WERE HERE. She's in scrubs, but still meticulous: brown hair cinched in a gleaming knot on the back of her head, understated makeup on her face, fingernails painted a soft salmon pink. (Meredith once told me that she always looks at people's fingers when she meets them. She said that you can tell a lot just by whether someone's nails are clean).

She glances up as I walk toward her, and I force my face to relax and let my shoulders drop. It's this automatic urge with her to prove that I am okay. To discount her unspoken assumption that she needs to fix me. That she, alone, knows what it takes to fix me.

I remind myself I have a plan. A cobbled-together road map that can maybe do the impossible: make something brand new. Time, myself, etc.

"How are you?" I ask before she can open her mouth.

She gives me a look, one eyebrow raised. I remember as a kid wishing I knew how to do that. "I'm fine," she says. "I'm trying to help you figure out next steps. I don't want you to hide from this, Alex."

"I know," I say. And then—before she can speak, before she can point us in any one direction—I flag down a server and order us beers. Red ale for me, a lager for Mere. When the drinks come back, they slosh over the side. Wet stains on the already splotched-up table. I press a napkin down into the wood. I take a sip.

"You want me to get tested," I say.

The eyebrow, again. "I want you to at least think about this. To see the therapist, to consider support groups. The last time you had a setback—"

"I know," I cut her off. I don't bother pointing out that a deadly illness qualifies as more than a setback. I don't think it will help my case.

"I'm just really worried about you, Alex. You can't pretend this isn't real."

"I agree. And I want to make a deal."

She leans back in her chair. "A deal?"

"We don't do anything about this for three months." Her mouth opens with one loud huff, and I raise my hand. "Let me finish. We take three months to slow down, to think this through. But in three months' time, no matter what, we start the counseling. That's the first step to getting tested. And I will do it. I'm promising you that right now."

"You'll go to the counseling? You'll start the process for getting tested?" she asks. "In three months."

I turn my head to the left. Toward a dartboard with Derek Jeter's face stuck to the center. He's grinning, but there's a dart stabbing through his left eye.

"I'm not promising to get the test. Most people don't, Mere; you know that." She presses her lips together but doesn't refute my words. I did my research. Less than 20 percent of people at risk get tested before they're symptomatic. Plenty of people feel how I feel right now: *Why find out if you're going to die when there's nothing you can do to stop it?*

Mere's recovered, though, and is shaking her head. "Fine, you're right," she allows. "And honestly, Alex, I believe that for some people, not getting the test makes sense."

"But not for me."

"No."

"Because you think I will get stuck."

She opens her mouth, then shuts it, biting back the words I can picture in her head.

Because you already are.

She leans forward, her eyes serious. "All I'm saying, Alex, is there's a difference between not finding out and burying your head in the sand."

We stare at each other, my fingers rubbing up against the beat-up table. "I know," I say at last. "I know. And that's why I'm saying that we do this. I am promising you that I *will* do the research. I'll talk to the counselor. I won't hide from this. And I will make a decision. In three months."

Mere picks up her phone and shakes her head. "Three months is Thanksgiving."

I blink back an eye roll. "A little over three months then."

"December third," she says, pointing at the calendar on her screen. "That's a Tuesday."

"Perfect, Mere. December third it is."

She meets my amused gaze, and something flickers at the corner of her mouth. "Okay," she says, "Okay." She takes a sip of her beer. "And what exactly will we do for the next few months? Besides not get tested."

I turn away from Jeter. "It's going to sound a bit cheesy."

"Okay. . ."

She's waiting patiently, but I still trip over the words. I remind myself that Meredith loves lists. I'm counting on that love.

"We make a list of three things we've always wanted," I say. "Things we haven't done because we don't have time or because we're scared, or, I don't know, whatever other excuse we give ourselves."

To her credit, Meredith resists rolling her eyes.

"Like, go skydiving?"

"No," I say. "I mean yes. If that is something you've wanted. But I mean bigger things." I hesitate. And then I tell her about Remy. About the court case and euthanasia and how I think that I can help. "I'm going to work with her. It's a pretty tough case, and if it goes well, I can probably drum up some media on it and use it to relaunch DogKind."

Meredith looks at me closely. "Are you ready for that?"

"I don't know," I say honestly. "But I think I'd like to find out."

There's a pause. The door opens, and a couple sits down behind us. It takes that long for Mere to smile. But when she does, she's half her age. We are half our age. Teenagers again.

"Okay," she says. "I'll do it. But can you tell me—why? Why do you want to do this?"

I think about the unused dating apps, and the feelings that I haven't felt in years. Feelings I'm realizing I still miss. I think about my standstill career at Kensington and the future I'm supposed to want. About my conversation with Deena, and how tempting it would be to become somebody else. Someone who does things like *Year of Yes* and *Eat, Pray, Love*. Who believes that change is easy. Who believes that anything so simple can work.

I think about all of that, and then I think about my sister. About what I want for her.

"I want to be happy," I say at last. "And you were right: I'm bad at going after what I want. And it seems like, now more than ever, it's probably time to change that. To be strong enough to choose things that make me happy. Does that make sense?"

Something flickers behind her eyes. A bright spot of longing I recognize but didn't expect.

She coughs. "Fair enough."

"Good," I say, seizing on this. Using it to push to the most important part. "And we both have to do it, Mere. We both have to focus on ourselves. On what makes us happy."

Meredith nods slowly. "Until December."

I lift a shoulder. "It's worth a shot. See where we end up."

She nods again. The smile tilts; it doesn't disappear so much as it morphs into something else. "If we do this, you should still think about it while we wait to get the counseling. At the very least, tell Holly."

She keeps going, keeps explaining how I should use my time wisely, but I'm watching the couple behind her. They're young—maybe twenty-three—and their faces are flushed with a glow that makes me feel older than I am. Because I remember being them. Being Boston and brand new. Boston and brand new and then everything that follows: First dates and first jobs. Cramped apartments that feel like milestones. The romance of discovering a dive bar. Thinking you are the first.

I look down at the table. At the words carved into the wood. Ally and Andy were here. I look back up at the couple, and I feel the oddest surge of protectiveness. An urge to stash them in a box and ship them somewhere safer.

"Three months," says Meredith. "December third. I can make the appointment?"

I lift my gaze. I don't hesitate.

"Yes."

Chapter 4

The problem with DogKind was that it never should have been me on that video. It should have been Holly all along.

The year after we launched, DogKind gained new clients every week. Holly got me on radio shows and, once, a local Boston news station. My face in front of thousands, flushed and splotchy as I stuttered over the words Holly had written out. That night, we drank champagne at the Top of the Hub. We toasted our future in delicate thin-stemmed glasses, the city sprawled at our feet with the Charles River reflecting back the sunset. Playful pink strands that Holly said looked like cotton candy. Beautiful. Her words made me see that, too.

I want to be the kind of person who belongs in the spotlight. The kind who can carry a brand on her shoulders. I think influencers are brave and bold. I think there's something magical about seeing cotton candy in a typical Boston sunset.

But I'm awkward and easily tongue-tied. And to me, pink is usually just pink.

I text Nathan and ask him to meet me at a café near my apartment on Wednesday after work. The heat has finally broken. Cool air filters through the city, making way for autumn.

On the train ride to Somerville, I get started on my list. My three things. The three things that will help me get at what I want to feel: Independent. Strong. The precursors to happiness that I think I've somehow always missed.

Remy is first, but I tap out *Kensington* next. There's a promotion opening on my team, and Deena's been pushing me to apply. To *step out of my comfort zone*. And maybe she is right. Maybe I've been holding back from Kensington because I am scared of moving forward, of realizing there's a path outside the one I'd once thought I'd follow.

I don't know. But when it comes to independence, figuring out my career—DogKind or Kensington—seems like a good place to start.

Two out of three.

I fiddle with my phone. I type out a third bullet, change a word, and frown. I try again.

Be open to a new relationship.

The words aren't right. Not quite. But they are the best that I can do. The best way I can explain what I'm becoming desperate to figure out: how to feel like I did with Nathan but not lose myself again. There has to be a way to do that, to love someone without making them my world. Without needing quite as much.

I'm aware that Huntington's complicates this part of the plan. That love and relationships require some level of honesty that I can't imagine giving yet. But I have three months. Just over that, in fact. Even if I meet someone tomorrow (which I won't), it will take at least that long to see what's there. To decide what they need to know. And this is one of the many reasons that, despite who I am going to see, I write down the word *new*. Not someone like Nathan, not someone with all our history, but someone new. A story we get to build from scratch. A first date where I can feel it: that little shiver of what might be. Of what could happen if I just stop hiding.

Strong. Independent. Tough.

We trundle across the Charles, sunlight splashing against the glass window behind my head, and my heart beating at a steady rate in my chest. Finally. Because I'm doing it: moving forward, even with the threat of Huntington's. This deadly disaster that might be hidden in my genes. (That's one of the weirdest parts of this: its inevitability. You can't pretend there's anything you can change at this point—no exercise, eating well, desperate prayers, or existential bargaining. And no regrets. Because you either have it or you don't. It's either always been there or it hasn't. And that, of course, pulls up the other part . . . the question begged if the faulty gene has always been there—about whether you could even be you without it.)

When I get to the café, Nathan's sitting at a table outside. He's not in a suit today, but he still looks formal: khaki pants and a blue button-up, the sleeves pulled back to reveal toned forearms tanned from the sun. I try to consider him objectively. Tall and fit and well dressed. Ray-Bans perched easily in his hair. His eyes scanning his phone with an intensity that stops servers from approaching, even as they keep sneaking peeks at him. He's always had the kind of confidence that intimidates even while it pulls you in. It's still there—only it's heightened by age and whatever has happened to him in these last seven years. Whatever made his cheekbones a little sharper, his eyes a little more shadowed.

He's grown up. And the adult Nathan is the kind of good looking that singes. The intensity of his eyes, the set of his cheekbones, all of it calling up sleek hotel rooms and stolen kisses and naked bodies intertwined in steaming showers. Everything sexy. Everything illicit.

I give myself a shake and remind myself that shower sex is overrated. And then, I'm walking toward him, my yellow sneakers flashing beneath me. I changed in the bathroom at work, swapping my wrap dress for clothes more suitable to training: black spandex and a loose cotton top. My hair is pulled back in a ponytail, but it's windy, and red curls keep escaping from the band and flapping around my face.

Nathan stands when I get to his table, making as if to hug me, but I stick out my hand instead. He gives me his signature smile—that deceivingly lazy confidence—and takes my hand in his, and the whole thing backfires, somehow becoming more intimate than a hug: his skin against my skin, the way he seems to hold on for a fraction of a second too long.

Hi, I'm Nathan.

I'm Alex.

Smart outfit choice.

I'd blushed then. It was the second day of freshman orientation. A weeklong canoe trip. I was already very sunburned and very over the wilderness, and I'd donned an oversize men's long-sleeve T-shirt to protect my skin. I'd assumed he was making fun of me, but on closer inspection, he seemed genuinely supportive.

And interested. He was interested in me.

I shake the memory away, even though I have a thousand others that are the same. Nathan was always like that, always direct about what he wanted. Always all-in once he decided something mattered.

"Do you work around here?" he asks, pushing a coffee toward me. Black. The same way I always ordered it in college. I want to add cream, to prove to him that I am not the same, but instead, I take a sip and scan the café. We're on a side street off Union Square. It's deceptively quiet; we can hear the breeze rustling in the leaves of the trees over our head, but if we walked around the block, we'd be hit with the noise of bars and commuters.

"No," I say. "But there's a park that's usually pretty empty around the corner. I thought we could take Remy there after we talk."

"Thank you," he says. His eyes catch mine across the table. "Thank you for doing this. I know it's—not ideal."

"Tell me about Remy," I say. "Tell me everything about her history."

He nods, following my lead to focus on her instead of us. He tells me that Remy is a mixed breed, but he doesn't have the specifics. Australian shepherd and lab and probably a few others. She's seven years old, which makes her a senior, and is also one more strike against her. Why take a chance on a dog who is already more than halfway through her life?

She had the same family until she was four. No incidents. And then, the family moved, and they left Remy in a shelter. When Nathan explains this part, he sounds thoughtful but not convinced. "I don't think they had any options," he says. "They didn't have any family who would take her."

I nod, but I catch him watching me. Nathan knows that Tessa left. He knows I probably share his lack of sympathy on this one.

"It happens," I say simply.

"Yeah, well. After that, things went downhill fast. She was in that shelter for a couple of months, and then—you said you read about the fire?"

I nod. The shelter fire in Billerica two years ago. More than half the animals had died. I'd been sitting at my desk at Kensington when I'd gotten the news alert on my phone.

"Remy made it out, but she's been skittish ever since. And there was that rush of adoptions afterward, so she got a home, but the family wasn't really ready for a dog. They just wanted to help; you know how people are. She bit the dad—I don't have much information on what happened, but it was nothing major, barely broke skin—but they sent her back. And then, she bit one of the shelter workers, too. He was trying to take her food bowl."

"And they were going to put her down?"

"Yes," said Nathan.

"So you rescued her."

It's not a question. We look at each other across the table, and I know we're both thinking the same thing. Nathan's mother had breast cancer twice when he was a kid, and it came back the summer after our sophomore year at CU Boulder. The cancer was nasty and fast growing, and the treatment plan was brutal. Nathan's dad, Aaron, was a commercial truck driver, so he was often gone on long-haul trips. And Kit, Nathan's little sister, was just a kid, still living at home, still needing rides to school. Someone to give her a hug at night. Aaron talked about taking leave from work, but financially that wasn't realistic. Nathan stepped in instead.

We were together at the lake, at the cabin his family rented, when he found out about his mom. He told me his plan the very next day. How he was taking a year off and going home, moving from Colorado back to Massachusetts. Two thousand miles from me. Thirty miles from the place I'd just left behind.

He held my hand when he told me, but for the first time in our relationship, he didn't look me in the eyes. We'd been together for two years, and that was the only time I saw him falter. And I knew, right then, that he needed me to lie.

"I love you," he said, rubbing the back of my hand with his thumb. "We love each other. And we're both practical people. We'll make it work. What's a few months of long distance?"

I nodded, because it was what he needed. And because I wanted him to be right. I wanted to be the kind of person who could commit to faith and ignore the facts: that long distance almost never works. That he would likely be gone more than a few months. That our plan was entirely hypothetical. And that better than anyone, I knew how quickly love and hard work stop being enough.

The wind surges at our table, and I take in the hazy sky. The weather app didn't call for rain, but the air feels full, like I can almost taste the coming storm. I look back at Nathan, into his eyes that match the gray-blue sky above.

"How is your mom?" I say, and Nathan hesitates, then smiles, his whole face softening. I've always loved this side of him. But it used to worry me how I was often the only one who got to see it.

"She's good," he says. "Still in remission. Has her hands full with Kit, who has been called up for two disciplinary hearings in her first two years of college."

"Well, something tells me your mom can handle that," I say. "Sue was always a toughie."

"She thought the same thing about you."

There's a pause. And not for the first time, I think this is a mistake. Being here.

I want Nathan to be a catalyst, a reminder of what I'm capable of feeling. Of what I can have with someone else, but not with him. Not this. Not how it feels just being near him. Everything neatly stitched together, all coming undone.

"You ready to meet Remy?" he asks, and I take another drink of my coffee.

Remy . . . The whole reason I am here.

"How's she been with you? You've had her for six months, you said?"

"Yes. Like I said, she's skittish. She hid in the corner of my apartment for the first week or so, but then she started to come out of her shell. At this point, she's fine as long as it's just the two of us. We hang on the couch, she sleeps at the foot of my bed. She loves fetch—I mean we really just play in my apartment, but she loves it. It's anything outside . . . dogs, people, cars, etc." He shrugs. "We haven't really ever had a successful introduction."

"And she's on antianxiety meds?" I ask.

"Yeah, for a couple of weeks now."

"They can take months to really kick in."

He clenches his jaw. The Nathan I remember hates inefficiencies; he has no patience for poor management.

"I know," he says. "But she doesn't have that long."

I nod. The system sucks.

"Okay." I start to stand. "I'll email you a questionnaire that I usually have clients fill out. But, yeah, in the meantime, I'd like to meet her."

We walk together from the café in the opposite direction of Union, toward an ugly part of the neighborhood dominated by old warehouse buildings and construction. Somerville is like anywhere else in the Boston area—one neighborhood after the next getting gentrified; abandoned buildings and dilapidated homes swapped for mixed-use developments and lab buildings. In another two years, these blocks will be unrecognizable.

I point at the abandoned dog park and tell Nathan to grab Remy and meet me there.

"She's in a muzzle?" I ask before he walks away.

"Yes, it was one of the requirements."

"And you said she'll come if you call her, so we can collect her easily if we need to?"

"Yes."

"Okay," I say. I tell him that I'll go into the park first. It's best to have Remy join me, rather than her feel like I'm invading her space.

"Keep her on the leash, but let her lead. If she wants to come to me, that's fine."

"She's going to bark at you," he says. "She can sound pretty vicious."

"It's fine," I say. He looks unconvinced, but I ignore him and walk into the park, picking my way across the unkempt grass until I'm standing in the middle of the field. I don't turn toward the entrance. I just sit there and I wait.

And then, there's the creak of the dog gate opening. The sound of running paws, and a bark so loud and deep, I bite my lip to keep from flinching. I register that she's panting even though it's not that warm; she's nervous. Nathan's letting her lead, but I can feel his anxiety, too. That bark again; it's something.

Remy is muzzled, though, and she's maybe sixty pounds at most. Even if she body slams me, I'll be fine. And I want to understand her. I need to understand her, and quickly. Will she attack unprovoked? Will she try to prove she's dominant? Or is her barking a warning, simply asking me to stay away?

She's close now, barreling toward me, and I give Nathan a look because I can tell he wants to pull up on the leash. And then she's right in my face, barking and snarling. I can smell her breath, feel the warmth of it against my cheek.

"Hey, girl," I say. My voice is low and steady. "Hey there, how're you doing? How're you feeling, sweet girl?"

I don't move; I just keep talking. Remy's still barking, but she never touches me. She gets close, barking right up in my face, but that is it. I never even feel the plastic of the muzzle. She runs out and then back in. She ignores me, and then a shadow or a shift in my posture and she's back. Those loud barks, and then retreating. Always retreating.

She's beautiful. Even with the muzzle. She has the half-bent ears of an Aussie, but the wide nose of a lab. And her fur is this strange mix of rust brown and white and mottled gray. I scatter treats in front of me, and she scarfs them down, her pink tongue flicking through the muzzle, while never taking her eyes off me. Skepticism spelled out in liquid topaz.

"I know, girl," I say. "I know."

I'm not sure how long I sit there. My legs stiffen beneath me, and I start to shiver as the wind picks up. The storm is coming, and I'm not wearing a raincoat, and I should get up. Give up. Except, I think that I can feel it: the shift. The next part. I am almost sure that it is coming.

Nathan makes a move, his mouth half opening with a question, and I give the smallest shake of my head. I can't feel my left foot. Shoots of half-dead grass are poking through my spandex. I can feel Nathan's confusion, and I'm starting to think he's right.

It happens then. The rain starts, heavy pounding on my shoulders. I close my eyes against the downpour, and I hear the soft padding of paws on wet grass. The jingle of a collar that Nathan must have purchased. Remy's name alongside a phone number and a name—her last chance at a family.

One minute, I am alone. And the next, a silky head presses against my shoulder.

There. Right there.

Hope.

"That was something," says Nathan.

The rain is over, passing by as quickly as it began. We're standing a half block from Nathan's car where Remy's waiting for him. Close enough that she can see him, but not so close that she starts to bark again.

"It's a start," I say, but inside, I'm quietly elated. I'd forgotten how much I missed this. With DogKind, I'd never been good at the business part or the promotions, but this: the dogs, the way their eyes widen when they're nervous, the careful stiffening of a tail, the feel of a wet nose on the back of your hand . . . this is the language I speak best. It's what I've always loved. It's the part that has always made sense.

And it seems possible, just then, that the list will work. That training Remy really is one part of the solution. A way to prove to Meredith and to myself that I can move forward. That I am tougher than I was before.

"Do you think she has a chance?" asks Nathan, just as I start to walk away.

I pause. I turn and look at him, standing on the sidewalk behind me. After we broke up, I never thought I'd see him again. And here he is, for the second time in five days, close enough that I can touch him.

"More than most," I say.

"Meaning?"

"She has you," I say. "And you don't do things halfway. You always have a foolproof plan, and ninety-nine percent of the time, it works."

I mean the words as a compliment, but they land sideways—both of us stiffen; his eyes dig into mine like he's trying to solve a puzzle.

"There's always that other one percent, though," he says, his eyes never leaving my face. I feel my heart thump under my still-damp shirt. "You were better at seeing that part than me."

I shiver. I try to lighten the mood. "I'm just not what one would call an optimist."

"And I am?" he asks.

Only because you think you have to be.

"Not an optimist, exactly . . ." And I find myself biting back a sudden smile. "You're an achiever, I guess. Kind of like a robot. If it can be done, it shall be done. And so on."

He lets out a snort of laughter, then glances at Remy, and his expression shifts—that uncertainty from the other night. Still wholly unfamiliar.

"You always told it to me straight," he says, his voice serious again. "So, tell me now. Do you think she has a chance?"

I don't say anything, but I can't hold his gaze. Because he's wrong. I didn't always tell him the truth. I didn't always tell him when I was scared or unsure. Or when I thought he was being shortsighted or expecting too much. I never wanted to cause him pain.

I still don't.

I look back up. I try a smile.

"There's always a chance."

Chapter 5

It was Meredith who suggested I go to one of Boulder's outdoor orientation trips before school started. I'm still surprised I listened to her. And I still can't decide if I'm glad or regretful that I did.

If I hadn't gone, I never would have met Nathan.

We were in a group of twenty other incoming students, all about to spend a week in the Rockies—hiking and canoeing and other adventurous activities I'd only read about in books. I was born and raised in the Boston suburbs, a city girl through and through.

On the second day of orientation, Nathan and I ended up in the same canoe. That's when he told me he liked my shirt and that slow blush spread from beneath my skin.

I'd had boyfriends before, but never guys like Nathan. The guys I dated were the kind who promised authenticity: would-be activists and artists who loved to talk about their ideals, and whose ideals made them seem like the type of people you can trust. The appeal of seemingly gritty honesty. Guys who I fell for over late-night conversations, but who I always ended up finding wearing in the daylight, their cynicism a little too predictable. A little less like honesty and too much like an act.

On the surface, Nathan was their opposite. He was all-American good looking, clean cut, and driven. Polite and slightly distant, but with a quiet intensity that made you lean in closer. When Nathan focused on something, he focused on it entirely. His whole being got wrapped up in his gaze.

He was the kind of guy people gravitated toward without meaning to. The kind of guy my ex-boyfriends would have hated on sight. But even by that second day, I could tell that Nathan didn't care what any of us thought. Often, I got the feeling he was friendly out of politeness rather than interest. Where the rest of us needed each other—for friendship, for validation—he was happy with himself. Confident in what he wanted and his plan to get it. He never tried to pretend or impress.

Later, I would source this in his priorities, how none of them started with himself. But back then, he was simply the most authentic person I'd ever met.

That day in the canoe, when he said he liked my outfit, I didn't know if he was making fun of me. But he gave me this look—intense, assessing—before saying he wished he'd thought to bring a long-sleeve shirt himself.

"Sun protection," he said. He swung himself around so we were facing each other, his paddle still in his hand. We were in no rush; everyone else was still packing. "My mom's already beaten cancer twice." He gave this shrug . . . this shrug that became familiar too fast. *It is what it is.* "The Brownings don't joke about UV rays or cigarettes."

"I'm sorry. Really."

Another shrug. "She's in remission."

I nodded, but I kept quiet. I understood how it felt to cling to bad news. To think the words aloud were worse than the story in your head. He stuck his paddle in and then out of the water. He looked at me and then away. And when he finally continued, he sounded almost surprised that he was speaking. "The doctors aren't optimistic. There's a good chance that it will come back."

"They told you that?"

He lifted a shoulder, the paddle shifting in his hand. "She was never supposed to survive in the first place. My parents are all about honesty. They told me the truth when I was a kid."

His tone was casual, a practiced nonchalance, but I had this flash of him as a child. The same decided chin and steady gray-blue eyes, but with cheekbones still rounded. Sitting in a chair, pulling back shoulders that belonged to a little boy. Pretending he was okay.

Long after we'd ended, of the thousand reminders of Nathan, the worst were the random quotes I'd see—in a book, on a T-shirt—that always kicked against my heart. These quotes that brought me right back to that canoe in Colorado because they reminded me so much of him, of all the reasons I worried about him. *Take it on the chin; don't blink; never let them see you sweat.* All of these expressions that added up to a type of strength I both admired and abhorred. Because Nathan *was* strong; he'd take on anything without blinking, but that was the problem. He never considered the consequences. He never considered what each of those promises would cost him. And it used to terrify me to consider what he'd have left when the bill was due.

"I don't believe in lost causes," I'd said, and then winced at the oversimplification.

His eyes tracked my expression. That intensity. "Because they're an excuse not to try?" he asked.

"Because they're an excuse to decide the trying part doesn't matter."

We stared at each other, the water slapping against the boat, his face quiet, waiting for me to continue. "The thing is," I said, "I'm not great about the future, about expecting the best . . ." I touched my tongue to the roof of my mouth. I chose my next words carefully. "But your mom? She's beaten it twice. That's the part that's already happened."

His head tilted. And there was this expression, this look that I'll never forget, as his eyes studied my face—like there was something special there. Like my slightly slanted way of seeing the world was better. Like I was better, just as I was. No one had ever looked at me like that. And sitting there, surrounded by blue water, my whole body buzzed.

After that conversation, we kept talking all day. I'd never felt so comfortable with anyone other than my sister. I liked the way he saw me, the way it made me feel. And I liked the way he talked about his mother . . . I'd never heard a guy talk about one of their parents, and definitely not their mother, that way, like she was smart and cool and clever. Like she was his friend.

Most of all, I liked the way he saw the world—all clean cuts and calculated decisions. And unflinchingly honest opinions. It was incredibly refreshing. Optimistic in its simplicity. And impossible not to trust.

By the time we dragged our canoe on land for lunch, I knew I was in trouble.

By the third day, I found myself looking for Nathan at meals so that I could sit beside him. By the fourth day, I was noticing how the other girls noticed him, the extent of his magnetism. By the fifth day, I started to wonder if I was imagining the intensity of that first conversation.

On the final day of the trip, I ended up in a canoe with a quiet guy named Steve, and Nathan ended up with Isabelle. Isabelle, who was pretty and cheerful and at home in a canoe. Not to mention very sweet. She made friendship bracelets for all of us, which sounds weird, but wasn't at the time. She was the kind of girl I expected Nathan would end up with, wholesome and adventurous, the perfect yin to his yang.

I, on the other hand, had discovered that a long-sleeve shirt was not enough to protect my pale Irish skin, and that the sunshine of Colorado hadn't turned me into a sunshiny kind of person.

That night, instead of watching the two of them and the romance I'd decided was inevitable, I sat near the fire and stared at the flames spitting orange sparks into the sky. It was windy, and my hair was blowing around my face, so I didn't see him walk over. I just felt a person settle on the log beside me, and I didn't need to turn to know that it was him. There was something about how he sat down—how he was just an inch closer than expected, how his arm brushed against mine and stayed there—that made my heart turn over in my chest. And I knew, right then, that Isabelle didn't matter. Nothing mattered but this.

"You ready to get back on campus?" Nathan asked. I could feel his breath next to my ear.

"I'm ready to shower."

He chuckled softly, and I fell in love with that sound. With how it loosened his shoulders. "Not a big nature person, are you?"

"Take the girl out of the city . . ."

He laughed again, and I wondered what it would be like to kiss him. To feel his mouth curve up beneath mine.

"Why did you choose Boulder of all places for school?" he asked. "Don't get me wrong, I'm glad you did, but . . ."

"I know." I nudged a rock with my toe. "I just—I wanted something different."

"Than Boston?"

"Than me."

He turned, then, so our faces were almost touching. I could see the fire reflecting in the corner of his eyes. And I was embarrassed by my honesty, but also something else: the smallest bit exhilarated. Because honesty had never felt this easy. Because I had never felt more sure that I could say the truth and he wouldn't leave.

"Why did you choose Boulder?" I asked.

"I got a scholarship," he said simply. "Covered more than half of the tuition."

"You must be smart."

He shrugged. "I have a plan." He said the words easily, but he couldn't quite mask the strength of his drive. Of his ambition.

"Why do you want to be different?" he said, shifting so our knees bumped together.

"I don't know," I said. I thought about Meredith, always worrying, and about my father, who never did. "I want to be . . . the kind of girl who can handle her own canoe. Who people don't assume needs help. Someone who takes up space. I just want to be more, I guess. I don't know. It probably sounds pretty silly to you."

"It doesn't," he said. He looked at me, really looked at me. "I don't think you are silly. I think you are . . ." he hesitated.

"Embarrassingly insecure?" I quipped.

"I was going to say brave."

"Because I want to be someone else?"

"Because you don't mind admitting that there are things you'd like to change."

I wanted to touch him then. I wanted to grab his hand, to pull him closer, to eliminate the small space between us. But I couldn't move. I was held in place by his eyes, by the way they took me in.

"Do you think it will work?" he said. "Coming here?"

I shook my head. "Honestly, no." A smile tugged at my lip. "I think I flew a couple thousand miles to find out that change is not that easy. That maybe I just am the way I am."

"I see," he said.

And then, he reached out and tucked a strand of hair behind my ear. Like it was the easiest thing in the world. Like it was a habit he'd just needed to start. "Not that it's any consolation," he said, "but I like you just the way you are."

Nathan wouldn't kiss me until the next day. We wouldn't give ourselves a label for another month. But right then, sitting on that log, his long fingers against my cheek, his eyes holding mine, it felt like the start of everything.

I send Nathan a training schedule for Remy. Three nights a week plus Saturday afternoons. Lois agrees to lend us her backyard for training so we can practice without a leash or muzzle, and when I get to her house on Tuesday, she corners me in her kitchen. Her blue eyes are wide and eager.

"So, who is this young man? When I spoke to him on the phone, he said he used to know you."

I pause, then decide the truth will come out eventually. "His name is Nathan." I steel myself for her enthusiasm. "He was my college boyfriend."

Lois blinks, and then a smile spills across her face. "Oh my, *yes*," she says. "Yes, I remember him. Or hearing about him." She's practically bouncing. "Whatever happened with you two?"

"He moved away. We didn't make it."

Lois narrows her eyes at my blasé tone, but I just shrug. She eyes me more closely, then touches my shoulder with her hand. The bouncing stops.

"Are you okay, Alex?"

"Yes," I say carefully, trying to follow her change in manner.

"Listen, sweetheart." She pauses, and I feel myself stiffen. My shoulders hiking up. "Meredith told me about your mother's death. I'm deeply sorry."

There they are. The words I don't want to hear and I don't even deserve. If anyone deserves sympathy, it's Lois. She was Tessa's friend for over two decades. She probably knew her better than I did.

I consider mentioning this, but don't.

The doorbell rings, and I give Lois an apologetic smile, then push gently past her toward the door. But I'm still thinking about Tessa, about how I don't want to think about her at all. I don't know if I'm supposed to mourn her, this woman who was my mother. (*Is* my mother? The tenses get weird with death.) And I'm so busy thinking about this that I forget to prepare for him. For Nathan. And then, he's standing in Lois's door, smiling down at me, a white shirt peeking out from under his half-zip blue-gray sweater. The sweater matches his eyes.

And this is what I notice. His eyes first. His eyes before everything else. His eyes, and not because of the color, but because of how I still feel when they're on me. Like I am being seen.

"Hi," I say. My voice sounds hoarse, and I bite my lip.

"Hey, there."

He steps closer, and I smell cinnamon again. Nathan used to love Big Red gum. I'd find the wrappers everywhere—in the pockets of his sweatshirts, on the floor under my bed. These little reminders of him that made me laugh right up until they didn't.

"You must be Nathan," says Lois from behind me, and I pull my eyes away from his.

"Yes, ma'am," he says, holding out his hand to Lois, who shakes it looking utterly charmed. "Thank you for all your help," he says. "You've really gone out of your way, letting us train here, and connecting me with Alex . . ."

"Alex is a very special girl," says Lois.

"I couldn't agree more," says Nathan.

I force myself to roll my eyes. To make all of this a joke. Because it has to be a joke. Because I can't be feeling these things again. I'm not that girl anymore. I'm not a romantic.

And I don't make the same mistakes twice.

And also—I might be a ticking time bomb. And I can't do that to him.

I thank Lois for her help, then direct Nathan on how to bring Remy around back. Like before, I'll wait for her in the middle of the grass. I'll let her come to me. This time, though, I tell Nathan to drop the leash and leave off the muzzle.

"Are you sure?" he asks.

I'm already walking away from him, but I stop and turn around. "She's scared," I say. "She's not going to attack me unless I come at her."

"How do you know that, though?" he asks. "How can you be sure?"

Because I am. Because I've worked with dogs like Remy before. Dogs called "aggressive." Dogs who bark at strangers on the street. Who lunge at children and anything on wheels. Angry growls and snapping leashes.

Aggressive. Dangerous.

Scared.

Scared first. That's the part that no one sees: how reactivity usually stems from fear—because they were too sheltered as a puppy, or because of their genetics, or just the dog's general disposition. They're scared.

And they bark and growl and lunge because they're telling you not to get too close. They're telling you that they are scared and to, please, stay away.

In a way, arguably, they are doing you both a favor.

I know all of this. I do, and so, I understand Remy. But I'm not sure Nathan ever will. He's never been built for it—understanding fear.

"Just trust me," I say. I hold his eyes with mine. "Please."

There's a pause, and then he gives me one stiff nod before walking back to his car. And again, I sit in damp grass and wait until I hear her running toward me. This time, I'm prepared for the bark, and this time, she stops sooner.

I was right to keep her off the leash. She feels safer knowing she can get away.

"You want an exit strategy, huh," I say. "I think that's pretty fair."

She's running around the fence line, but at my voice, she pauses and fixes me with a look. Her gaze is cool and assessing. There's something regal about her, not just the eyes, but the way she lifts her chin, the heft of her tail. Even her posture.

"Remy queen," I say. She takes a step toward me, then stops.

"You're not sure about me, hmm? You're not sure about any of us."

She shifts her weight. And she's a dog, so, of course, she cannot speak. But I get the feeling that she wouldn't say anything even if she could. I get the feeling that it's still my turn. Still my job to convince her.

Because she's the one who was left. She's the one who had to teach herself to be strong. And look at her; she did it. She's beautiful.

"It's okay, Remy queen. I'll wait."

She stares at me, those eyes scanning my face, while I sit quietly in the grass. And then, she wags her tail. One wag. Like it's a gift.

Which, of course, it is.

"She likes you," says Nathan. We're standing in Lois's driveway. He's so much taller than me; his shoulders block the sun setting behind him.

"We're making progress," I say.

"I've never seen her like this with anyone. Not even me."

I don't like the way he's studying me, like I have some secret talent, when I haven't really done much of anything at all.

"It's just about being patient. And that's probably easier for me."

"Why?"

I shrug. "Because I don't have any expectations. She's not my dog."

Nathan considers this. "You know, when I went to the shelter, I had this idea in my head about the dog I'd bring home. A boy. He'd have a silly streak but also be well trained, the kind of dog I can take on walks without a leash. And kind of ugly, too, but with some redeeming feature, like a funny spot on his nose, a crooked ear. I had it all in my head . . ."

"And then you saw Remy."

Nathan gives me his half smile. "And then I saw Remy. She was sitting in her cage, just quietly watching me. Back straight. Those eyes. I could tell she didn't expect me to stop. It was like she saw me and dismissed me. Like she thought, *There goes another basic guy looking for another basic dog.*"

My mouth twitches. "And here I was, thinking you took her home to save her. But it was really to prove you are not basic."

He lifts his shoulders in mock defeat. "You know, sometimes, I see golden retrievers at the dog park or just walking around the city, and everyone is always smiling at them, petting them, letting their kids 'meet their first dog.'" He rolls his eyes. "I watch them and I think—"

"Show-offs," I jump in.

There's a pause, and then he starts to laugh. And it's exactly like I remember. A little slow to start, a little stilted, but then it tumbles into the real thing. Like he can't help himself.

"Yes," he says, his eyes glinting. "Yes, that is *exactly* what I think."

We're both laughing, and I feel lighter than I have all week. All year, maybe. The sun has almost set, and Nathan's face is steeped in shadows, so that everything is blurred. And maybe that's what makes all of this easier: the laughter, the undeniable energy between us. Our ability to forget our history, not just how we ended but why we will never work.

And then Lois's driveway light flicks on, and our eyes catch in the sudden light. Blue on green. And before I can step back, he does the opposite, closing the distance between us in two long steps. He's so close, the hairs on my forearms rise up to meet him. Static electricity.

"Come have dinner with me."

"No."

He cocks his head. "Not even going to make up an excuse there?"

"I thought we didn't lie to each other." My voice comes out as a whisper, and the whole mood changes in an instant. He leans in closer. There's no more laughter now. There's everything else, instead.

"We don't," he says.

He reaches out and grabs my hand. And it only lasts a second—just the briefest moment, the pressure of his fingers around mine—but then, it's a memory of another second, on another day. The very first beginning of a beginning. And there's a band tightening just below my chest, and my heart and lungs seem, suddenly, in danger of exploding.

"Do you remember three-penny hockey?" he asks.

A scratched wooden table. His pinkie finger, two freckles on his left hand. We used to play together when we first started dating. One evening after the next, sitting at an old coffee shop that doubled as a secondhand bookstore. Shelves and shelves of paperbacks behind us. Pennies, pinging back and forth. Us talking. My eyes on the table and then back up to his face, and all that talking. I used to think he knew me better than anyone.

I fell in love with Nathan over pennies. I still think of him when I see one on the ground. Every single time. Every single penny.

It's been seven years.

"Alex?" he prompts, and I step back. The cool night air fills up the space between us.

"I remember a lot of things," I say.

I remember everything. From the day we met, to the day he left Boulder, to the day he called me and told me he wasn't coming back.

My list flashes through my mind.

Be open to a new relationship.

But it wasn't supposed to be with him. Because I want to feel something real, but our history is already too heavy. Because someone as sure as Nathan should not be with someone as lost as me.

Because I might be dying.

I might be dying, and despite everything, he is the last person I want to hurt.

I might be dying, and he is the person who will most easily hurt me.

And still. And still. And still. I cannot shake this feeling. Half-formed hopes that I shouldn't allow to spread.

"What do you want, Nathan?"

He shifts at my tone. At the directness of my question. He's not used to that from me. "I want to talk to you. To find out how you are doing." He drags one hand through his hair, the gesture oddly stiff. "I'd like to be friends."

Friends.

Rejection washes over me like ice water.

"Why, though, what's the point?" I can't keep the frustration out of my voice. But I can't do what he's asking, and suddenly, I want him to admit that he can't, either. "We're not friends. We never really were, and even now"—I gesture between us—"can you honestly tell me this feels like friends right now?"

There's a pause that lengthens. I can still feel where his hand touched mine. The outline of his fingers.

“Of course it doesn’t,” he says at last. “It’s you and me, Alex. Of course, it doesn’t feel like friends.” The distance in his voice resets. “You’re right; that’s never what we were.”

I nod as if I’m satisfied, as if being right is what matters. But something cracks inside my chest—the whole thing splitting open. Because it’s all between us now: our whole story. How we once thought that we were epic. How it turned out we were wrong.

“I have to go,” I say.

And this time, when I walk past him, he doesn’t stop me.

Chapter 6

Reactive dogs—dogs like Remy—they're the hardest to train. The best way is through slow and positive exposure to the things that scare them. Sit twenty feet from a bike path and give the dog treats when strangers walk by. Go every day, and day by day, get a little closer. Move back if the dog gets at all nervous. Stop and start again. It's painstakingly slow work. It's one step forward, two steps back. It's stressful and overwhelming—your dog barking, people staring, you feeling like a failure. And it's almost never a complete fix; typically, the dog will always need extra training, extra precautions.

And because it is so very hard, and because it can feel hopeless (and sometimes it is), people often give up. They give up; they choose avoidance, and their dog's world gets so small. They miss so much.

I'm not saying all of this with any judgment. I've worked with people who have eventually given up; I know they love their dogs. I know how hard they tried. And I know that, sometimes, avoidance really is the only and best option left.

No, I don't say any of this from judgment. I say it because I get it. I get the relief of sitting in your living room with your dog and feeling, finally, finally, relaxed and happy. Feeling safe. I get wondering, why should we go outside? Why should we go face these things that lead to nothing but stress? Why should we put either of us through all this pain?

I understand how intoxicating it can be: to build a life in a bubble, to ignore everything outside of it, to believe that this is how you can make sure everything turns out okay—not just for you, but for whoever you love, for whoever you are trying to protect.

For the rest of the week, Nathan and I are painstakingly professional. We talk about Remy's city council date, which is scheduled for November 28. I'll testify on her behalf, but we'll need Remy's veterinarian on our side, with documented improvement, and, ideally, her own testimony. I explain all of this to Nathan while we stand on opposite sides of Lois's fence. I tell him this is Remy's best shot. Which is true.

What I don't say is that this is her only shot.

Even if Remy improves. Even if her veterinarian agrees to help. Even if we jump through every hoop, we don't know how the hearing will go. If they rule to euthanize her, there's nothing we can do.

Remy watches me with her soft topaz eyes, and I get the feeling that somehow she knows. That she knows what's at stake, and still, she doesn't bend. She's nervous—unsure of us, unsure of her environment—but she's not unsure of herself. She won't be rushed into giving up her ground. And as scared as I am for her, I find her attitude kind of admirable.

Sometimes, when I'm watching her, I catch Nathan watching me. I feel his gaze against my back, against my hair, an intensity that makes my insides twist. But he doesn't ask me to grab dinner again. And he doesn't joke around. Other than those moments—the heat of his gaze, strong enough that there are nights I cannot fall asleep—he acts like any other client. Which confirms that he has, in fact, moved on. That the spark between us is a memory that we shouldn't try to reignite.

I tell myself this is a good thing. I remind myself of my list, of my plan for independence and the reason I added *a new relationship* in the first place. A fresh start. A fresh me.

And time.

The following Friday, Holly texts me to come out with her for her boyfriend's birthday. She mentions one of James's friends is single, and I send a laughing emoji back. I haven't seen her all week, and I feel a pang of guilt about all the things I haven't told her.

Nathan. My mom. Remy and the business.

HD, and how my body might be on a fast track toward destruction.

I freeze. I'm standing in my bathroom, my hand holding a mascara wand, and I'm frozen. I'm trying to understand when I started using the acronym from Mere's emails—Huntington's disease, HD—like I'm someone who can match her calm, like this has become normal enough for abbreviations. I'm trying to remember, and then, without warning, I'm crouched on the cold tiles of my bathroom: my elbows on the toilet bowl, my forehead sticking to my hands, beads of sweat running down my face and dripping, with this horrible pinging noise, into the water below.

Eventually, I push myself off my knees. I wash my face, and I reapply my makeup. I empty my mind, and dress carefully. Short black dress, bright-blue suede heels, my hair in red waves all down my back. I meet my eyes in the mirror, and I nod.

I am good. I am perfectly fine.

But when the Uber drops me at the bar, I catch my reflection in the window as I get out, and I stop. I'm suspended on the street, my hand clenched against the thin fabric of my dress, my eyes locked on my reflection. Because it feels fake, somehow, like false advertising, pretending this body will hold up. And for a moment, I am stuck there, on the street, the crush of the city on a Friday night holding me in its fist, but then the Uber is gone. It's gone, and there's another car in its place, beeping at me, this crazy woman standing in the middle of the street.

I let go of the dress.

And I'm walking now, hardly aware of my feet following one another, pushing toward Murphy's. Toward a half-formed solution that crystalizes into a name.

Holly. I want to tell Holly.

I want to tell her everything. It doesn't matter that we've barely seen each other lately, or that I can't remember our last real conversation. She's still the only person I can tell. The only person I can imagine saying the words to. *Huntington's disease.* Because she's seen everything else; *we've* seen everything else. Holly and I are each other's twenties—the pain and shame of breakups and lost credit cards and too many hangovers to count. She held me after Nathan left, and again after it ended. She knows I didn't judge her when she dated the married man, or when she got sloppy drunk at one of our college roommate's weddings. Because we don't judge each other. We never have.

She's my best friend. And whatever else has happened, I need her one more time.

Murphy's is crowded and loud in that way Faneuil Hall spots always are. The floor is already sticky with spilled beer, and there's a band pushed up against the back corner playing something poppy. I hear a roar of laughter and find Holly, sparkling in a shockingly purple jumpsuit, blond hair piled on top of her head. Even from here, I can feel her energy—boundless, spilling all over the room.

Back before Holly quit DogKind, we used to have weekly meetings. Weekly sessions in front of her whiteboard, mapping out revenue goals and projections, a bottle of wine between us. It always amazed me how she did it. Sketched out our future in blue and green markers, somehow making it possible.

She catches my eye across the room and smiles, but she must see it on my face because she puts down her drink and elbows her way toward me.

"Are you okay?" she asks, her blue eyes wide and worried, one hand half reaching toward me.

"No, I—"

But James is coming up behind her. And I remember, suddenly, that it's his birthday. That we are supposed to be celebrating. And I see her glance at him and back at me, trying to assess, to decide, and I look away, embarrassed. Because what am I doing? I've known about this for days, and I'm choosing to cause a scene now? To be that kind of asshole?

"I'm fine," I say. "I'm sorry."

"No, come on," she says, even as James throws an arm around her shoulders. "We can run to the bathroom."

"No, really." I force a smile. "Someone slammed into me when I got inside, and I'm tired. Complete overreaction. Ignore me."

It's a lame excuse, and she doesn't buy it. But I feel dramatic and uncomfortable, so I wave at the bartender and order a round of shots for James's birthday, and he takes his, and then kisses Holly—long and slow. And by the time they come up for air, I've managed to make my smile convincing. I down my own shot, and let the whiskey burn through me, trading the shame for a cold clarity: I just need to get through this night.

James introduces me to the promised single friend, a guy named Kyle, who does something with city planning, and has a doughy face. *Be open to a new relationship.* I sip my drink and try to pay attention while he talks about permits and building codes and the bastards on the city council. He laughs after almost every sentence, and he keeps leaning in too closely, so I can feel his hot breath on my cheek, so I can smell, not just the breath mint he's popped, but a hint at whatever it's hiding. I wonder what made Holly think that I would like him, that he is my type.

When he touches the small of my back, two fingers above what would qualify as groping, my stomach rolls. It takes another ten minutes to beg off and make it to the other side of the dance floor. I hide against a window, the cold draft a welcome breath across my skin. Holly and James sway in a half embrace on the dance floor.

The night ambles along in a haze of music and low lighting and laughter mixing with the ever-present tinkle of glass on glass. When I realize that Holly and James left—that she left without saying goodbye—the air momentarily constricts. But I press the feeling down, because at least this means that I am free to go, that I made it through this ill-advised evening.

I push outside, already picturing my bed, and I'm five steps from the door when a passing car swears at a biker and the biker swears right back. And then, that same biker yells at me, risking the Boston streets to point at the ground in front of me. "You dropped something," he calls, and I look down, and there's my wallet. Lying in the street.

I pick it up, staring at the black leather clenched in my hand, and then I start to laugh. The cold evening air washing over me, and my melancholy switching to relief. Because this is why I love this city: rough, unfiltered. Honesty that still makes room for kindness. An undeniable toughness. You almost believe it will rub off on you.

When I left Boston, I always knew I would come back here. I needed space; I needed time. But of all the things I am unsure of, I have always been certain of this city. And as I walk through the busy streets, the bright lights flashing against the dark sky, my body still bothering to do what it's supposed to, this small truth warms me. I breathe in and out and go through the same three points I've gone through again and again since I last saw Meredith. *I don't need to think about HD right now. I might not even have it. And who knows what treatments might exist in another couple of decades.*

I take the red line from State Street and then get out a few stops early because I don't feel like being underground. I want cold air on my cheeks, again. I want angry bikers and beeping cars.

I walk almost a mile along Broadway, before cutting onto the side streets toward my apartment, but when I turn onto my block, I stop short. Because there is someone sitting on my front stoop. Tall and long and lean. Slightly floppy hair, always the only relaxed thing about him.

Nathan.

My heart is thumping, a racehorse galloping in my chest. I make myself walk slowly toward my apartment. When he doesn't say anything, I climb the steps and sit down beside him. The wind rustles the leaves in the tree outside my building. Its colors are just starting to turn.

"I'm not sure I ever caught up," he says into the quiet night. Like we're continuing a conversation. "After I took that semester off, I always felt rushed. Always felt behind. And sometimes . . ." He shakes his head and lets out a gust of air. "Sometimes, I blame her."

I lean back. I know what he is doing. It's one of our things. To always tell each other the truths that most people don't want to see.

For Nathan, unloading was a rare relief. He learned as a kid to keep a tight lid on his emotions.

For me, it was terrifying. But I tried to do it. I tried for him.

"My mom died," I say. "It's been almost a week since I found out."

"Alex—"

"No," I cut him off. "Wait." I press my fingers into the wood stairs beneath me. "I don't think I'm even sad."

A leaf falls from the tree above me. And it's dangerous, this conversation. Our bodies this close together. The temporality attached to this time of night. No filter needed because somehow nothing feels like it will count. I know it's dangerous, but I don't care. Sitting here, I miss him so much it hurts. I miss him enough that even one more conversation is worth whatever pain will come next.

"She's sick again," he says. "It came back. Again. We found out two months ago. I lied to you before."

I turn toward him. "Why?" I ask. "Why did you lie?" It's not what matters. I know it's not what matters. Except . . . it's not like him to lie. And without warning, I am worried about him. I'm worried in a way that I haven't been for years.

He shakes his head, though, ignoring my question. "That's why I'm back here. I've been living in DC, but she got sick, and I didn't want to be so far away, so I came back. My life is now a bit of a mess, actually. I still haven't even unpacked. I had to switch law firms—"

"You're a lawyer?" I break in. It was always Nathan's plan. He's always been openly ambitious. Certain about the kind of life he wanted, and willing to do whatever it took to get it. It wasn't about status, though. It was about security. It was always about security for Nathan.

He didn't grow up with a lot of money—his parents seemed to have a good enough relationship but they'd argue about finances, and when his mom got sick, they struggled. His dad, Aaron, was gone all the time, taking extra shifts to keep up with the medical bills. And I know the whole situation weighed on Nathan. He didn't want that for himself. He wanted a job that guaranteed financial stability. I remember him telling me that we wouldn't have to worry. That our kids wouldn't have to hear us fight. He made it seem possible: to plan enough to keep out pain.

He nods. "I was on track for partner. But now . . . I'm starting—not over, but a couple of years behind where I was. I'm behind, again. And I'm angry. I'm angry a lot of the time."

He shakes his head, calmly disgusted, his eyes on the empty street. "It's a shit thing to feel. I'm not even the one who's sick."

"Yeah, well, that's the trick, I think," I say. "Find a way to choose your feelings."

The bitterness in my voice punctures the air, and I want to take the words back. Because of all the things I used to be, bitter wasn't one of them. And now he's looking at me. Really looking at me. And it's my turn to tell him something more. Something true. It's my turn. I think of the pamphlets in my desk drawer and an acronym I've come to hate and the memory of me hunched against the toilet. Cold sweat.

I start to open my mouth. I really do. But then he moves. He moves toward me, and the words dry up somewhere below my throat.

He reaches out and touches my face. Three fingers just below my cheekbone. And he's so close, I can smell him: plain bar soap, shaving cream, and cinnamon. I'm afraid to consider why he's here. I'm afraid to consider what I might want it to mean. *Friends, he said friends.* And that's for the best. It's better that way.

But his fingers don't leave my face.

"I miss this," he murmurs. "Ten minutes just to be shitty. To not try to make someone else comfortable. Just admit the level of shitty I've reached these days."

I am not sure that it's a good thing: that I am his safe space for what is horrible. I always thought he made me better, but I wonder what this means that I make him.

"Is she going to be okay?" I ask.

"I don't know." He closes his eyes, then opens them. "She wasn't supposed to get better the other times."

I study him in the shadows. I take in the dark circles under his eyes. The five o'clock shadow on his cheeks.

"You can't be everything for everyone," I say softly.

"I know that."

But you're still going to try.

The blue of his eyes is darker than usual. Stormy skies.

"I've been trying to convince myself I was over you," he says suddenly. So suddenly that I don't see the words coming. I am not ready for how they tighten around my heart. "I thought I'd moved on," he says. "Which is illogical, really, because I loved you from almost our very first conversation. Right from the start, I thought you were the sweetest, most sincere girl I'd ever met. Brutal, even. These adjectives that I never would have thought to put together until I met you."

"Nathan—" I try, but he keeps going.

"I spent years trying to forget that, to forget you. To pretend that what we had was not actually rare. But then, I saw that video . . ." He shakes his head and gives a bitter laugh. "I saw you with that dog, doing what you always do: believing in everyone but yourself. And I was angry at you all over again, which is how I knew I had to come here. Because as it turns out, I'm not over any of it.

"Alex, I can't see you and not want to tell you every good and shitty thing that has happened. You are still the person I want to tell."

His words are naked honesty, and I shiver. Goose bumps all over my arms and legs.

This cannot happen. *I cannot let this happen.*

"It's been years," I say. The control in my voice does not match how I feel. "We might not—we don't even really know each other anymore."

His eyes search my face. “Do you really believe that?”

No. No, I don’t.

That’s the thing about endings that were never really endings. When the person comes back, it’s like they never left.

I’m shaking my head, though, leaning away, my body ahead of my brain. Because it doesn’t matter what we feel. Not really. This is wrong for a thousand reasons. Nathan moves too quickly; he always has. And he’s missing the risk here. Not just for me, but for him.

I had a plan. I had a list. I had an idea of how I would be.

I don’t know how to be that person with him.

“What happened to us, Alex?” he asks. And the question unlocks something in my chest. A well of anger and pain, so sharp it freezes every other thought. Because his question is not fair. Because he’s the one who left. He’s the one who left and never came back. He’s the reason I cannot breathe—not just tonight, but every single time I see a penny.

So, I stand up, breaking the moment while searching for air. But he stands with me, and he’s too close, and I make the mistake of lifting my head, tilting my chin back, so our eyes end up locked together. And every good intention falls away.

I don’t know who leans in first. All I know is that when his lips press against mine, I forget everything I’m scared of. I forget everything but this.

One of his hands is in my hair, the other tightens around my waist.

We are still standing on my stoop. I find myself thinking, *We are a relationship built on stoops*, and I almost laugh. I almost tell him because I know he would laugh, too.

But he’s pressing me up against the door now, and I forget what was funny. My hand is on his cheek, on the rough shadow of his cheekbone. And it’s time to open the door, but I don’t want to go in my apartment.

I don't want him in my bedroom, where there are pamphlets in a desk drawer. Where there are not yet memories of him.

I tell him that my place is a shoebox. I tell him Holly has something planned with James. Half truths and half lies, depending on how you look at it, but I'm not sure he's even listening. His eyes are all over me.

We take an Uber to his apartment, and I feel bad for the driver. We are not polite. We are not making a movie, but we are not polite. I make a mental note to ask Nathan to add an extra tip, and then, the Uber has stopped in front of Nathan's building, and we get out, and his hand finds mine and we are nearly running up the path, and just before we get to the door, I realize that the building overlooks the statehouse. And I inhale. Because we've come back to where my night started. The bar—Murphy's—and maybe even Kyle are just a few blocks east. But they feel like another night entirely. Almost another world.

I let out the breath; I focus on the feel of his hand against mine.

Almost as soon as we're through his door, he pulls my dress up and off me. That confidence. And then, there's something else: the way he pauses. The way he pauses and looks at me, like he's seeing something in me that I don't recognize. Something beautiful.

I shiver and lift my chin. In all the things I remember, I forgot about this part. The *feeling* naked part. The intimacy that has nothing to do with the dress on the ground between us. I get to him before he gets to me, cinching my leg around him so he's forced to hold me, to pick me up and press my body to the kitchen wall. The plaster is cold and hard against my bare back, but I don't care. I lean into the roughness.

Remy's in his bedroom, but that doesn't matter. We wouldn't make it there, anyway.

I gasp and grip his shoulders.

These weeks have been anesthesia. An emptiness I've refused to name.

But this.

This is everything.

Chapter 7

"Stay the night."

I'm sitting on the ground, wrapped in a throw I pulled off his couch. Moonlight trickles across the wooden beams of his apartment. It's a large one-bedroom, with a nearly floor-to-ceiling window in the back, long, dark curtains pushed aside to let in the night. Everything is gray or white or black. Unpacked boxes line the wall.

"What are you looking for?" Nathan's watching me curiously.

"Even just a little color."

"Let me guess, your apartment is full of colors."

I think about the owls. "My apartment would hurt your eyes."

He laughs. And I want to close my eyes and listen. To pretend for one more minute that our worlds never got this far apart. To pretend that something that feels this good can be fair to keep.

"Stay the night," he says again.

I pull my knees up to my chest. My dress is still on the ground by the door.

"Why?"

When his eyes meet mine, they're serious. "Because I don't want you to leave."

Later, I'll think about those words. About him asking me to stay because he didn't want me to leave. As opposed to him wanting me to stay. Later, I'll wonder if his words were a warning. Not about what we were doing, but about what we both could stand.

Nathan's living room seems different in the pale-gray light of dawn. I notice things I didn't notice last night. Like the half-unpacked suitcases in the corner, or the framed photo peeking out of one: half of Nathan and a woman who looks about my age. My eyes scan the unadorned walls, empty, every one, except the one behind the couch where we slept, tangled together. This wall is devoted to a built-in bookcase. I lean forward and turn around, taking in the four shelves stacked one on top of the other, each one completely full. Heavy tomes that I'm guessing are from law school are squeezed in the corner of one shelf, but otherwise, the books seem like a completely random assortment, this wonderful, haphazard collection, so out of place with everything else in his bare, almost spartan apartment. *To Kill a Mockingbird* next to a collection of Jane Austen, all seven Harry Potters beside a book I recognize from Oprah's Book Club list. American classics, fantasy hits, recent bestsellers, and tens more I've never heard of—all here, all right above our heads this whole time. All these great adventures, just an arm's reach away.

Nathan shifts beside me, and I freeze, my hand halfway to *East of Eden*.

Last night was perfect. Like every memory I had, but set on fire. How our bodies, so mismatched in size, so easily seemed to fit together. How he held me when it was over, and then until I fell asleep. The way he said my name, not during the sex, but after. After there was no reason to pretend.

Nathan Browning. The boy in the canoe. It was years. It took me years to feel like something near myself again.

I feel him shift beside me and I stiffen. I need to leave.

Last night was perfect, but I am not an idiot. There's a secret between us—dark and muddy and all mine—and he is not the person to tell. Because there is no point. Because the only ending is pain. Because with or without HD, we don't work. A fact evidenced by how, even now, I don't know what Nathan wants. A week ago, it was friends, but now I'm naked on his couch; and then, there's the reality that his actual life is in DC, and I can't leave Boston. And it's all just a little too familiar. Him making grand, sweeping statements that ignore the practicalities; him only focusing on feelings instead of the facts.

All of it, a reminder of what I already knew: how dangerous it is to feel this much, especially with him.

In college, our friends used to be jealous of us, how instinctively we navigated around each other. How even the way we organized our bodies accounted for the other.

But the part they missed was how untenable, how dangerous that kind of love is. How irresponsible it is to let your happiness rely so much on one other person. And I should have known better. I saw how my dad was after my mother left. I saw how the soulmate story can end, and I knew it wasn't pretty. And still, I fell in love with Nathan.

I fell in love, and then, I fell apart.

"Thinking about sneaking out?" His voice is low. Throaty. There's a new roughness to him that wasn't there when we were in college.

And I like it—I *more* than like it—but it's different. And I wonder if that's a sign. If I want it to be a sign.

"I wish you wouldn't do that." He's sitting up beside me now. One hand covering my whole knee. My entire body shifts toward him, like a magnet.

"Do what?" I ask.

"Worry about what comes next."

I try a smile, but it's shaky.

"Alex, whatever you're worried about, we'll figure it out," he says.

He's not being dismissive, he's being Nathan. Certain. No explanation needed. But I've never been great with blind trust. And I can't do it again: leap without a net. Especially not now.

I turn around. I force out the words I should have said last night.

"This won't work. You and me and whatever we are doing . . . it's a bad idea. And it won't work."

"Why not?"

Because I want to do things differently. Because I'm trying to go forward. Because I might be sick and you don't even know.

I stare at him, at his steady gray-blue eyes. He looks even more tired today. More tired, but also happy. Even now, even with me saying what I'm saying, he looks happy, just sitting next to me.

I drop my eyes to his hands. "Because you didn't come back."

When Nathan moved from Boulder back to Boston, he mapped out a plan. He'd fly out for a long weekend in October. I'd go back to Boston for Thanksgiving. We'd talk on the phone almost every day. He'd take some courses at one of the local universities—it wasn't as if Boston had a shortage—and then, a year later, his mom would be in remission. And we'd be back in school together. He didn't entertain any other option.

I cried the night he left, but I told myself we'd be okay. Because he was doing the right thing. And because I loved Sue, too. I wanted her to have Nathan. And so, I tried to ignore the small but persistent voice in the back of my head. The one that reminded me that love rarely lasts even if you are in the same house. That the odds had been stacked against us, even when we were together. And that while maybe Nathan could do it, that was because he was often described with words like *dependable* and *determined*—words that not a single person would use to describe me.

At first, it went okay, though. Even better than planned. Halfway through the fall semester, Sue went into remission, and Nathan started talking about coming back to Boulder that spring. At night, I'd lie in my bed under the pale-green comforter Meredith had bought me, and I'd stare at the calendar app on my phone. I was obsessed with the idea of February.

But then Nathan got invited to participate in a special policy seminar at Boston University in the spring. He'd taken a couple of courses there during the fall, and had been informally adopted by a law professor with connections at firms all over Boston. The seminar was a big deal, and we both agreed that Nathan had to stay. It was just one more semester.

But still. I stopped looking at the calendar on my phone. I think, maybe, I knew right then what was coming.

By February, I could feel it, the distance growing between us. I started to worry he wasn't coming back, and we started to argue more and more. Always about stupid things: missed phone calls and Facebook photos posted of him with people I didn't recognize. Never about the truth. Never about how much I needed him to come back. How much I needed a plan. A timeline.

But Nathan was busy; he was building a life in Boston—which belonged to each of us separately, but had never been ours together—and I was still in Boulder, where everything reminded me of him. I was surrounded by Nathan's ghost, and even if I wanted to be independent, it didn't feel like I could.

When he called to tell me that he wanted to finish school at BU—that he was applying to transfer all his credits there—I was standing in my apartment, the one I'd expected to share with him the next year. I felt myself sink down onto the cool tile in the kitchen. I pressed my fingers into the black divots, as Nathan talked and talked. As he explained how this was better for both of us. How we'd always planned to settle in Boston, and Professor Rodriguez could help him. Help us.

I put the phone on speaker, lay back onto the tile, and let his words wash over my head.

"Alex," he said. "This doesn't change anything. I love you."

I knew that. The same way I knew that if I told him to come back, he would.

But I wanted him to miss me. And it didn't feel like he did.

Nathan talked, and I lay on the floor of that kitchen that I'd never used in the apartment that would never be ours. The one I'd only picked because of the kitchen in the first place. Because Nathan loved to cook. I lay there, and I stared wide-eyed at the ceiling, and I pictured another fifteen months of missing him. Fifteen more months of wondering what he was thinking, of worrying about what he hadn't said, of trying to figure out the formula for staying close to someone who was two thousand miles away.

Fifteen more months and then what? There was law school and both of our careers. There were so many pieces of our lives left unaccounted for. Nathan talked about the future, but he never dug into what came in between. And in the back of my mind, quiet but persistent, was the voice that asked why he was staying with me. Whether it was because he wanted to, or because he'd once told me that he would. Whether he even knew the difference.

Whether, in fact, I'd always loved him more than he loved me.

I lay there as silent tears slipped out of my eyes and down into my ears and onto the tiles. And I knew I couldn't do it. I couldn't keep feeling like this.

Nathan's staring at me, his hand still heavy on my knee. I wonder what he remembers. And not for the first time, I wonder if he wishes he had fallen for someone else. For someone who was a little more like him.

I wanted to become that kind of person. I'm trying to become her: tougher, stronger, a little more resilient.

"I left," he says. "But I wouldn't have ended things."

"I know that," I say. "I know that was me. But it wasn't working. It wasn't working for me." I hesitate. "And I don't understand how it was working for you."

He gives me a look. "It wasn't perfect, fine. But I loved you."

"But you didn't come back."

His eyes bore into mine. "I know."

"And it's not like you ever—" The embarrassing words come out sticky. "It's not like you asked me to come with you."

"I didn't want to take you away from your college, from your friends. And I knew we'd be okay. I never doubted us, Alex."

He glances toward the window, but I think I see frustration before he turns. And I know what he is thinking: that it's the same old argument. The one that always lingered under the surface—me thinking he should want to come back, him thinking it didn't matter when we had our whole lives to be together. But I never understood that line of thinking. I never understood how he could be okay staying away. How the constant ache of missing us only seemed to affect me. What was it about me that was so easy to put to the side?

I used to ask myself that question all the time. I used to think, if I understood the answer, then maybe I could fix it. Whatever part of me was wrong.

I stare down at Nathan's hand, ignoring the heat rising in my cheeks. I don't want to ask that question anymore. I don't want to be that girl.

And I should walk away, except I can't. I can't move his hand from my knee. I can't forget last night. I can't go back to life where every romantic movie makes me think of him.

I don't want to.

I just want to do things differently.

The truth of this filters through my veins, cooling my cheeks, slowing my breathing. I take a steadying breath—in through my nose and out through my mouth, one, two, and so on—and I think about relationships. The ones that fizzle and the ones that linger more than they last, and reality rises up, two fingers snapping in my face.

This feeling, right now: no one gets to keep it for eighty years.

I couldn't admit that seven years ago. But now, I think I'm ready. To be okay with it not being forever. To accept that everything has an expiration date.

To risk breaking my own heart again, but find a way to do it cleaner.

He turns back to me, and his expression sharpens. He reaches out, one hand gently pushing my chin up, so I can see his face.

"This thing between us . . . it's still here," he says. "But I don't want to make the same mistakes. And I am telling you right now that I am different."

I am not.

But maybe I can be.

His hand moves from my chin to cup my face. "We don't have to figure out everything at once," he says. "So just tell me, what do you need to know right now?"

That this doesn't mean more to me than it does to you.

I bite back the words. I bite back all of it. I kiss him instead. I kiss him, because I want to see if I can do it. If I can be here, with him. Even if just for one minute.

One minute.

His mouth is already familiar. All of him, familiar, his chest pressed against my chest, our bodies automatically getting rid of any space, the weight of his hands on my shoulders, real and firm and sure.

And it is everything.

It is something.

It is something to remember even if it is not something to keep.

Maybe, I can do this.

One minute.

And then, the minute ends, and the rest of the story slides back into focus. Not about me—about what I can handle—but about him, too. About the part of this that I've been ignoring, the part that makes me undeniably selfish. Because maybe, this minute could turn into another and another, until I learned how to do it: make each minute enough all on its own.

Maybe I could do that. Maybe I could be stronger this time around. But in the end, it doesn't matter. Because Google results are circling in the air in front of me, and there's a terrible taste rising in my throat, even as he kisses me.

Selfish.

I might not have the gene. And even if I do, there might someday be a cure. But none of that changes that right now I am at risk. And Nathan doesn't know. He doesn't know that out of all the ways we've already hurt each other before, there are still bigger ways left.

I try and fail to swallow the terrible taste. If I stay in this room for one more minute, I am going to puke. Actual vomit on his gray-and-white carpet. And I don't want him to see that. I don't want him to see any of this. So, I stand, and I yank on my dress, and I say something that I hope makes sense, an excuse about calling him later, seeing him later. Something that is later. And then I'm through his door and on his stairs and pushing out onto the Boston streets.

Chapter 8

The weather takes me by surprise—it's drizzly and gray, and not what I remember seeing through the window from Nathan's living room. I could have sworn that there was sunshine. I take a few deep breaths, but I don't stop walking. I don't want to wait to see if he will follow.

It takes me fifteen minutes to get home, and when I do, Holly's sitting on our couch, blond hair in a ponytail, last night's makeup on her face, and a McDonald's wrapper in front of her. She notices me noticing and smiles ruefully. She only eats fast food when she's hungover.

"James went out to buy something more nutritious," she says.

"Nothing wrong with a little greasy magic." I'm trying for jocular, but I'm distracted. I keep seeing Nathan's face when he told me how he felt. And if I try, I can almost feel it: the way his fingers gently grazed my collarbone, the softest whisper of his breath lingering in my ear. Cinnamon, sweet and spicy.

I shake my head. My fingers are touching my own cheek.

I feel selfish and terrible and terrified. I shouldn't have done that.

I want to do it again.

A car backfires outside our window, the cracking noise making both of us jump. Holly's left the window open, and the cold, damp air is now impossible to ignore. It takes me a minute to get up and shove it closed, the latch catching like it always does, and when I look back, she's watching me with a narrowed expression.

"Were you out all night?" she asks, eyeing my dress. "We didn't hear you come home."

I give a noncommittal shrug, but even in my haze, it strikes me that she didn't text me. It shouldn't matter. She was with James, and I hadn't texted her, either. It shouldn't matter, except it's a departure from how we used to be. How we used to always know where the other one was. How that knowledge used to mean something.

I start to sit, but accidentally drop my purse, and a pack of dog treats skids across the floor. My hands are shaky; everything is all over the place, turned around and inside out and overflowing.

"What's with the treats?" asks Holly, and I pause. For the first time, I stop thinking about Nathan.

"A dog," I say, carefully. "I'm helping train her, actually."

Holly glances at her hands. "You're starting up the business again?"

I hesitate.

When Holly stepped back from DogKind, it wasn't a big conversation. It didn't happen overnight. It was one of our Friday meetings missed because of a work deadline. A Saturday spent with James instead of taking photos for our socials. This series of small steps, inconsequential until they weren't. Until I realized they added up to something more long term. And by then, by the time I realized this, it felt too late to say anything. It felt unfair. Because she had told me about every step. Each one, every time. So, what was there to say?

And also, there was this: that it felt unfair to stop her from doing it, the thing I kept finding so difficult. Moving on. Making her life big instead of small.

I shrug, keeping my voice light. "I mean, not really. It's one client. It was an urgent thing. She might get euthanized by the state."

Holly nods slowly. "Is that what was happening last night? When you got to the bar. Something with the dog? I know how hard training can be when the stakes are this high. I remember how it was for you."

I bend down to tug my shoes off, trying to find the words to bridge the space between last night and today. But the impulse from the bar is gone, and I am awkward again. Tongue-tied and not sure where to begin with the person who used to be the person I could tell anything to.

"Yeah," I say at last. "Her name is Remy. It's going to be a tough few months, but she's really special."

"Like Cliff?" Holly asks.

Cliff.

That last day at the clinic. I still remember holding him. The rough underside of his paw pad against my palm.

"A little like Cliff."

There's a beat of silence, and then she gets off the couch and grabs a glass owl from a shelf behind the door. Pale blue. "Here," she says. "For Remy." And I feel a smile tug at my mouth. It's a game we've played for years: hold an owl, get wisdom, get good luck. Just like that.

"This is just an added precaution," she says. "Because if anyone can help her, it's you. I believe that. One hundred and seventy-five percent."

"Thanks," I say, meaning it. Because I know that she is trying. We are always both trying. That might be the worst part.

I clear my throat. "How's James?" I ask. "You guys seemed really good last night."

"We are good. *Really* good." She moves toward the coffee maker, giving me a smile, her usually sparkling blue eyes soft. "It's going to sound silly, but we just, we never run out of things to say. I'm really happy with him; it's honestly a little freaky."

"That much talking?"

She wags her coffee spoon at me across the counter. "Cynic."

"Kidding, kidding," I say, and she shakes her head.

"The other day, he brought up marriage . . ." She looks down and adds another lump of sugar to her coffee, stirring it carefully. And there's something about the movement, an unaccustomed shyness, that slows my heart. That reminds me of all the guys before James. The ones who left her in tears and made her swear off men for a month or a week or however long it took her to remember the thing that made her her: how much she loved to love. How good at it she was.

I shift closer to the kitchen, so I can see her fully.

"What did you say?"

"That I loved him. That I can't imagine my life without him." She puts her spoon on the counter, letting the coffee drip around it. She bites her lip, her forehead creased. "Do you think I'm crazy?"

I think of Nathan. Of the things he's unafraid to say.

"I think you're brave," I say.

"You mean it?"

"I really do."

Our eyes catch over the counter, and something passes between us. The outline of our friendship pressed like fingerprints into this counter. Remnants of countless morning conversations giving each other exactly what we need.

She exhales into a smile. She gives herself a little shake. The moment passes.

"How about you and Kyle?" she asks. Her voice is teasing. "Is he where you ended up last night . . ."

She waggles her eyebrows, and I roll my eyes, but smile, too. Because she's being Holly. All energy and enthusiasm. Making jokes about double dates, and eventual couples' trips. Her energy, this conversation . . . all of it so familiar, it feels like it could be three years ago. Like we're still twenty-five, and it's still us against the world. Gossiping and giggling and utterly in sync.

And it could be three years ago, it could, apart from the blue pamphlets in my desk drawer. Apart from Nathan, the man I actually spent the night with. Apart from the fact that Meredith is picking me up in ten minutes, and I still haven't told Holly why.

And I should tell her. I really should. But it's not three years ago. It's not three years ago, and she's talking and talking about Kyle, this guy who I don't even like, but who she is convinced will make me happy. And I can't escape this little voice, asking if her enthusiasm is for me or something else. Something closer to relief.

Relief that I might have found someone else to rely on. Relief that it won't all be on her, to know where I am if I don't come home.

I don't want to meet up with Meredith. I want to go into my room and spend the rest of the day in bed. To curl up and map out a strategy for Nathan and HD and the things I am not ready to say. The things I need to figure out myself before I figure them out with him.

The smart move is to stop this now. I know that.

And yet.

Already, I miss him. A fact that seems incredibly unfair. To miss someone you only just got back. I've had a whole life without him; I have everything I've built over the last seven years. So how is it possible that one night can do this? Make everything else suddenly more incomplete.

I want to curl up under the covers and remember how it felt sitting on his couch in his apartment. That one minute. I want to live there—in that minute—for just a little longer. To see what might be there to find.

But instead, I'm sitting in a car with Meredith, driving out to Lexington to a yellow house that I only visit on select holidays. Driving out to engage in an exercise that's far more hopeless than the one I started last night.

Lexington, Massachusetts. The town where I grew up. And the place where he still lives. Shane Bailey. Hospital administrator. Patriots fan. Dad.

I haven't seen him since Christmas. I haven't seen him because there isn't really anyone to see.

The thing about our dad is that he wasn't a terrible father. He was never mean, never even yelled. He took care of us after Tessa left. He made sure we had nice food and nice clothes and nice toys. That we lived in a nice house in a nice neighborhood with nice schools.

So much niceness, it hurt your teeth to look at it.

He's my dad, and I'm grateful that he hung around. I'm grateful for the niceness. But that's where it ends. That's where he wants it to end, and I'm careful not to forget that. But Meredith is still Meredith. And she can't help but try to fix things. Even for him.

When we walk into the kitchen, he's reading the newspaper at the long oak table that's featured in all our old photos. He's sitting under the same clock that's hung on the wall since I was six. Everything here is the same. A museum to our history. To her. Almost twenty years of marriage, frozen in time.

I hate coming here.

Meredith does the talking while I fiddle with my hands. He looks the same as he did last Christmas. Thick brown hair with the barest streaks of gray; broad shoulders that are only just starting to stoop forward; white teeth that flash against weathered, dark Irish skin. Meredith takes after him—same hair, same eyes—while I've always been all Tessa.

He's handsome, my father, his looks barely touched by age. Good genes, I remember an aunt saying.

He's perfectly polite. *Nice.* He asks about Meredith's job (he works in health care, too). He asks me if I've thought more about grad school (I haven't). We get all of this out in the first five minutes, and then he mentions he has a meeting. He has a meeting, and we'll need to move this along.

Never mind that it's a Saturday. I used to believe him about the meetings.

Mere's eyes flash to mine; a careful check: *Are you okay?* I give her a pointed stare, and then, she's back to him. Using her doctor voice, gentle but clear. She doesn't waste time. She's direct, just like I knew she would be. I know the words before she says them, and still: I feel my hands curl into fists in my lap.

"I'm sorry, Tessa passed away."

Five words. Five words that make something that already happened real. Five words that I've already moved on from, but I know he never wanted to hear.

My heart. That's what he used to call her. It was Meredith who took their wedding photo down after Tessa left. I remember when he looked at the wall and saw that it was missing.

I'm sorry, Tessa passed away.

I try not to watch him now. I try not to see it: how his hand holding his coffee stops halfway to his mouth. How his face shrinks, an instant aging. How his fingers clench too tightly on his cup, and it tips. Black liquid pooling onto the table, running up against the paper and then dripping down onto his leg.

I jerk toward him, and then away. It's automatic, my reach.

He doesn't flinch. He just grabs the paper and starts mopping up the coffee. Brown stains across black-and-white words that bleed and run together. His hands are steady. The mess is covered. There's nothing left to see.

I lean backward in my chair.

"How? How did she die?" he asks.

"A brain condition." Mere sidesteps the implications for us. "It's something she was dealing with for years."

I count to six into the silence. I count to six to stop myself from doing what I know I should not do. From what I still end up doing next. Which is look up and into his face, and into those familiar eyes. The ones that always crinkled with a smile every time I used to walk into a room. Every single time. Do you know how good that feels? To know you are the constant reason for a smile.

Because I do. I remember.

I look up and into those eyes. The ones that used to watch me patiently from across this same table—this stupid table—while helping me with my math homework. I look up and catch his gaze, and I feel his name slide toward my lips. *Dad.* The word that used to bring him running. The word that was always a guarantee. I'm staring into his eyes, his name on my tongue, and I almost do it. I almost ask for what I know he cannot give.

And then I blink, and my father is staring at the wall. Like he's already forgotten we are here. Like the last stretch of seconds didn't happen.

But I could have sworn I saw it. I could have sworn he wanted to reach for me, too.

I wrap my arms around my stomach while we walk back to the car.

Meredith and I are both quiet on the ride home. The suburbs pass by outside my window. The houses are farther apart here than in the city, each one as neat and well maintained as the one I grew up in. Two girls drawing with chalk in their driveway wave as we drive past. They make me think about Mere and me as kids. Her neat braids and my messy curls. Her hand on mine before we crossed a street; me laughing at her carefulness.

As we drive, I rub my fingers against the divots in my elbows from where they pressed into the table, wishing I could rub away my feelings, anger and frustration and this barely concealed hint of shame. Because the worst part isn't our dad's indifference—I had known how it would go—it's that, for one second, for the space of a memory, I regressed entirely. I let myself imagine that this news could change things. That Tessa's death would do what her departure didn't: bring us together. Turn us into something like a family.

I became fifteen again. Fifteen and desperate, waiting for a hug, a look, a smile.

Anything, really. Back then, I would have taken anything at all.

I think of Nathan, and I wince, then shake my head. Because there has to be a way. There has to be a way to handle this without turning back into her.

When Mere finally speaks, we're back on the highway, our old neighborhood falling away behind us, past green exit signs.

"You know what? I think at least one of us won't have the gene." She checks her rearview mirror, her hands neatly in the ten and two position. "I mean, I think we deserve that, right? There's only so much terrible stuff someone should be dealt—nearly catatonic dad, absent mom followed by dead mom, and now HD. I mean that's . . . that's—"

"I think *bullshit* is the word you're looking for."

"Yes." She nods vigorously. "Exactly that. It is bullshit, and we deserve a break somewhere. It's only fair."

Despite everything, despite the fear that steals my breath whenever she mentions HD, despite my frustration with myself, I find myself smiling at her indignation. She's doing what she always does: She's willing things to change. Vintage Meredith. Always a force. Polite and well mannered, sure, but also incredibly determined. Always unafraid.

"What's that terrible saying that I think proves the opposite of your point?" I ask. "It never rains, but it pours?"

"Stupid," Mere proclaims. "But you're right. There are tons of them. Tons of crappy sayings to make you think the crappy stuff is okay."

"Bad luck comes in threes."

"God never gives you more than you can handle."

"Oh, that one might be the worst!"

We're both laughing now.

"The point," says Meredith, "is that we've been dealt enough bullshit, as you neatly put it. The point is that we deserve a break."

I'm still smiling, but I don't say anything. Because I'm thinking about tonsillitis. When I was thirteen, I had a fever for days, and I couldn't speak without crying. Meredith went with Tessa and me to the doctor. She sat next to me in the exam room, holding a purple notebook with a list of my symptoms written out line by line. She didn't leave my side for the next two days, except to microwave tomato soup—the only thing I could swallow.

And sitting here, next to her, watching as she presses her hands into the steering wheel, ten and two, and wills our lives to change, I think about tonsillitis. I look at my sister and I think about tonsillitis, and I consider the very real possibility that I already got my break.

Chapter 9

The night of Remy's next training, I get to Lois's early. It's cold out for the first week of September: maybe fifty degrees, and cloudy. A sharp wind whips my hair around my head as I rush from my car to her front door. I catch a glimpse of myself in the mirror over her entryway table, and I wince. My cheeks and nose are red, which, with my red curls, makes me look like a tomato. I'm in my usual uniform of spandex and a long-sleeve cotton T-shirt. I fish a blue headband out of my pocket and try to tame my hair into a ponytail.

Lois trots up beside me and smiles over my shoulder. She lifts a hand and gently smooths my hair, the gesture so motherly, so automatic, I stiffen.

"You look perfect, honey," she says.

"I look like I just woke up," I deadpan.

She shakes her head, her blue eyes piercing. "You're too hard on yourself."

The doorbell rings then, saving me from having to answer, but I quickly squeeze her hand as I walk by. I open the door, and Nathan's standing there, the cool light of the day behind him. I'm still not used to seeing him. I'm still not used to how he grew up: long and lean like I remember, but also all around more solid; still focused and direct with a casual sense of humor, but a little more polished. A little more reserved. And somehow more handsome than I remember.

"We have to stop meeting like this," he says, gesturing at the stoop. And I can't help but smile. Even though I still don't know how I'm going to do it—turn this mess into something that might work.

We go outside, letting Remy out of Nathan's car and beginning the usual routine. She warms up quicker every day. She still won't let me touch her, but she'll bump me with her nose, and she seems to like to walk beside me. When she pants now, it's not from nerves, but from excitement, her pink tongue lolling over her sharp teeth. At the end of the last couple of sessions, when Nathan's put her in his car, she's kept her topaz eyes on me. She's a herding dog with a pack mentality, and I get the feeling she doesn't want us to separate. Even though she's still unsure of me, she wants to make sure that I'm safe.

After an hour or so, I duck under the fence and stand by Nathan. He's watching Remy, his eyes bright with hope.

"She really seems to be improving," he says.

I nod, but I don't respond. She *is* doing well. But she's doing well in a bubble, and as far as the city ruling goes, a bubble doesn't count for much.

He studies my face, resting his elbows easily onto the top of the fence.

"You don't agree?" he asks.

"I do," I say. "I just think she still has a long way to go. We shouldn't get ahead of ourselves."

"Ever the optimist."

"Always the overly confident."

"You know there are studies that say confident people are kinder," he says.

I join him on the fence, so I can tap the wood beside his hand. "I guess that means you're the kindest?"

That shrug. One shoulder. "Your words . . ."

"Cocky."

"Never," he says with a sudden grin. The kind from him that I never expect, utterly unrestrained. And his eyes collide with mine, and there's a moment, right then, when it's as if the fence rail buckles between us. When it's all I can do to resist gravity. To keep myself from falling into him.

This. This right here. I want to stay right here.

There has to be a way to stay here.

"So," he says, his tone shifting slightly. His eyes focused fully on me. "You left pretty abruptly the other day. Makes a guy feel good."

I try a laugh, but we both know it's forced. The wind is picking up strength, blowing the red-and-white mottled fur back on Remy's face. She reminds me of a lion. Fierce and without anything to prove. I think about telling him that we should just be friends, stay focused on Remy, but every sentence sounds flimsy. Embarrassingly insincere.

I stick my hand through the fence. I've done this move a thousand times already, and I'm not expecting Remy to come. I'm not expecting anything at all. So when she shifts, her eyes flicking from my hand up to my face, I freeze. I took her muzzle off before I ducked behind the fence. Stupid.

And yet.

I take a breath, and lean forward. I don't move my hands. "Whenever you're ready, Remy queen."

And I know she doesn't understand the words, not really. But I also don't believe that it's coincidence that she chooses to drop her guard only after I drop mine.

I press my fingers into the silky strands that hug her neck. I shift my gaze to Nathan and then back to her.

"Tell me something true," I say.

I can feel his eyes scan my face, that meticulous gaze, and then he nods. He gestures at Remy. "It's my fault that they might euthanize her." His voice is matter-of-fact. Not an ounce of self-pity. "I'm the reason she's in this situation. I'd been training her, working with her, and I let her meet my neighbor. I thought she was ready. I was sure . . ."

He rubs his face with his hand, and I notice the shadows under his eyes again. They seem to have taken up permanent residence. It has to be tiring always believing you can make things right. Always finding your way back to certainty even after the shittiest things.

"It's my fault," he says again, standing up straighter, pressing his hand into the fence. "I was wrong, and now she has to pay for that. Because of me."

"It's also because of you that she's not still stuck in a shelter. Not everything is black and white." I nudge his hand with my pinkie. "You wanted her to be ready. You wanted her to be okay. There are worse things than that."

We stand there, quietly, together. Our hands touching. My pinkie against his pinkie. The smallest contact that somehow still ends here: with this feeling between us. So big, I imagine anyone looking at us could see it, and I think of the expression *weak in the knees*, and I press mine together. My skin is hot, every cell standing at attention, waiting for what's coming.

Because it is coming: all of it. Dinner, tonight. The two of us, squished side by side at a corner table at Lucca in the North End. Parmesan and tomato sauce. One of those low, flickery candles. Paper napkins and red wine. His bed, afterward. His hands in my hair, my tongue tracing lines up his neck. His body, so familiar and still new. And then, tomorrow morning, breakfast burritos at my favorite diner. Laughing, leaning in, his face almost touching mine. Leaning in and laughing at something only the two of us can hear.

These are the things that will happen if I say nothing. A hundred perfect moments. Each one, so easy, if I just forget the rest. Not just Huntington's, but our history.

Start over. Be brand new. This could be my plan. And I think that I could do it. I think that I could try to focus on being happy for a while.

On finding something real that does not have to last. I think knowing how to do that might just be the trick.

And when it comes to Huntington's, isn't there an argument that he doesn't have the right to know just yet? That this is my life, my body. And I deserve some time?

Start over. Be brand new.

I feel Remy press her weight against my hand.

I could do it. I am almost sure that I could do it.

But as it turns out, I can't do it to him.

"I told you that my mother died. But I didn't tell you how." My voice is rough. It creates immediate distance between us. "It was Huntington's disease. That's how she died. It's hereditary, and its untreatable, and Mere and I each have a fifty-percent chance of inheritance."

My heart is doing cartwheels in my chest. But the words come out surprisingly clear. Almost nonchalant. So casual that it takes a second for them to land. One frozen second. And then, his hand grabs mine, his fingers pressing hard into my palm. He grabs my hand before anything else. Before his eyes widen. Before his sharp intake of breath. And it's probably instinct, nothing more, but I think that years from now, that's the part of this conversation I'll remember most. Him moving toward me instead of moving away.

I don't wait for him to respond. Instead, I channel Meredith: sharing the rest of the facts quickly and without emotion. I sprinkle in the good parts, the research and medical innovations, how my mom was relatively old. That it might be years, decades, really, before I even need to worry.

And, of course, that I might not even be sick.

"There's plenty to be hopeful about," I finish lamely. He gives me a look, and I can tell he's not convinced. He knows me too well. But I can also tell he's thrown. That he's not sure what to say. His eyes are pinging from my face to Remy, and back again. I've never seen him this unsure.

"Don't look at me like that," I say.

"Like what."

"Like you are scared for me."

He lifts his eyes to the sky, then back to me. "Shit, Alex. I am."

"Well I don't want to be."

"Is that how this works?"

"It's how it works today."

The sun is starting to fall, orange and pink fingers reaching across fading blue. Nathan's jaw is clenched. He's back to studying the sky.

When he finally turns his face to me, it's rigid. A mask I recognize from all the other times I've seen him prepare to fight for something—for his mother, for his scholarships, for his sister. For Remy.

"Okay," he says. "Okay. What can I do? I'm here, Alex. I'm right here. I'm with you on this." His voice is ragged. Full of all the things he's about to say. The right things. The things you say to someone who is facing something like this. Not *let's see what's here*, but instead, *I will stay*.

But I don't want to hear those words. And the thought crashes in my brain that this, right here, is the biggest reason I didn't want to tell him. I don't want him to choose me for the wrong reasons. Not again.

If we are going to do this, if we are going to try for something, then I don't want to go backward. I don't want to have to wonder, again, about his feelings. I made this mistake before, and I don't want to do it again. I don't want to have to figure out if he's fighting because he loves me or because I am an obligation. I am afraid that I will settle for either one.

I don't want to be a person who accepts that kind of love. It's not fair to either one of us.

But suddenly, I am afraid that's exactly who I am. Who I *still* am.

I take a step away from the fence, feeling for stable ground. Casting around for anything. I will take anything over this. I think back to my plan. And I grab on to what remains, little pieces cobbled together.

"What if we just pause," I say. "Just pause us, right now."

A muscle ticks in his cheek. "You mean stop seeing each other?"

"No," I say. "I mean, yes, if that's what you want."

"That's not what I want."

I let out a breath. "Okay," I say. "Me neither. I'm just saying, let's not get ahead of ourselves. I mean, it's just . . . It's all a lot. You and me. Our history, this whole thing with my health. It's all a lot. That's what I'm saying."

"Yes," he says slowly. "But it's also the reality."

"I know that." Obviously, I know that. "But can't we just take the pressure off? If I'm sick, it probably won't affect me for years. Decades, really. And there could be a cure. It's, you know, the time of medical breakthroughs. They say."

He stares at me, and I don't blame him. "Who the fuck says that, Alex?"

"I don't know. Them. That's not the point." I take a breath. "The point is that we don't need to get into all of this yet. You said it yourself: We don't need to figure out everything at once. We don't even know what we want from each other yet . . ."

"I do know. I told you, I—"

"No," I cut him off. "You said you missed me. That's all. I pushed you to say more. I pushed you for explanations about something that happened years ago. And even now, I'm pushing you into declarations about a future that you might not even be around for."

There's a painful beat of silence. But it's true. It's all true. I don't know what Nathan wants, not really. I just know what he currently feels obligated to say. And I think again about how I didn't want special treatment. How I want to be strong. Tougher this time around.

"Whatever this is, Nathan, there's a long list of reasons it might not work," I say firmly. "I might be sick, and it's too soon to process that. For both of us. And either way, you have a life in DC that you need to consider." He opens his mouth, but I press on. "You said you wanted to do things differently, so let's do things differently. Instead of making commitments, jumping in headfirst again, let's just see what's here. No pressure. No expectations. We have almost three months until Remy's trial, right? Let's just take those to be us. You can process this, and we . . . we can just have a few months of being us."

"And what happens after three months?"

"We reassess," I say simply. "No hard feelings either way."

"And, what, you think I'm going to walk out in three months' time?"

"I don't know. Maybe. Maybe I will." I try for a smile, but he doesn't laugh.

I lean toward him. I can hear the urgency in my voice. "You wouldn't be walking out," I say. "That's my point. We are not a couple. We are just two people who were something once, and are seeing what might be there now. I want to promise that we make no promises. That we just be us."

His eyes narrow. "Why?"

And this time I am honest. "I need to know that I can do this. I need to know that I can be happy without any guarantees."

The words settle like a blanket over my shoulders, steady and absolute. Right in a way that I don't question. Because this is what I want: no promises, no guarantees. Just us, right now. Happy. If I can't learn to do that with him, we will never make it. I have never been as sure of anything as I am of this.

He doesn't answer for the longest time. The temperature is dropping, and I shiver. I want to wrap my arms around myself, but I don't want him to notice.

Finally, he turns to me, and his eyes swallow mine, and just like that, the cold is gone. Because there is nothing else. Just us. My whole heart, wrapped up along this fence line.

"We just be us," he says. "See what's here. And then, deal with the rest."

"Yes," I say. "We deal with the rest only if we have to."

He nods once. I stiffen. "Okay," he says.

Exhale.

There. Done. It's what I wanted.

It's what I wanted, and I'm relieved he gave in so quickly. I'm relieved—*I am*—except that for the space of a breath I forget not to think about the future. I forget; I jump ahead to the place where his agreeing now means him leaving later. And despite what I just said, despite everything I just reasoned, that thought makes it hard to stand.

Chapter 10

Now that I'm out of school, September is marked by annoyances. At least in the city. The end of summer beckons a flood of returning college students. Crowded trains and worse traffic. Longer lines at bars, dirtier streets on Saturday and Sunday mornings. A whole new level of line at Trader Joe's. Students running wild with all this energy, all this forward momentum. Students who, without warning, one day look younger than me.

This year, September is different. It feels different. The energy is still there, but now, I'm moving with it. We're moving with it. We sneak picnic dinners on the beach in Southie, our eyes snagging as my lips press against a cold beer bottle, gray waves and a too quickly setting sun. Nathan gets us exploring the best brunch spots in Boston, flaky croissants at my favorite bakery in the North End, runny eggs that melt in my mouth at a tiny Charlestown diner that he frequented as a kid. We spend Fridays at crowded concerts—Brighton Music Hall and the House of Blues—listening to bands who are only just starting to play at bigger venues. They're filled with joy and the manic energy of having maybe made it, and I keep thinking that their gratitude matches mine. For finding him, finding this, again.

Because here's the part that I am too afraid to say aloud: *It works*. Putting everything to the side, freezing time. It works. We are happy in a way that I don't recognize. Always, all my life, every good moment has been marked by this quiet assumption that the other shoe will drop. That it will never be fair to keep something that feels this good. Happiness is a finite resource. Appreciate it, but don't assume that it will stick.

I never imagined I could turn that thinking off. I never imagined that I could simply stop my brain before it goes there.

But I do. We stay right here. And we are happy. Even Nathan, always so intense, so focused, is lighter than I've ever seen him. More playful. It reminds me of the time in college when we pooled our money for a three-day trip to California wine country. Three days of idyllic vacation. Of rest.

Don't we deserve to just rest? To see what that will give us?

At the end of September, he asks me to go away with him, a line that makes me want to giggle, and I am not a giggler. I picture old movies with the girl and guy in a red convertible, top thrown back. The girl's hair getting messier than she means. A useless scarf trailing behind her.

I bribe another trainer to stay with Remy, and we drive Nathan's Jeep north, up to Ogunquit, a little coastal town in southern Maine. It rains the whole way there. When we stop at a rest area, I brave the weather and end up soaked. My clothes stick to my skin. The storm's only getting worse, so we wait there, in the lot, watching as the rain shifts to a downpour, until we can't even see the cars around us. Steam clouds our windows.

"It could be an apocalypse," I say. I'm still on a high from racing through the rain.

Nathan grins. "You and me against the world."

"Tempted?" I joke, and his smile widens.

"I love seeing you like this."

"Wet?"

He hesitates. "Happy."

"That actually goes both ways."

His eyes drill into mine, and everything slows. The blood in my veins is thrumming with the beat of the rain on the car's roof. And when he kisses me, it's like an answer to a question I haven't asked.

I'm thankful for my wet clothes. I'm thankful that I have an excuse to shiver.

The rain settles down into a steady pounding, heavy but consistent. It continues that way for the rest of the drive and well into the night. Our hotel is on the water, so Nathan buys champagne, and we sit on the covered balcony watching the rain pound against the rocks while the angry colors of the sea and sky swirl together, almost interchangeable. We talk about old friends from college, speculating about who ended up in what jobs, who ended up married, and where they are now.

"What about you and Holly?" he asks. "I can't believe it's been a month, and I haven't seen your other half yet."

I shrug. "We're both so busy," I say. "And I think college is different than real life. It's tough to keep that kind of friendship up."

"I guess, but you two used to be inseparable."

"She's still my best friend; it's just, people grow apart. I think that's normal. These things happen."

"People let things happen."

I shake my head. "Don't do that," I say. "Don't imagine you know her better."

The wind lashes against our balcony, and Nathan lifts a hand. "Fair enough." And then he coughs out a laugh. "I always forget that you get protective."

I roll my eyes, and he nudges me with his knee. And it's over, barely half an argument. And still, it feels almost bigger than anything else that's happened.

When he notices goose bumps on my arms, he gives me his sweater. It swallows me, the hem sitting just above my knees. He looks at me in it and smiles, direct and warm and mine. And then he leans back, his eyes following the moving water.

"Tell me about dog training. What's the best and the worst part."

It's late. The other balconies nearby are quiet. It's just us and all this water, the rain making the ocean seem like it could overflow and pull us under.

Or maybe that's just the champagne.

"The best part is easy," I say. "It's almost exactly what you'd think."

"The dogs?"

"Almost." His mouth tips up, and I duck my head. "It's the moments when they get it," I say. "The dogs. The owners. When they both get what the other one wants. When, suddenly, they're not alone."

"Such a secret softie," he murmurs, and I laugh. He always used to call me that.

He pulls my feet into his lap. "And the worst part?"

I was going to make a joke, to keep it light, but there's something in his voice—that earnestness—that gives me pause. That makes me want to be honest.

The worst part.

I think about DogKind. About the money and the anxiety that bubbles in my chest when I admit I'm too afraid to do it on my own.

I think about Cliff, and a stupid video filled with promises I couldn't keep. I think about the other dogs I've tried and failed to save.

And then, for some reason, my thoughts jump to Lois. Lois, two Halloweens ago, when she called me to help with a foster dog.

The dog was fine. That's not what I remember.

What I remember most is it being Halloween. I remember Lois's decorations: spooky spiderwebs and cornstalks, and rows and rows of pumpkins. All for her granddaughters. She does it every year.

But last year, the girls didn't come because they'd moved away. It had been sudden, Lois said, something with their mother's job. She was diplomatic, calm—but I remember noticing how thin the skin around her wrist looked in the fading light. The blue of her veins, exposed, matching the spiderwebs that those girls would never see. Before I left, I watched her and the dog walk up the driveway, Lois's spine ramrod straight, her hand holding tightly to the leash.

The two of them, alone. The decorated house, dark and silent behind them. I remember how the shadow of it nearly swallowed them whole.

The worst part.

I lean my head back and close my eyes. I listen to the steady thumping of the rain.

"The worst part is this," I say, "no matter what you do, there's always something left to fix."

I feel his grip tighten around my legs. I let myself feel this and nothing else. And when I open my eyes, he doesn't try to spin my words. He leaves them where they are, and just keeps holding me.

We stay there until the rain stops. Sometimes, we're quiet; sometimes, we talk. And when we do, the honesty continues.

"I used to want to start a rescue center. For dogs like Remy."

"I can see that."

"It's silly. Just a dream."

"Lots of people get their dreams. Why not you?"

And:

"I think part of the reason I went to DC was to avoid you. To avoid reminders of the life we'd planned."

"I used to look for you. On street corners in the financial district. In the bars the law crowd frequented. I'd look for you."

He touches my face. I run my fingers through his hair. We are honest in a way that I might regret in the morning. But right now, I don't care. Right now, I am flying.

The rain slows to a trickle and then, nothing at all. And when the silence gets too loud, he leans forward and picks me up. One smooth movement. His lips crashing into mine. The smell of saltwater. My fingers in his hair, my legs wrapped around his waist. He holds me like a secret. Like something worth protecting.

I fly and fly and fly.

It's a perfect weekend. The kind that, even as I'm living it, I'm already trying to commit to memory.

Sunshine spills out on Saturday morning, glinting off the wet puddles that the storm left behind. Refracted light landing in unexpected places.

We spend the morning walking the beach, each of us daring the other to brave the icy water. I point at my green cotton dress, using it as an excuse, and Nathan's eyes rove across my body before he runs in, waist deep. Without warning, he dunks his head all the way in. And the genuine shock on his face knocks me down. Literally. I sit in the sand and laugh and laugh, holding my belly. My dress flutters around my ankles.

I wish we didn't have to go back home.

We wind our way from the sand up to the streets of Ogunquit, and we end up at a pop-up brewery. It's turned into one of those absurdly gorgeous autumn New England days. The snappy breeze dancing off the water, off Nathan's hair. The sun beating warm against my cheeks, my chest, my arms; a pulse of happiness, echoed by the people laughing all around us.

We find a table on the patio. It's painted bright yellow, sunflower or buttercup, something that tells anyone who sits there that this is a place for happiness. Nathan hardly fits between the bench and tabletop, his long body jostling against the painted wood as he leans across it, his lips grazing the left side of my temple, leaving heat behind.

Despite these last few weeks, despite last night, I'm still not used to it: the way my whole body comes alive around him.

The day fades into late afternoon, and our conversation barely pauses. We talk about Remy, about her progress, which is not as much as I'd like. I feel guilty that we went away this weekend, that we've wasted thirty-six hours on each other when we could have spent it all on her. Because I want to help her, and also . . . I love her. Somehow, already, that is true.

She's completely comfortable with me now. I can run into Nathan's apartment unannounced, and she starts yelping with excitement from her crate. When I let her out, she runs back and forth between my legs, then, as if she's embarrassed by her outburst, she sits directly in front of me, nose in the air, and waits for me to pet her. I still like to call her queen.

She's silly smart, and I think she knows that we're both girls, because sometimes when Nathan does something ridiculous—explains something to me in his "lawyer voice" or tells her not to drip water on the floor—she will give me a look, as if to say, *Men*, and I find myself snorting with laughter. Nathan will raise his hands in the air in defeat and mutter about being ganged up on. In those moments, we feel like our own small family.

But there is a world outside of us three. And it's there where she still struggles.

"Eventually, we'll be able to take her on these kinds of trips," says Nathan, and I smile at him. He does this, I've noticed. Throws general future dates into the air between us. No specifics. Nothing so sharp as to prick our bubble, but just enough that a splash of longing rises in my chest. For that undefined future.

He reaches out, and touches my cheek where it must be red. My awful blushes.

"You're beautiful."

He doesn't say it like a compliment, or like he's trying for any kind of reaction. He says it the way he says everything: straightforward and without agenda. Simply sharing what he thinks.

Beautiful. My dad used to call me beautiful. One hand smoothing my red hair. *Her* hair. He loved how much I looked like her, right up until he didn't.

"You seem happy," I say, moving the subject away from my face. "Dare I say relaxed. A whole new Nathan Browning."

"Very funny," he deadpans.

"You remind me of Mere sometimes. Both of you always with an agenda."

"You sound like my mother," he says. And then he laughs at my expression. "Hey, it's not a bad thing. She's always on me about relaxing. She thinks it's her fault I won't slow down."

"Because she got sick," I say. It's not a question. Nathan spent most of his early teenage years with his mom in and out of the hospital. Even those first two years of college, he worked another job so he could send money back home to his family. Just in case.

He lifts his head up, looking at the pale-blue sky.

"People die," he says bluntly. "She wasn't supposed to get better." A muscle ticks in his jaw. "Not the first time, and not the second time or the third. And probably not this time. My mom has cheated death three times already, which by any standards qualifies as a miracle. And I'm not going to act like I'm not grateful. Like the world doesn't deserve a whole lot better than a half-ass version of myself."

He's staring studiously ahead now, that muscle ticking in his jaw. I adjust my gaze, giving him a minute, and my eyes land on another brewery visitor. A guy with orange moppy hair and in a blue T-shirt with gold embossed letters on the front: A GOOD MAN IN A STORM.

Nathan. One of those phrases that always makes me think of Nathan.

He's spent most of his life waiting for his mother to die. Holding his emotions tightly in check, refusing to be bowled over. Refusing to give an inch. And for every bit of our relationship, even when we were apart, even when the sight of a T-shirt like this one kicked my heart, I just want him to feel softness.

I picture Tessa. Her red curls and the sound of her laughter echoing across the kitchen table. The silver of her car. Her cello left behind, sitting in the corner of her studio. I think of Mere. Of a test that I'm not sure either of us is ready to take.

There are countless reasons I cannot be the person Nathan needs. Countless reasons I can never be a soft place to land. Not in the long run.

But right now, we are here. Right now, I can decide that that's enough.

I lean forward, and his blue eyes snap back to mine, as if he was waiting for me to move. As if he is always waiting for me to move. I take my hand, and, deliberately, I smooth out the crinkles on his forehead.

I smooth downward until my hands land on his shoulders, broad and straight and sure. And when I lean in, I kiss him tenderly. I kiss him like a promise. Not of a future, but of this, right here. Of what he means to me, right here, on a sunny day, at a buttercup table when I don't need him for one single thing.

I kiss him and I feel his lips part beneath mine. I feel his shoulders loosen under my fingers, his breathing slow.

Softness.

There are hundreds of pages in someone's story, but I read a two-line poem once that stuck with me for years.

The length doesn't have to be the part that matters.

Chapter 11

It's the Tuesday after Ogunquit. In a rare move, Holly's not with James. She'd asked if I wanted to get dinner, instead, and we're at Kentro's: this tiny Greek restaurant three blocks from our apartment. No reservations. Tables crowded together, one stacked nearly on top of the next. No privacy, except that everyone is too busy focusing on their partner to focus on you. It's a strange kind of intimacy.

There was a time when we'd come here almost every week.

"I still can't believe he's back. Nathan. You and Nathan."

I told her about him weeks ago, before Ogunquit, but this is the first time we've really been able to talk. She brushes her long blond hair out of her eyes, which are trained on me. "Are you sure about this, Alex?"

An unapologetic romantic, Holly used to be Nathan's biggest fan, even when he first left. "The world is shrinking," she said. "Long distance doesn't have to be a death sentence. And it's you two. It's you and Nathan. Meant to be."

Her optimism carried me through those first months. But as the winter months went by, I'd catch her watching me, a small worry line creasing her forehead.

"I just want him to know that this is hard," I'd said to her after another one of our fights. "To admit that it is hard. I don't want to keep fighting with him."

She looked back at me, her blue eyes uncharacteristically serious. "Maybe you do, though. Maybe, you want to know that he will fight back."

I remember feeling the smallest bit embarrassed, but mainly relieved that she understood. That she understood my fear and didn't judge me for it.

And looking at her now, I know she's remembering those same conversations. And I wonder if she is not just remembering Nathan, but also remembering us. How open we used to be. How we used to let each other in.

I swallow and stare down at my plate. I spear a piece of feta, and by the time I'm finished chewing, my eyes are no longer stinging.

"It's been pretty amazing," I say. "I don't think I realized how much I missed him."

"Have you talked about it?" asks Holly. "About why you two ended."

I shrug. "We know why we ended. We were twenty-one and trying to do long distance. It didn't work. That doesn't need to mean anything more than that."

Holly narrows her eyes but lets this go. "And what are you guys now? Is he your boyfriend?"

"We haven't talked about labels. We're just enjoying what we have right now. We're taking it day by day."

"Alex—" she starts. And suddenly, I'm annoyed. She's known about this for weeks, and now, out of the blue, she's decided to have an opinion. And, yes, I know she cares. But this isn't what I need.

"We're taking things slow, Holls," I say. "Don't read into it. Don't make it something that it's not."

Holly raises her eyebrows, but she doesn't answer right away. She's chewing, taking her time. She read a book about this in college, I think. Something about eating with intention. She'd quote passages of it to me while I made pizza rolls in the microwave.

"Do you still love him?" she asks.

Her words thump against my chest. Heavy and uncomfortable. I imagine she can see my sharp intake of breath. But she doesn't understand. She doesn't understand that it's not about whether I love him; it's about not making the same mistakes.

"It's complicated," I say at last. And Holly shakes her head.

"That sounds a lot like a yes."

It's such a role reversal: my sparkly best friend telling me to be careful. And I have a flash of us at twenty-two, our first year in Boston. It's summer, sweltering city heat, and we don't have AC. Holly's standing next to our ratty gray futon wearing a red polka dot bikini. A lime-green cooler swings in her hand, and she's begging me to get off the couch, where I'm reading a magazine, a fan blasting muggy air on my face.

No part of me wants to get anywhere near the sun, but Holly made margaritas, and she's bouncing there beside me, practically on the balls of her feet, her energy threatening to overflow. To turn into the kind that gets her into trouble, that leaves her somewhere low. And so, I get up, and we get into her car and drive to Southie, the windows down, our noses pointed toward salty air. We lie on the sand in the too-hot sun, and the beach is empty—which makes no sense, which makes it magic—and our joy feels endless, as tangible as the sand beneath my toes. And I am almost consumed with this rush of certainty that it will always be this way with us. That we will always give each other exactly what we need. That whatever else goes on outside this stretch of sand, we two will always be enough.

And now, I'm sitting across the table from her, all our old roles reversed, and that's not even the part that matters. All I can think is that I miss her. I miss her so much it hurts.

"I don't think it's possible," she says at last, "to take it slow with someone you used to love. With someone you thought would be your everything. I think you are going to get hurt."

"I'm happy," I say. "I'm happy now. And I'll deal with later, later."

"Are you?" she asks. "Are you really happy?"

"What's that supposed to mean?"

She puts down her fork and wipes her mouth. "Just that you do this. Ignore your feelings," she says. "Jesus, Alex. Your mom died a month ago, and I only know about it because Lois sent you flowers."

I shift in my chair. "What does that have to do with anything?"

"It has to do with being honest. With yourself. With everyone. I think, sometimes, you think you are protecting people—keeping everything inside—but you aren't. That's not how love works."

There's a question behind her eyes, and for a second, I am not sure if we are still talking about me and Nathan. I push my hair behind my ear. One strand keeps falling forward into my stuffed eggplant. I keep my voice calm.

"I haven't seen Tessa in over a decade. She could have been dead for years, for all I knew. This is just confirmation."

"She's your mother, Alex. You can't just decide this isn't a big deal. She's dead. And you and Nathan? Whatever you are not calling yourselves? It's a big deal, too."

The couple next to us gets up to leave. When they stand, one of their chairs hits our table, and a bowl of olives tumbles to the ground. Small green and brown balls rolling everywhere. No one even notices. I meet Holly's eye, and I expect her to laugh, to make an inappropriate joke. To do anything other than what she does, which is to keep looking at me seriously.

"Even Meredith's worried about you. She texted me the other day."

I snort. "She's not worried about me. Well, not about this."

"Then what?"

I hesitate. I should tell her. I should have told her weeks ago. But I can't shake the niggling question of what this will mean for us, for me and Holly and wherever we go next. Of what happens if an unknown defective gene does what I can't do. If it brings us back to where we used to be, but for all the wrong reasons.

I take a sip of my drink and start again. "It doesn't matter, Holls; it's stupid sister stuff. Can we please just change the subject? I'm happy. I'm good. Just be happy for me, okay?"

She opens her mouth to argue. And I imagine, for a minute, her bulldozing her way through all the secrets we've buried. Upturned earth. There's a lessening, a lifting—that constriction that happens just before relief.

But then, she cuts herself off short.

"Fine." She takes a sip of water. She does what I asked her to do, instead—she takes us somewhere else. "James asked me to move in with him."

Oh.

I wonder if they will play the same game with her owls.

And then: I wonder if they already do.

"Wow, that's . . . wow. That's amazing." Three seconds. Three pathetically long seconds to get over myself and get to her. To her news—such good news, news that's brought something bright and vivid to her face. And underneath that, a wariness that I almost overlook.

My food feels heavy in my stomach.

"This is big. This is huge. Congratulations. Wow." I'm babbling. My mouth keeps moving of its own volition. "You're going to do it, I assume. I mean you have to, right? It's James."

I gulp some water, if only to get myself to stop talking. And then, I wish I was still talking. Because now, we're looking at each other across the table, and the noise and people have fallen back. And it's just us two. Just us two, and this endless instant watching our friendship of a decade, everything between the beginning and tonight. Salty margaritas at college dorm parties. Mascara wands passed in dirty bar bathrooms. Cheap flights and cheaper hotel rooms. Endless trips to Home Depot to replace lost apartment keys. The first time we bought a real tree for Christmas—we forgot to get a topper. Shared clothes and shared closets. Secrets told only in the dark.

The constellation of moments that make up a friendship like ours. Best friends. The childish words that are still the only ones that fit.

"It wouldn't be right away," she says. Her voice is quiet. "Our lease is up in January, so, I was thinking. Maybe then."

January.

Just over three months. One hundred days. We've lived together for almost ten years. Over three thousand mornings. Nearly that many times that I've moved her coffee spoon from the counter to the sink.

"But I could stay longer, too," she adds. She must catch something on my face. The wariness on hers flickers. "I figured you and I would talk it through, see what makes sense—"

"January makes sense," I say, cutting her off. "You're right; it's good timing."

It's good that I didn't tell her about HD. I don't want to get in her way. I don't want this to be the reason that she stays.

We both look down at our now-empty plates. There's a piece of spinach stuck to the side of my spoon, drying in the open air. A new party has sat down at the table opposite ours. Three women, close to our age, tap together raised glasses. A tinkling that sparkles. One laughs so loud, the sound echoes across the restaurant. I can almost swear that I see the water in my own glass vibrate.

Holly pushes her food across her plate.

"This is it, isn't it?" she says. "The hard part, I mean."

I look back at her. She shrugs her shoulders.

"About growing up."

We follow the familiar streets back to the apartment, slowly. Quietly. I wonder how many more times we will do this walk. And I wonder if she sees it, too: that we've already moved into the time of last times.

It's beautiful out. One of those perfectly mild, late-September nights in New England. The leaves are just starting to change. The trees fan out in yellow, orange, and green arches over our heads, the setting sun creating shadows that make the colors more interesting than they are. Almost like mid-October.

"I'm happy for you, you know." I need to say it. I need her to see it's true. "This really is amazing news. I can't wait to pick out a housewarming present for you. I suspect it might have wings."

She chuckles, and bumps my hip with hers. "Thanks," she says. And then, "I'm happy for you, too—about Nathan. About whatever it turns out to be."

We're back outside our apartment now. The sun has dipped out of view, and it's getting colder, a reminder that winter is closer than it seemed when we left the restaurant. I can see Holly start to shiver under her long gray trench, but neither of us makes a move to open the door. We just stand there, together, as the sky shifts from gray to deepest blue. We stand there and we wait.

Chapter 12

October sneaks up on me. It's usually my favorite month, the one I wait for. But this year, it comes when I'm still convinced we're in September. Meredith texts me that she set up the appointment with the genetic counselor. December 3 on the nose. Five days after Remy's hearing. All of it, just two months away.

But still: two months away.

Nathan and I have long, lazy mornings in his apartment, more in his bed than out of it. It's sex and something else. Something softer. He tells me about his life in DC. About his eccentric neighbor and the capital balls and the endless social climbing that defines the city. I share funny stories about the dogs I used to train and, more often, their parents—the big, muscular man who brought his two pugs everywhere in a stroller, the woman who was convinced her cocker spaniel's anxiety stemmed from a past life. I try to put these people into words: how they made me laugh with their awkwardness, but how I also wanted to squeeze their hands. To tell them that I see them.

I like the way Nathan listens to me, how his whole body seems to pay attention.

We sneak kisses. His lips pressing against mine when I crawl over him to grab a glass of water. We've already had sex, and still, the kisses are thrilling. The best of the butterflies.

We aren't traveling in a straight line. We're jumping from one place to the next. We're picking and choosing where we want to go, which parts we want to skip over.

Every once in a while, Holly's words trickle into my head, and sometimes, I step back. I tell myself not to text him, or not to go over when he asks. And I last for a morning or an afternoon, sometimes half a weekend. But Holly is never home, and the apartment air is stale, and the simple truth is that I miss him. I miss him when I am not with him.

But it is okay, I think. Because I'm figuring out how to do it: how to not get too far ahead. How to be happy with this. One minute, multiplied, for as long as I can.

And I think, for me, with him, that's the only way to do it, to learn how to make it last.

On the first Saturday of October, Meredith invites me over for lunch. I read her text while lying in Nathan's bed. He's making breakfast and singing along to a nineties station, skipping over the words he doesn't know, his voice crackly and off key. He sounds light, easy, and listening to him, I'm hit with this overwhelming wave of belonging. I lean back into the pillows, letting the wave wash over me, my arms spread wide in comfort, and I realize it's all starting to feel like ours. The pillows. The bed, the sheets.

Mornings. Mornings are starting to feel like ours.

A few hours later, I get off the T in Back Bay and walk straight into a downpour. It's not exactly surprising—our wet summer has been followed by an even wetter fall—but I don't have a rain jacket, so I end up running the three blocks to Meredith's house. Strategically ducking under storefronts at crosswalks, as if that might help. And the whole thing reminds me of driving to Ogunquit, and I'm laughing when I get to her doorstep, my red face matching my frizzy hair and cheeks that feel too warm. I stand under the awning to catch my breath and listen to the gentle thumping of the rain against the cobblestones. A cat walks across the empty street, unbothered by the rain.

It's Syed who answers when I ring the doorbell. He's holding out an iced coffee like an apology, and he laughs when he takes in my appearance. "Well maybe it's for the best that Meredith isn't here yet."

"What, you don't think she'll like the drowned look?"

He raises an eyebrow, still smiling. "Let me get you a towel."

Syed and Meredith met a year after she graduated from college. He proposed on their fourth anniversary, and they got married on their fifth. Meredith liked the neatness of the dates. Of the timing. I was the maid of honor at their wedding. A big reception, filled with Syed's family. Kind and overbearing women, good-naturedly questioning who I was dating and when I was getting married. After all the toasts—the speeches talking about the beautiful wedding and the beautiful bride who planned it all—Syed's friend leaned across her seat and gestured toward me. Her voice was sweet with wine and slightly slurring. She gave me a conspiratorial nudge and asked me if Meredith was a bit of a bridezilla. "It must be tough, being the little sister. Living up to everything she wants."

I'm thinking about this, about Syed's friend and what she saw and what she missed, when Meredith strides into the room. She takes in my appearance, the blue towel I'm using to wring out my hair. She purses her lips, but doesn't comment.

"You've been avoiding me," she says.

"You've been texting my best friend."

She doesn't bat an eye. "You should tell Holly what's going on."

"It's not up to you, Mere. When I tell her. What I tell her."

"Or what you tell yourself?"

My anger rolls in with a vengeance. "Just because I'm not processing your way doesn't mean I'm not processing. We had a deal. I'm trying to move forward."

"Is that really what you're doing?"

"Yes," I say. I lift my chin. "And I am. I met someone. I'm happy."

She shoots me a look, but I hold her gaze until she turns away. I don't tell her that the someone is Nathan. One way or the other, we'll get there eventually.

She walks over to the fire in the corner and nudges it with the poker, harder than necessary. Rather than watch her, I scan the collage of photos on the adjacent wall—all joy, and happiness, and promise of the future—and suddenly, I'm nervous. Because I can see my sister everywhere, not just in the photos, but in the neatly decorated room. My sister and Nathan are both planners, but they come at it in such different ways. Nathan plans because he believes he can make it all go right; Mere is simply trying to make sure nothing goes wrong.

"I just want you to handle this the right way," she says. I look from the photos back to her. She's ended up on the couch.

"Your way," I say, quietly.

"Yes."

There's a stilted silence, and then, her lips twitch. The gears in my chest loosen.

"Always so modest," I mutter, and her smile cracks open all the way. She throws a pillow from the couch in my direction, and I bat it down, then sit on top of it on the ground.

For a few minutes, neither of us talks. I pull the knit throw from her couch over my knees and listen to the crackling of her fire. And when I turn back to Meredith, she's staring at the kitchen door where I can hear Syed moving around. And I realize she's wearing a small, bright smile on her face. I can't put my finger on why, but it's maybe the sweetest smile I've ever seen.

"So," I say, "why did you want me to come over? Syed's practically pacing out there, and despite your nagging, you look . . . happy. Really happy."

She startles, and the smile slips, but comes right back. She inhales and the smile widens. "Well, actually, we've been thinking about the whole 'pick three things' thing. And I'm hoping you might settle for me just picking one."

"Okay . . ." I say, slowly. She's wearing a sly look, a joking to her I almost never see, but none of it masks a new softness to her face. It leaves it open. And I have a sudden urge to move the blanket from my knees onto hers. To give her one more layer of protection.

"We want to have a baby," says Mere. Her words cascade together. "Syed and I. We're going to try. And it's going to be hard because of everything, so I wanted you to know."

Her face. That smile. Waiting right there at the corner.

"A baby," I say softly.

"Yeah," she says. "Yeah."

A baby.

A baby.

A small pink bundle. Tiny perfect fingers. *Goodnight Moon*, over and over again.

Meredith. A mother.

Me, an aunt.

It is unreal; we are still children. Still sisters, frozen at twelve and fifteen. But there can be nothing more real than the expression on her face. That openness. Her naked want. Her dream. And it's too dangerous for dreaming, everything too dangerous, but I forget that for a minute. I let the force of her hope fill the room, fill every breath, creating pictures in the air over her head and over mine. I have to swallow the excess, the tears rising in my throat.

We look at each other across the coffee table. Fear and joy that match my own are playing tic-tac-toe across her face. I love you I love you I love you.

I grab her hand across the coffee table and squeeze.

I don't ask about HD, but she brings it up right away.

She can make sure the baby does not have the gene, she explains. They will do IVF, fertilizing her eggs in a lab rather than in her body.

The lab will test the embryos—the fertilized eggs—for the defective gene, and then only implant the embryos that aren't affected.

The doctor wouldn't need to tell her if the other embryos were positive. Meredith would never have to know if she doesn't want to.

"We'll do the test," she says. "We will make absolutely certain that our baby is safe."

If my mother had done that test, there's a possibility that Mere and I wouldn't exist.

I shiver. I push that thought away.

"It's a weird coincidence," she says. "Because we were always planning to do IVF. With my endometriosis . . . it left scarring. I think I told you about that once."

I nod. She did, maybe a year ago. The last time I'd asked her about kids. Even then, she had a plan. And I realize she's doing it again: believing that if she follows a certain set of steps, she can fix what needs fixing. So she can get the life she wants.

The magnitude of her exposure steals my breath.

I take a sip of water from my Nalgene. I use the time it takes to recap the bottle to let my lungs refill.

"When will you start the process?" I ask.

"I'm not sure. We were always planning to wait another year or two, but now . . ." She lets her voice trail off. She looks at me. And I know what she is going to say before she says it. "I think I want to find out first. About whether I have the gene. Not tomorrow; we can stick with our timeline, but eventually, I think I'm going to find out."

I force my head to nod. It makes sense, her wanting to find out more. Having a baby means there's more at stake. Of course, it makes sense. But there's a twisting in my gut.

"If you have the gene, will you not . . . ?" my voice trails off.

She taps her finger against the armrest. "I've done a lot of research, and we know more now than we did before. There's something called CAG repeats. HD is caused by these repeats, by there being too many. Forty or higher means you'll develop HD. But the higher the number, the worse it often gets—earlier onset, faster progression. It's not an absolute rule, but . . . it's something."

"So if you find out you are sick, they'll tell you how many you have?"

"Yes." She shifts. She's sliding her watchband round and round her wrist. "If I have a lower number, it's more likely that I won't develop symptoms until well into my forties, even early fifties. If that's the case . . ." She shrugs. "Our child could have a normal childhood. That's what I want."

"And if your number is higher?" I ask.

"Then we will talk about it." She glances toward the kitchen, where I can hear Syed typing on his laptop. I imagine him making a registry. *Small, soft blankets. Pacifiers. Diaper bag.* "In those last few years, it will get nasty. And if our child is still at home, then Syed will have to care for both of us. Both of them will have to watch me suffer. Never mind the judgment and the stigma we'll face. People staring at me, at us. People making assumptions about my health, about my choices . . . I've read all the chat rooms. I've seen what could be waiting for me."

I know what she's talking about. I read about it, too: how people mistake HD patients for alcoholics, drug addicts. How they're frightened by the tremors, the jerky movements. Stories on chat rooms about mothers walking their children to the other side of the street. People saying it's a mistake to bring a child into a home that will one day be filled with pain.

People who have never met my sister. Who can't understand how much love she'll bring.

"Screw other people," I say. "Asshats. Every one. Any of us could die tomorrow, right? There are people all over the world at risk of horrible things. And no one is telling them not to have children."

Meredith gives me a tight smile. And then she shrugs. She takes us somewhere else. "I keep thinking about Tessa. I keep thinking about why she left. If maybe she would have done things differently, if she'd known she had the gene."

My head shoots up. There's a metallic taste in my mouth. Bitter. We never talk about Tessa.

"Done what differently?"

Meredith looks at me. She stops spinning the watch. "I think it would be hard," she says. "To have a child if you knew you were going to die. If you knew they were going to have to watch you die. I think maybe it was hard for Tessa. That part of why she left might have been to protect us."

Bullshit.

I can feel Meredith's eyes on my face, and I keep mine blank. I'm not doing this. I'm not breaking our old deal and trying to understand Tessa. Because what's the point? I don't really think there's any excuse to make your children feel abandoned. Did Tessa leave because she loved us? I don't know. I doubt it. All I know is that as soon as we ask that question, we become the women we never wanted to be: the women who care about the answer.

I don't need an answer. I don't need anything from her at all.

I take a breath, adjusting the blanket on my leg. I don't need Tessa, but I hate that she is making Meredith doubt herself. Making my sister—my annoyingly strong and steady sister—question her abilities.

Such a legacy she left.

"You're not like Tessa," I say firmly. I want to get back to where we were at the beginning, when Meredith was happy. I don't want her to create a problem that does not exist. "You wouldn't leave. You would never leave your kid, Mere."

"I don't know," she says quietly. "I've never been a mom before. I don't know what I'll be like."

Her voice snags on the last word, and something flickers behind her eyes, a fear so acute it steals my breath. And for a minute, there is silence. Not because I agree, but because of how deeply I do not. My brain scrambles for words, and I scan the photos on the walls. The ones from Meredith's wedding. And again, I think about Syed's friend asking if I felt smothered by my sister. And I did; I do, but it's nothing beside the part that matters more—Meredith's constant presence. The kind of love that's absolute.

I look back and into Meredith's face. I know each one of its angles, and she knows each one of mine.

"But, I mean . . . I do," I say. "I know, Mere. I know what you'll be like."

I stay at Meredith's for another hour. She tells me she'll let me know when she finds out if she's eligible for IVF. She reminds me that it's not a sure thing. She reminds me not to get ahead of myself. Every reminder at odds with the hand unconsciously resting on her lower abdomen. Her body already dreaming for her.

When I leave, I walk, aimlessly at first, eventually cutting left on Irving and popping out on Cambridge Street, picking my way toward the Charles. This morning's rain has collected on the leaves that pile on the ground at my feet. The sunlight that touches the water transforms them, restoring some of their vibrancy—muddy red becomes deep auburn, dull brown is overshadowed by bright speckled yellow spots.

A baby. Meredith, Syed, and a baby. My chest is warm and full. Because regardless of everything else, this good news, this one good thing, is real. There is a future out there that is beautiful. One that my sister is brave enough to believe in. One that I want to help protect.

I stop and stand near the water and watch as people rush by, children skipping, couples rollerblading, a group of women passing a Frisbee. Everything is moving forward, and for the first time in ages, I don't feel like they are all passing me by.

I pull out my phone and text Nathan. I tell him I'll pick up tacos at our favorite place in East Cambridge, and I start walking again. Picking up my pace with every step. I think about how I used to love to run. How maybe I'll start again.

Chapter 13

When I first started dog training, I learned about two fear responses. The two we always hear—fight or flight. Fear that leads to aggression or fear that leads to a retreat. Both, an action. One moving forward, and one moving away.

But the two options aren't accurate. Because there's actually a third. Fight, flight, or freeze.

I've never worked with a dog who freezes. But I've read the studies. There's an argument that freezing is synonymous with logic: taking the time to examine your surroundings, weigh the threat, and decide what to do next. Freezing not as unconscious numbing, but as cool calculation. When you put it that way, it doesn't sound that bad.

But I worry that's what makes it dangerous. Its seeming innocuousness. Us thinking it's smart. Us forgetting how rarely anything good stems from fear.

On the second weekend of October, two of Nathan's buddies from BU come to visit, and we all go to a Sox game. We drink expensive crappy beer, and I spill mustard down my front. Nathan makes fun of me in his dry, understated way, calling me messy while his hands keep playing with my hair, with the bottom of my sweatshirt. He makes fun of me in that way you do with someone you're dating. With someone you've been dating for a while. And I notice how his friends watch us talk and joke around—watch how we are with each other. I notice how they exchange looks: half amused, and half something else.

"Your friends seem . . . friendly," I say to him the next day. We're on the bike path in Somerville, somewhere east of Davis Square. It's gray but not rainy. One of those Saturdays where, despite the grayness, you feel like you should be outside. Not because it's nice, but because the next day might be worse.

We're with Remy, the three of us sitting in the grass, ten yards from the main path. We're practicing. Trying to work on her exposure to people, dogs, and things on wheels. Whenever something scary gets near, I toss her a treat. That's the essential piece: slowing her heart before it has a chance to escalate. Recreating a bad experience as good. Doing it over and over again, until she can do it—forget that she ever needed to be scared.

"My friends think I'm in trouble," he says, lightly. He's joking, but evasive. It's not a move I recognize on him.

"Is that why they were looking at me like that?" I ask.

"Like what?"

I eye him, and he lifts a shoulder. He's running one finger up and down the inside of my arm. It's distracting enough that I have to move away. To try to remember what we were talking about.

He sighs. "They're just . . . curious. They know I always planned to move back to DC. Being here . . . it was supposed to be temporary."

I nod. We've gone through this already—I know he was trying to work out something with his old firm. He hasn't brought it up since, but now, I'm thinking about the unpacked boxes. This life in Boston. The one he hasn't really started.

What am I going to do if he leaves?

The thought is a boot across my throat. Unexpected violence. One minute, I am fine. The next, I am unable to breathe. The world sways. I can't hear the people from the path.

No promises. No commitments that are forced because of how much he thinks I need him. If he stays, it's because he chooses to be here.

That is what I wanted.

But the boot is pressing harder. My chest is so tight, something is bound to break.

And then it's over. Nathan is still staring at the bike path while scratching Remy behind the ears. The air tastes cool and wet.

"It's good to have options," I say, carefully. It is shocking how steady my voice sounds.

Nathan gives a noncommittal nod, then slowly, his gaze zeroes in on my face. Which must not be as calm as my voice. His eyes narrow, and he shakes his head.

"I'm not saying I want options." He reaches a hand out and presses on my knee. It's all I can do not to flinch away. "I'm saying that nothing about us looks temporary. I'm saying that's why they're confused."

My head buzzes; hot hope flares so quickly that I do a poor job of hiding it. He stands up, pulling me and Remy with him farther off the path, behind a boulder, so we get some semblance of privacy. He kisses me. Hard and fast.

I want to stop time. I want this moment to stretch for another day. For a week. For as long as I can keep it.

He leans back before pulling us both gently to the ground. Remy's cocked ears are pointed in our direction, her golden eyes curious. But Nathan's eyes are intent on mine. Searching. And then he starts a conversation we haven't touched.

"I think you think that I took us for granted."

My heart picks up speed in my chest. He's watching me, that question on his face, our history between us. The people on the path behind the rock have faded far enough into the background, I can imagine we are alone. Just the two of us, and Remy. The gentle rustling of leaves. My fingers digging into the cool earth, feeling the dirt wedge beneath my nails, the action acting like a time machine, making me feel younger than I am. Braver.

"No," I say, quietly. "That's not it, exactly." I poke at a rock with my pinkie. "You had so much going on back then—with your mom and your sister, and with school—and I wanted to be the one person you didn't have to worry about. I didn't want to be another obligation you were trying to balance."

"You weren't," he says quickly.

I was, though. Phone calls and extra visits and constant reassurance. All of which he gave, all of which got in our way. Grated on him. Made him feel further away. Resentful. Which made me want to hold on even harder.

That wasn't the worst part, though. The worst part was that he didn't end it. Despite everything. Despite how obvious our unhappiness was. He would not end it. Could not end it. And maybe that should have meant something—about his love. About the depth of it. Except I could never be sure of his motives. If they were for us, or for him. For what he thought we might get back, or for an image of himself he couldn't lose.

As someone who wouldn't break a promise.

I reach out. I press my fingers against his cheek, locking our gazes together. "I started to be," I say softly. "Eventually."

Someone shrieks from the path. I give Remy a treat and then drop my hand back to the ground.

"Even if that's true," he starts, and I bite back a shiver. *It is true.* "It's not on you. I didn't want to admit that I was failing with us. With everything, really. I knew you were having a hard time. And instead of dealing with it, I ignored it."

"I didn't want to be something you had to deal with." My voice comes out shaky, teetering on the edge of what I can control. I am, without warning, too close to losing it. "That's the point. I didn't want you to come back because it was hard for me. Or because you were trying to take care of me. I wanted you to come back because it was hard for you. Because you wanted me the way that I wanted you. Because you missed me the way I missed you."

"I loved you. Of course, I missed you."

"But I didn't know it."

I press my hands farther into the dirt. Nathan has never understood what it meant to question something once the boundaries had been defined. *I loved you.* To him, once said, those words were set in stone. He never considered that they might change.

That maybe they did change. For him.

I look back up.

"You didn't argue when I ended it. Tell me, honestly, were you relieved?"

"No," he says, but his face is stiff. Everything frozen. Waiting for whatever he will say next.

"You were twenty-one years old." My voice sounds distant. "It's okay, you know."

"I missed you," he says again. Fiercer this time. "I missed you every goddamn day."

But that's not an answer, and we both know it. He rubs his hand across his face, and I wait. I am steady. I am stone.

"I wasn't relieved," he says, but his voice holds too much defeat. And more than ever, I wish we weren't having this conversation. Not for me, but for him.

"I wasn't relieved," he says, "but I thought that maybe it was for the best. I knew you, Alex. I knew about your family and how fucked up all of it was. And I knew you needed a plan. You deserved a plan. You deserved guarantees with actual weight behind them, and my life was too messy. Too unstable. I couldn't give you what you needed."

My throat is numb. Words won't work, and I am shaking. The muscles of my arms quiver under my weight. Because his voice cuts like the truth, which only makes all of this worse. More proof of what we could have had.

If I hadn't needed so much reassurance. If I'd been strong enough to wait.

For a long time, no one speaks. We've shifted, somehow, and we can see the path again. The world going on about their morning.

"It's not your fault," I say eventually. And I sound strong. My voice propped up by all the things that I have learned. "It's timing. Needing the same things from each other at the same time."

He smooths the dirt next to my hand. "I don't know if that's always possible. Relationships are sometimes compromise."

"Sometimes. But not always. There has to be balance. One person can't always need more than the other."

He nudges the tips of his fingers against the tips of mine, and I glance down. His hands dwarf mine. It's almost comical. Almost sweet. Fifty-fifty, depending on the angle.

"Is that really what you think?" he asks. "That you needed more than me?"

Yes.

"I needed you, too, Alex." He nudges my finger again, but I'm looking straight ahead.

"It was a long time ago," I say. "We can both do better now."

"By making no commitments?"

"I think that relationships that don't rely on promises are more likely to last."

He opens his mouth, to argue, I suspect, but his phone starts ringing, and the noise startles Remy. So I stand up automatically, moving away from him toward her, getting her to focus on me instead of the noise. We practice sit over and over again, while Nathan watches, the phone already back in his pocket. The earlier moment is lost, though. I've moved us even farther out from behind the rock.

"How do you think she's doing?" he says eventually. She's settled back on the ground, her one red paw folded over her white one, like she's trying to be ladylike. Like she's trying to prove that she's all set. *I don't need your help.*

I know what Nathan means by his question. We progressed in leaps during those first few sessions, but now, it feels like Remy's gotten stuck. She's good in enclosed spaces, but her confidence still flips to defensiveness in public. That's normal, though. It's always harder outside the bubble.

"Remy's independent," I say. "It's hard for her to believe that we have this under control. She still thinks she needs to protect herself."

"So what do we do?" he asks.

"Exactly what we're doing. We follow her cues. We don't rush her. We give her every single reason to trust us, no matter how illogical her concerns might seem. We go at her speed."

"I can do that," Nathan says. "I can take it slow."

There's a double meaning in his words that I don't miss, and for some reason, it annoys me. I don't want us to go backward, where he can't give me what he thinks I need.

"Do you want to go back to DC?" I ask. I'm trying to be blunt, to face it head-on. To prove that I don't need to be protected.

Nathan looks down at me, like he's trying to read something in my expression. Like he's trying to read everything.

"What do *you* want?" The softness of his voice does nothing to mask the intensity. "Because I am here and I am in this. But it would be really great if you could tell me the truth this time. Tell me what you want."

I drag my eyes across his face. All these years, I don't think I ever forgot a single detail. Those eyes, the sharp lines of his cheekbones, the serious way he sets his jaw. Each feature is a landmark on a map I memorized.

I want you. I have always wanted you.

He's trying to make a point. To prove that this time, we can do it: be honest with each other. And I am so close to saying the words. I am so close to not caring about the consequences. To forgetting my plan altogether. Because his eyes are asking me a question, and maybe it's time to answer. Because if I tell the truth this time, then maybe he will stay.

The words are in my throat, my heart pounding just beneath them. And suddenly, I picture my sister. My sister, worrying about being like our mother who chose herself instead of us. I picture my sister, and I feel my hands clench at my side.

I don't want to be selfish. I don't want to be like Tessa. I don't want to choose myself over the people I'm supposed to love.

This time *is* different. This time, there is HD. And Nathan deserves options. He deserves all of his choices without me getting in the way.

And if I'm going to get in the way, I better be damn sure that I won't screw it up.

I take a breath. I wait for my heart to slow down in my chest. I arrange my face into something like a smile.

"What I want is to not get soaked in the rain that is definitely coming," I say, standing, wiping grass from my pants rather than look at Nathan's face. "We'll just add this to our list of things to talk about when we're ready."

"Quite the list," Nathan says dryly, but I just shrug.

We need more time. I need more time. And we have it. It's only the middle of October. We haven't even hit November yet.

The Friday before Halloween, Meredith calls when I'm in bed with Nathan. When I see her face on my screen, it's comical how quickly I leap up, yanking the blanket with me, like she might somehow see us through the phone. Nathan yelps at the cold air, and I shoot him a glare as if it is his fault that I am crazy.

"Hello, Mere?"

"I was wondering if you wanted to play hooky this afternoon. We could do some shopping for your birthday."

I let out a breath. I smile into the phone. "You couldn't have texted?"

"I thought we might try to get out of the habit of phone calls always signaling bad news."

We meet at Torrisi in Beacon Hill, a few blocks from her apartment. The appetizers are already on the table when I arrive: bruschetta with garden-fresh crushed tomatoes, spicy calamari with a lemon zest, creamy burrata alongside chunky golden bread. All of my favorites. Seeing my sister's face, happy and bright above them, I feel lighter than I have all week.

This used to be our thing, random languorous lunches on a Friday afternoon. Meredith acting like they were spontaneous and irresponsible; me not having the heart to point out that nothing on a Friday afternoon could qualify as such. Or remind her that neither one of us was particularly prone to spontaneity. They were fun, the lunches. One of the few times when Mere would stop nagging and just be my sister. (And, in fairness, one of the few times I didn't jump down her throat at every perceived slight).

It's been months, though, since the last one. Even before we found out about Tessa, we'd been letting them slide. Meredith was busy, and I was . . . something else. Tired. Bored. Anxiously bored. Anxiously tired. Take your pick.

So, it's good to be back with her across the table. Rich food on my plate, and white wine in my glass. This week has been endless. The extra sessions with Remy, and interview prep with Deena. The Associate Director job has finally been posted. *Item two on my list.*

Mere and I eat our way through the appetizers and then split a heaving plate of spaghetti and puttanesca sauce that bursts with garlic. Over desserts, she asks me about Nathan. I finally told her about him last week. I try to keep the conversation light: silly little nonstories that I laugh over while Mere smiles curiously. Somewhere along the way, it registers that I am talking just to say his name, and I peter out, embarrassed.

I know she's worried. I know that, like Holly, she remembers how I acted when it ended. How I quit soccer and could barely drag myself to class. How I didn't bother to go on a date for almost another year. Facts that I am embarrassed to remember and I really wish she didn't.

"We're keeping it light," I tell her. "It's just dating."

"Good," she says. She taps her finger to her glass. "But light or not, you sound like someone who is falling in love."

There's a pause. And I want to laugh, because I've said the phrase in my head, but on her it comes out sweet. Old fashioned: *falling in love.*

Like it's an accident. *Head over heels.*

I want to laugh, to minimize everything. But regardless of the delivery, the word itself arrests me. Love. It sounds almost simple here, in this crowded restaurant, in this afternoon from another era. Even though we haven't said it.

I take a sip of my wine. "I'm careful," I said. "Don't worry about me."

She gives me a look that tells me that's impossible. "He's coming to your birthday?"

It's more a demand than a question, but I agree.

"Good," she says. "I'm glad I'll get to see him again."

I ignore the implication behind the words. "I'm excited for that, too."

We wander down Charles Street, grabbing a coffee at a little bakery that smells like fresh bread, then keep going, poking our heads into one boutique after the next. The clothes are all more than I can afford, but Meredith reminds me it's her gift, and so I keep trying on dresses that look like they belong on someone else. Bright colors. Bold patterns. Even the most relaxed piece comes with dangerous cutouts.

Eventually, I find a jumpsuit that's deceivingly simple. Black and high necked but fitted with a flare at the knee that somehow makes my legs look long. The material drags on the floor, so when I leave the dressing room to show Meredith, I have to walk on tiptoe. I circle the whole store before I find her, in a side corner, almost hidden. It takes me a minute to realize what she's looking at: a tiny white vest with a yellow duck stitched along the side of it. The beak opened over a button in the shape of a flower.

"Probably would have been a bit harsh to make the button a fish, hmm."

Meredith jumps at my voice and almost drops the vest. She gives me a look. And then she looks again. "Hey, I like that." She gestures at the suit. "You need heels, but . . . it's really good."

"I like that, too." I nod at the vest. "And gender neutral, I see."

She bites her lip. "I had an appointment this morning, actually."

"And?"

"And everything looked good."

I feel my eyes widen. "So that means?"

"It means if we were ready, we could start as early as next week."

"Meredith," I say. "Mere."

She looks at the vest, then back at me. And then, she smiles. Her whole face opens up. "I know," she says. "I know."

Only two words, but there's a fierce joy behind them. So fierce, it spreads to me, my cheeks stretching automatically, and our eyes connect, and for a minute, we are children again. Ten and seven years old, lying underneath her bed, staring at the stars she stuck to the baseboards. We're plotting out our lives, imagining where we will go and who we will be. The endless potential of our futures, as easy to grasp as the stars over our heads.

I start to take a step toward her—toward her and the vest and the future I'm suddenly impatient to watch her seize—but then, the shop door opens. It bangs open from the wind, and the noise and cold air from the street gusts inside and blows between us. I shiver and Meredith startles. She blinks, then looks away, squaring her shoulders before gingerly placing the vest back on its tiny hanger.

"We shouldn't get ahead of ourselves," she says. "My insurance is covering IVF, so that helps a lot, but still. There are no guarantees. And the genetic test is expensive. Typically, you operate with a thirty percent success rate, and we can't afford too many tries."

I watch her spout off the statistic without emotion. I watch her rearrange her face until the happiness is still there, but more contained. The earlier openness is now a memory. And it's like someone's pressing on my heart. Because I know my sister. She doesn't dream; she achieves.

She is checklists and five-year plans. But this won't work that way. This is one thing she cannot control. And in this moment, I know she knows that. In this moment, her fear is palpable.

She tells me she'll meet me at the register, and I go back in the changing room and peel off the jumpsuit, but before I put my clothes back on, I study myself in the mirror; I stare at the space between my hip bones, and I think about Nathan, and I try to imagine what I want now and what I'll want later. I think about my friends, and their jokes about aching wombs, and whether it's a mistake to conflate emptiness with want. To believe children can fill the space.

I am not sure I am meant to be a mother. But right here, with my sister waiting outside, I don't care what I want. Even Nathan feels smaller. Our future is secondary to this thing we only just discovered: a small vest that my sister is too afraid to buy.

I slip the jumpsuit on the hanger and put it back where I found it. It seems suddenly a waste of money. I tell Meredith there was a hole in the sleeve.

Outside, the weather has shifted; there's a rawness to the air that reminds me of snowy nights and frost-filled mornings. It's still October, but autumn is short. The shift to winter will sneak up on us, and soon it will be December. Remy's hearing, the visit with the counselor, both coming swiftly toward us.

But right now, here, in the crisp October air, I don't want this to matter. I want to duck under the bed, again my fingers grasping at stars my sister made sure that I could see.

Later, after we hug goodbye, I go back to the store. I go back, and I buy the vest.

Chapter 14

Here is the thing I am learning that I didn't understand before. We get moments. You know the kind . . . when you're late and running out the door, your keys jammed in one hand while your other checks your pocket for your phone, everything moving forward, forward. And you're moving with it, with all of it. You're moving with it instead of against it because that's easier, the path of least resistance; and so, you're moving and then something catches your eye, at just the right time. Just when you're most likely to stop and see it. So, you do; you pause. You pause, and you turn and there it is, spread out in front of you—your life. Beautiful.

You want to catch it. To hold on and not let go. To pause a little longer. But you can't, because it's just a moment. A ripple barely reflecting off the water. Gone with the slightest angle of your head. There, and then gone.

It's loud in this restaurant. This is what I notice first. Not the high top where everyone waits. Not even Nathan sitting among them like he belongs. Just the noise. The crashing of plates coming through the swinging doors into the kitchen, the band in the corner that includes a woman with what looks like a cowbell in her hand, the laughter and shrieks echoing from the tables all around me. It's boisterous, bold. It makes me want to drink too much wine and pretend I am a person who dances on tables. It feels, somehow, familiar.

I love it.

"What do you think?" Holly is at my side, a vision in high-waisted dark jeans and a black-silk crop that shows just a sliver of her stomach. She asked me if she could choose the restaurant this year. It's a gesture, I think. An attempt to ease the residual weirdness between us. I automatically reach out and squeeze her arm.

"I know we've never been here, but I thought maybe something new?" Her smile's wide across her face because she already knows. She can see it written all over my face.

"It's perfect," I say, and I give her a hug, breathing in Pond's face cream and Miss Dior, the same perfume she's worn since we were twenty.

She leads me to the table where I take turns hugging everyone else: Meredith and Syed, James, and then Deena, who gives me a wink while introducing a curvy woman who calls herself Bean.

Nathan's last, waiting patiently next to the only empty chair. When he hugs me, I get this crazy urge to grab his hand and pull us both out the door. Back to his bed. Back to the safety of his room. Up until now, we've avoided hanging out with my friends and family. I've avoided it. I've liked our bubble. But I can feel Holly's concerned eyes on the back of my head, and so I grasp the energy of this place with both hands, and I sit down and smile and scan the wine menu. And when he whispers, "You okay?" into my ear, his right hand covering my knee, the warmth of his fingers traveling through my jeans, I'm not even lying when I say yes.

I've never been big on my birthday. It's not that I mind getting older (although har-har to that attitude now); it's that I don't like the expectations that surround birthdays. The requirement to turn them into evidence of others' willingness and energy to celebrate you. The Instagram and Facebook posts, the comments and likes—this fleeting proof that matters more if you don't get it than if you do. I started doing the dinners because they were easier than anything else. Easier even than doing nothing, which raises expectations just the same. The dinners were small, sometimes just Holly and Mere. And they were flexible; I never minded if we went on a day that wasn't actually my birthday. Low key, low pressure.

This one feels different, though. Maybe it's that Holly picked the spot, so it's infused with her boundless energy. Maybe it's that more people came than usual. Maybe it's Nathan, who flashes like lightning beside me. I imagine everyone can feel the crackling in the air. This thing, too big, between us.

"Twenty-nine," says James, once we're all seated and the wine is poured. He raises his glass toward me. "The last year of your twenties—all old age from here on out, so you better make this year count."

There's the shortest of pauses. Meredith and I aren't looking at each other, and it's Nathan who speaks up, his voice easy. Always knowing how to redirect a room. "What's that expression, that youth is wasted on the young?"

I let out a breath and wrinkle my nose. "I'm not sure that I count as youthful anymore."

"Tell that to those of us already in our thirties," Deena grumbles.

"I like that expression, actually," Bean pipes up. She has a soft, lilting voice, comforting and kind. When she speaks, the harsh angles of Deena's face seem to soften. "I don't think it's about age as much as appreciation. Appreciating where we are. Right now."

She registers my skeptical gaze and grins. It's a little bit mischievous. "You disagree?"

I take a sip of the wine in front of me. It's a deep red and feels rich behind my tongue. "No . . . I just think it's easier said than done."

"True." Bean nods seriously. She puts a weight behind her words that draws everyone in. That invites listening instead of laughter. I realize that I like her already.

"We all worry and think ahead, to varying degrees," she says. "We're programmed that way, right? To think in what-ifs. But appreciation allows us to overcome our programming. By seeing more, by appreciating more, we become more."

"It's transcendent," Syed murmurs. Bean tips her glass in his direction.

"Bean's a writer," says Deena.

Bean's cheeks flush. "I'm a waitress. Who writes on the side. But one day . . ." She shrugs. "Well, you never know."

"She's talented," Deena says. "Really." And you can't miss the fondness in her voice. My heart squeezes for her. For Bean. For these most fragile of beginnings.

"What about you, Nathan?" Holly pipes up. There's a challenge in her voice. "Do you think you've mastered the art of appreciation?"

I fight the urge to kick her under the table, but Nathan doesn't flinch. He turns the full force of his eyes on her, a whole conversation passing silently between them. They used to be close, back in college. Real friends in their own right.

"I'm better at focusing on the future, on how to get what I want in that future," he says bluntly. He won't pretend for anyone. It's something Holly and I both used to admire.

"Doesn't that run the risk of losing what you have now," she says.

"Yes," he says without hesitation. He stares at her across the table, his eyebrows knit together. There's something like an apology on his face. "Yes, it does."

There's a pause, and then she gives the smallest nod, and Nathan leans back in his chair, his fingers curling into mine, and I exhale.

"It's your golden birthday this year, you know," she says, turning back to me.

"Her what?" asks Deena.

"When your birthday is on the same day as your age," Meredith explains. "Alex's birthday is on the twenty-ninth, and she's turning twenty-nine."

"It's a big deal," adds Holly.

Deena raises her eyebrows, and I shake my head. "I'm not sure a coincidence of dates makes it big, exactly."

"Of course, it does," says Holly. "It means this will be your year. Your golden year. But you've got to believe it; you have to go into this year expecting only beautiful things."

I find Meredith's face, and something seizes in my stomach. She's not drinking. She's not pregnant yet, but she's not drinking. Because she wants to be as healthy as possible. Just in case.

Expect beautiful things. Bean whispers something in Deena's ear. Nathan touches two fingers against the inside of my wrist. Holly smiles. And whatever's gripping my stomach flips over. Hope. Hope. Hope. The word forms a rough chant in my head.

And I can see it: how maybe everything will be okay.

The server comes to share the specials, and low, buzzy chatter spreads around the table. Nathan takes the opportunity to angle his body toward me, speaking in a voice only we two can hear. "You look unfairly attractive in that dress."

A pink warmth spreads from behind by ears, through my cheeks and down my neck. I cover his hand with mine before I can stop myself. I don't want to be careful tonight. I want to believe in magic.

"Do you still not allow singing?" he asks. His eyes are tight on my face, curious.

I love that he remembers things about me, too.

"I am strongly against it," I say.

"What about your wish?"

"Hard to wish when there's usually no candle-and-cake situation."

Nathan leans in closer to me. Close enough that there's less than six inches between our mouths. "You still get a wish."

I can't think when he looks at me like that. Like I am the sum total of what he's seeing. Like I am big enough to take up that much space.

"What would you wish for?" I say, flipping it around. "If it was your birthday." He hesitates, and I edge just the smallest bit closer. "Tell the truth. One wish, right now. Don't think."

His hand brushes up against my cheek. "That you'll keep saying yes."

Somewhere, someone drops a plate, and someone else laughs. But all I see is green forests and blue water. The boy in the canoe. Honest and sure and mine. Somehow mine.

I let my head rest against his palm.

"Your turn," he whispers, and then, "One wish, right now. Don't think."

I catch Holly's eye behind his head. I look back at Nathan. "That we could all stay right here."

He leans in then, and kisses my bare shoulder. It's so quick, the pressure of his lips gone before it begins, that no one else notices. But my heart plays at double time in my chest. And I have to remind myself that we aren't alone. I have to remember that my world extends beyond the corner of this table.

It keeps happening all night, though: us forgetting that we're here, in a group. Forgetting that it's not just us two. But, somehow, it's okay. It's okay because everyone at the table is doing the same thing. Meredith and Syed, Deena and Bean, Holly and James—all pairings filled up with possibility, with this tender slice of hope. Hope that's happening here; hope that's not about tomorrow.

And when Nathan tucks a piece of my hair behind my ear, his hand lingering on my neck, my whole body seems to hum. He leans in and then pauses. His smile settles into an evil grin.

Our server's standing at my elbow. She's carrying a slice of rich chocolate cake with one candle on the top. A slice of birthday cake.

It's Nathan who starts to sing first.

When they're done, when it's over, and I'm every shade of red, I look down at the candle. I look down and then back up at Nathan and his smile, so sure. So full. He raises his eyebrows, nodding encouragingly. And I see it there, in the hazy air traveling up from the candle's flame to his face. I see the other birthdays, the other moments. The beginning of all the other memories we could make together. I see all of it, for an instant. I forget to stay right here.

I look back down at the candle, and as I bend my head to blow it out, I catch a glimpse of everyone else at the table. All these people who are here for me. And at the very last second, I catch Meredith's eye. I catch her eye, and salty water sparkles, glassy, across my vision.

I blow out the candle. One long breath.

Chapter 15

We all tumble out of the restaurant together. There are hugs and smiles and promises to get together again soon. To do this kind of thing more often.

It's chilly out, but clear. If we weren't in the city, we could see the stars. I look up at the dark sky overhead and imagine them, twinkling somewhere above me. Matching the magic thrumming through me. It's hard to believe, just now, that sometimes I forget that there are stars I never see.

I'm turning to say goodnight to Holly when Nathan grabs my hand and pulls me back against the door frame. He tilts my head up. The kiss is short and firm and sure. Like a habit. So routine, my head spins, and I find myself grabbing on to the mundanity as proof.

Proof that what we have is more than magic. That what we feel right now will last.

His lips taste like chocolate.

"Let's go to your place," I whisper, pressing my body against his. He runs one finger down the back of my ear, and I shiver.

"As quickly as possible," he says. His voice is husky, his breath warm against my cheek.

"Alex." We spring apart. Meredith is standing behind me. I can see Syed hovering by the corner of the building. "Can we talk for a minute?" She gestures to a small park—really a patch of grass—on the other side of the street.

The dimmest sense of caution brushes up against my bubble. Nathan walks over to wait beside Syed, and I pause, wondering what they'll talk about, but Meredith is already halfway across the street. Specks of dirt and mud kick up from her feet as she walks, dark spots that cling to the back of her pale, beige trench. I make myself follow.

"Tonight was really good," she says. She leans against the one tree in the park.

"You were quiet." I realize the words are true as soon as I say them.

"I was taking it all in."

"Transcending?" I ask, only half sarcastic.

Mere smiles and crosses her arms over her chest. "Something like that."

The wind whistles through the branches over our heads. The colors on the leaves are fading quickly; a few branches are already bare. Peak foliage in New England is elusive. Some people pretend it lasts for a month, but it's really one big weekend, two if you're lucky. If you aren't sure when to go, choose earlier over later. It always fades away faster than anyone expects.

Meredith clears her throat. "So, it was good to see Nathan."

I don't want to care what she thinks, but my shoulders tense automatically.

"You two are exactly how I remember," she says quietly. "In love."

I exhale. Something warm and bright wriggles in my chest at Meredith's words.

"I'm not sure about that," I say lightly. "But we are happy. We're good."

"Have you told him?" she asks. "Have you two talked about HD?"

The wriggling stops. A strong gust of wind blows the fallen leaves around our feet. I clench my jaw to keep from shivering.

"He knows," I say. "He's taking time to digest. I've asked him to take time to digest."

Meredith narrows her eyes. "What does that mean?"

"It means we are taking it slow. We are not making decisions about the future right now." She opens her mouth, but I jump in before she can speak, my hands clasped together. "Meredith, there is no 'right way' to handle this kind of thing when you are dating. If I waited to tell him, that would be unfair. But right now, it's too much. It's asking too much. So, this was the best I could do. I'm just trying to do what's right."

"What's right for him or what's right for you?" she asks. "What do you want, Alex?"

I want to give us the best chance at making it.

"You and Syed . . ." I wrap my arms around my stomach. "Do you ever—I mean, through all of this, I've never heard you worry about why he stays."

Meredith tilts her head. "He stays because he loves me. And for what it's worth, that's also why I stay with him."

I nod. I press my fingers together. "That's what I want. To know that if he stays, it's for me. It's not for this. It's not because he feels guilty."

"You don't want to be an obligation."

"I *can't* be an obligation."

And suddenly, she looks sad. More sad than I've ever seen. "But you will be," she says, at last, her voice too quiet. "Regardless of HD. Sometimes, love is an obligation. It can be an obligation and still be love."

But that's not the kind of love I want. That's not the kind that I can handle.

"I just . . ." She pauses, then starts again. "I sometimes worry that this is how you stay happy. I worry that maybe you're too good at avoiding what you don't want to deal with."

"Nothing wrong with a little compartmentalization," I joke.

"Except it can't last." Her voice is too urgent, and I step back automatically. "Not forever. Not even for very long."

The stars seem farther away than ever. I look across the street. I can barely make out Nathan's outline against the dark brick of the restaurant. And it hits me that tonight was perfect. Perfect enough that I was almost carried away by it. I almost believed that life—that *living*—could really be this simple. Grow up, move to a city, bring together new and old friends, fall in lust or love or something in between. Sit around a table and toast each other. Toast the people we've become. Toast the moment, the here and now. Loud music, bright lights, twinkly magic spreading through the air.

I almost believed it. Except as good as it felt, it looked even better. And that's the thing that's getting harder to ignore: the look of it. The look of us, of all of us, together. Picture perfect. Because what if it felt so good because it looked so good? What if it was all four steps removed, and that's what made it easy? Easy, but not real. Because I can't help but think, if it were real, it would be the other way around. If it were real, I wouldn't even notice what it looked like. I'd be too far in it to see.

"Come on, Mere. Let's not do this tonight." I start to walk away, one foot already on the sidewalk. One more step and I'm on the road.

"I'm doing it. I'm finding out."

I stop. I close my eyes. I see her face behind my lids. Meredith, but fourteen instead of thirty-two. Two straight braids down her back. The straightest posture of any teenager in the world.

It seems to take forever, the part when I turn around.

"So you decided?" I say, carefully.

"Yes, I saw the counselor. I've done the steps. And now I'm just waiting for the results."

So much, so fast. I'm blinking, trying to catch up. And then, I try too hard, and I end up jumping ahead. So that I can see it like it's already happened, like the future is already set. The two of us, sitting in a cold, sterile clinic. Mere, with her chin held up, calmly waiting. Me, trying not to shiver in the hard plastic seat. Someone brisk and faceless walks in and moves soundlessly toward us. Their silence beckons what comes next.

They tell us that Meredith is positive. My sister has HD.

The clock starts. The world fades from color to black and white.

"I can't have a baby and not know," Meredith is saying. "And I know we said we'd do the counselor together, and I can still go with you. In December."

I stare at her lips, moving rapidly. Trying to take care of me. Still trying to take care of everyone else.

"When?" The word half chokes me on its way out. "When do you find out?"

"November tenth."

Less than two weeks. Twelve days. We were supposed to have five more weeks. I want to care about the deadline. I want to be angry. I want to be anything but this.

She's not looking at me now. She's looking somewhere over my head. She wore her hair down tonight; brown toffee ringlets fall down her back. Her face is pale in the moonlight.

She's stunning, my sister. I was jealous when we were kids.

"I can come. If you want."

The offer hangs between us like a deflated balloon—thin and unconvincing. Mere shakes her head. "No, it's okay. They don't recommend siblings go together for this part."

"Are you going with Syed?"

She looks down at her feet. When her eyes lift, they're defiant.

"I need to do this alone."

A memory flickers, then solidifies. Meredith. The day we dropped her off at college, a two-hour drive into Connecticut. We'd hardly finished unloading the car—there were still unpacked boxes everywhere—when our dad said it was time to leave. He stalked back outside without waiting for an answer. He left, and then it was just the two of us, alone in this alien place, this place where neither of us belonged. The room looked and smelled dusty. Forgotten. Strange girls were running up and down the halls, screaming and laughing. It seemed impossible that I could leave my sister there.

But Mere gave me a hug, made a joke, and pushed me gently out the door. She made it look easy. And there's everything that happened next—the silent car ride home, the unbearably empty house, the dull pain whenever I walked by Mere's empty room. There's all of that, but it's not what I remember most. It's not what I remember now . . . I remember Mere and how she looked when I snuck back for one more goodbye. How she didn't see me, standing in her doorway. I remember my sister, alone, surrounded by her things, her face ghostly pale, her body stiff to the point of snapping, and her fists clenching and unclenching. Clenching and unclenching.

"I hate this," I say to the tree branch behind Mere's head. She sighs, leans toward me, and then stops.

"It's life. It's never easy."

"I know that." I'm not a child.

I want to ask her if she is scared, which is an impossibly stupid question. I want to ask if she can sleep. I want to understand how she can breathe. How she's still standing.

Instead, I count to four. I give an exaggerated shrug. "I suppose it could be worse," I say. I pause. "One of us could have been named Patrick."

It's an old game. And it takes a minute, but then a slow smile starts at the corner of Mere's mouth. When we were kids, Tessa told us she loved the name Patrick. She loved it so much, she considered it for each of us, even though we were girls. We'd shrieked in horror when she told us, as if a boy's name was the worst possible thing. And as we got older, it became our favorite joke. The most inconsequential touchstone.

"You know, Pattie could have been cute," says Mere. "Maybe, who knows, if I have a girl."

We smile at each other. And for a second, it's all the tiniest bit better. It's the tiniest bit better, until I look down. I look down at her hands, and I register their motion: clenching and unclenching in fists at her side.

A strangled voice in my head whispers: Is this really what you want?

◆ ◆ ◆

Nathan and I take our time that night. We undress each other slowly. We savor how the undressing feels, clothes sliding off skin, his hands against my rib cage, just below my breasts, my lips in the hollow underneath his collarbone, the cool night air against the nape of my neck when he lifts up my hair.

If one of us grows impatient, the other slows us down. We move with purpose. We take our time.

So, when he pushes himself inside me, I gasp at the change. The abruptness of our becoming. My eyes find the ceiling fan above his head, where the blades whirl round and round. Movement that gets them nowhere. I push myself up so our bodies are knit together, so I can barely see over the top of his shoulder. Until I can't feel anything except the way we move together.

I am with him. I am fully there.

I am everywhere else.

When it's over, he kisses me gently. The softest press of his lips on mine. Not like he's being careful, but as if he's still trying to slow us down. But it's too late. I can see him realize this. I can see it, all of it, on his face, right in front of me. I can see it because it's a reflection of what's on mine. We've reached the end of the beginning.

And sometimes, the beginning is all you get.

"Are you going to the appointment?" Nathan asks me. I'm curled beside him in a ball. Dawn light trickles through the windows, past the curtains we never closed. I feel a sudden urge to get up and yank them together. I'm afraid of what will happen when we leave this room. I want to stay here, to forget about what I remembered: that I've just been pretending to be brave.

I told him about Meredith the night before. I told him she was getting tested, and then I told him not to ask me anything else.

He's asking now, though. I pull my knees up closer to my chest.

"No."

When he doesn't answer, I flip over so I can see his face. "I offered."

His eyebrows knit together. "Did you mean it?"

No.

Nathan sighs. He doesn't need me to say it. He ruffles his hair with one hand. "When we were in college, you told me that your sister was your best friend. Your first friend."

The air leaves my lungs in one breath. And then it comes back in another. It comes back with an anger that I welcome. I let it take up all the space it can.

"You don't understand," I say, coldly. "You can't."

"Then help me to."

Somehow, I've ended up out of his bed. Cold air bristles against my skin, and I start pulling on my clothes, moving roughly around his room. I like the noise my feet make as they slap against his floor.

"My being there wouldn't help. She doesn't want help, from anyone. And she's never once wanted mine." I shake my head. "If I go, she will end up trying to protect me. Trying to make this easier for me."

"Maybe," he says. "Or, she will see that you don't need protecting. She will see what I know, which is you are already stronger than most of us."

I snort. "I'm not."

"You are," he says. He's standing in front of me, his hands on each of my arms. His voice is urgent; every bit of his intensity is focused on me.

"Do you know how many people in this world are full of shit? People who never consider their own shortcomings. People who never want to sit with pain—theirs or anyone else's." He clenches his jaw, a look of disgust rippling across his features. "When I came home from school to see my mom, I never wanted to hear about her fear. I was always positive. I was always certain that it would be okay. I thought that's what she needed." He squares his shoulders. "Three months in, she stopped letting me come to the appointments."

"Nathan," I say. I reach toward him to tell him it's okay. To tell him it's understandable. But he shakes his head. His smile is tight but true.

"You and my mom, you both taught me the same thing," he says. "That being strong isn't standing there and acting like everything will be okay. It's knowing that it won't be, and staying just the same. I think you always miss that. I think you miss that seeing the danger and staying is harder than deciding not to see it. What you do is harder than what I do. What you do makes you stronger."

I wrap my arms around my elbows. I turn and step back so he can't see my face, the wetness starting to spill over and onto my cheeks.

I close my eyes.

I want to be the person he's describing. I want to be her so badly—for him and for Meredith and for all the people I love. But he's only seeing half of me. He's missing the other part. The truer part.

And again, I'm in that waiting room. Meredith finding out. The positive result. The very worst option.

And maybe he is right. Maybe I could handle that.

But I squeeze my eyes together tighter. And it's the same waiting room. The same doctor with the results. But this time, it is negative. The very best news.

Except . . . except.

All along, I've thought that HD has been about me and Meredith. Our shared burden. But what if it's not? What if I am alone?

And I see it behind my eyelids: Huntington's and Tessa and the choices we've made and the things we inherit and what comes after everything stops. I love my sister. Love all capitalized. LOVE. Full stop. It is the one thing I am most certain of in this world. But it is not enough to overcome the truth: that whatever I pretend, I am still my mother's daughter. That I am always, always so afraid.

Of being left. Of losing.

I press my knuckles against my eyes. Which explains how I don't see him coming. I don't see him move in my direction. Until he's there, right in front of me again, his hands on my shoulders.

"Alex." He says my name differently than he's ever said it before. He says it like an apology. I wish I didn't have to hear it. "Slow down. Just for a second."

But we've already tried that.

"It's not going to be okay." My voice is hoarse.

"It might be." He shifts his hands, tilting me up, so I can see his face. "People step up. All the time. They do the thing that once seemed unimaginable. They do it for a day and then a week and then, one day, they wake up, and it stops being unimaginable. It just starts being part of their life. Not their whole life. Just one piece."

He pauses. "You do it," he says softly. "You've been doing it for years."

I can hear the sound of his heart, steady in his chest. I match my breaths to the rhythm. The gentle thud and thumps. I count the beat until my own heart rate slows. Until the sunlight turns from gray dawn to hazy yellow. Nathan presses his lips against the top of my forehead, and I imagine a world where I can stay right here. Where I can pretend it might somehow be okay, that I let things get this far.

"I'm here, okay? I'm here for you."

My eyes flit to the unpacked boxes. The ones that haven't moved in the past six weeks.

He's here. For now.

Chapter 16

The dog in the video, the one that went viral, his name was Cliff. A couple found him on the side of Highway 93, five miles north of the city. The first thing I thought when Lois called me was that the slim cuts across his back looked like pie crust. Strangely neat. Purposeful. I remember how his whole large body shook, how even the whiskers on his muzzle quivered with the endless shaking. I remember knowing, right away, that he needed more help than I could give.

It took months to get off the wait list for a veterinarian behaviorist, and then more months spent trying different medications. Month after month, with Cliff lying flat on Lois's kitchen tiles, shaking. Months of us hoping that what we tried would be worth it. For him, and also for us.

And here's the part that still makes me sick, actual bile rising in my throat. It almost was. Enough, I mean. We almost did it. Cliff started to get better. One afternoon, he pressed his nose into my hand, and his tail thumped against my leg. I still remember the noise, the way I counted the beats.

One. Two. Three.

Holly and I made the video that day. We let ourselves forget; I let myself forget . . . that moving forward means only so much. That the ground you gain is never guaranteed.

Just over a year later, Cliff regressed and then never recovered. And we made the only choice we could.

He was a king shepherd. Big and regal with silky brown hair and wide eyes that drooped at the corners. A white spot on the tip of his left ear.

Afterward, Lois told me she didn't regret trying. She told me that trying always counts for something, and Cliff got a year he'd never have had. Words that used to be mine, but now sounded alien. Naive. Because I looked at the new wrinkles under her eyes, and I pictured Cliff's face and that endless shaking, and all I could think was that maybe we'd gotten this one wrong. For months, I couldn't sleep without nightmares, so I stopped sleeping at all. For months, I could barely look in the mirror.

And then, another six months later, I opened my email, and there was Deena, telling me about the job at Kensington. A fresh start with far less pain. I read the email twice, and then I hit "Apply."

The beginning of November goes by in fits and starts. Every night, I look at my calendar. I watch as the days between now and November 10 tick away. I wonder if Meredith is watching them, too. I wonder what she is feeling, if she regrets choosing to go by herself. If she is looking at her phone, waiting for me to tell her that I'm coming. That I won't let her go through this alone.

I make it through the first round of interviews at Kensington, largely thanks to Deena. She runs through questions with me each morning when the office is still empty. I appreciate her motivation. I appreciate her unexpected patience more. I read the notes she jots down about predictive ROI and evaluating price elasticity. I pretend that I'm not pretending to care.

Holly's hardly home; she's swamped with work deadlines and spends most of her nights at James's. The empty apartment isn't unordinary, but I still find myself looking for her when I walk through the door. One afternoon, I come home to find a snowy owl figurine on the kitchen table with a note in her familiar scrawl. *You're hootiful. xx.*

I wonder if I will miss her more or less when she is officially gone.

Nathan and I don't talk about my meltdown. I'm embarrassed by my descent into self-pity and I don't want to revisit it. Nathan follows my lead, but the air is thick with everything we aren't saying. About Meredith's test. About what the results will mean for her and what they will mean for me.

About what they will mean for us.

Rather than talk about that, we stay focused on Remy. We have a visit with the veterinarian behaviorist a week before the trial, and it's critical that she shows improvement by then. She needs to be manageable in public. We need the vet to say she is not a threat.

On a Tuesday, we take her for a walk on Broadway, and it starts off well—I keep my body between her and the passersby, showing her she's safe, and I give her treats for encouragement. Her tail is relaxed behind her, and I'm swallowing pride, this cautious hope. But after a few blocks, I notice her start to stiffen, the tail inching upward. And I realize people are staring at us, their eyes taking in her muzzle, scanning her long, lean body. Stepping away. And Remy notices. She notices their fear and she responds with fear of her own.

It's that self-fulfilling prophecy. Fear inviting fear. That fear turning into aggression. Sparking more fear in return.

I try to move us down a side street, but a man jumps back, and Remy lunges, a blur of red and white and gray. It happens quickly, but I'm ready with the leash. She doesn't touch him. And still, the dirty looks, the yells from bystanders. Remy, golden eyes wide, her silky body twitching with anxiety beside me.

When we bring her back to Nathan's, she immediately drops down on the soft blue rug in his living room. She's relieved, but she wears an air of defeat that latches like a weight around my chest. That tells me she knows. *She knows. She knows.* I lie down, curled up directly across from her, so we are face-to-face. Her red-and-white paws are splayed out, one of them resting on my knee. I watch her chest rise and fall. I count her breaths until she falls asleep.

Her trial is in less than a month. If it were tomorrow, I'm almost sure she'd lose. I press my palm on top of her head, holding steady.

"I'm not giving up," I tell her softly. "I promise."

The day before Meredith's appointment, I leave work early, ignoring Deena's pointed stare. I leave work early, and I go for a run, across the channel where I walked with Nathan two months ago, then up through Downtown Crossing, straight on past the statehouse.

It's early evening. The streets fill up as offices empty out—harried moms and dads rushing to daycare, commuters jostling to catch the T, polished young men and women laughing in beer gardens, groups of frazzled colleagues gathering for forced networking events. Every step I take the city matches breath for breath with energy, becoming alive in the way I know it best. There's an electric feeling in the air that's magnified by the rush that always comes with mid-November, with the final bustling weeks before the holiday season claims the city.

The longer I run, the better I feel. It is the smallest act of rebellion. Of refusing to let go of the hope I found these last few weeks. My thoughts stay hidden beneath the steady rhythm of my feet hitting the pavement. I watch them cycle beneath me—bright-yellow sneakers flashing by, propelling me forward with every step.

A block away from Nathan's apartment, I let my feet slow. I jog, then walk, then slowly come to a stop. Like I've simply petered out. I sit on a bench under a bare, spindly tree. I consider the chances of him walking by me. I wonder if I could count our meeting as fate, even though I'd come this far on my own.

I want to believe that after tomorrow—after the test, after Mere's results—things between us can go back to how they were. Happy.

Butterflies. A smooth barrier between now and later. Everything on one side easier. Everything on the other easy to ignore.

Except, it's all caught up with us, I think. Huntington's. His life, waiting for him in DC. The time for deciding what we will become is inching closer.

And knowing all that, I'm still here: a block from his apartment. Close enough to tempt fate, but far enough to make its influence unlikely.

My phone buzzes, and my chest lurches when I see his name across my screen. *Good luck tomorrow. I'm here.*

Nathan. The boy I fell in love with at eighteen.

When do you make enough new memories? How can you tell when you have enough to last?

I push my head back and roll my shoulders. My eyes follow the lines of the branches overhead. My sweat cooled too quickly, and I'm cold. I need to move. I need to decide what to do next.

I look back down at Nathan's text. I picture his eyes, clear and confident on my face. Annoyingly sure of who I am. Of what I can and cannot stand. I'd thought he was oversimplifying everything. Assuming I was better than I am. But what if I was wrong? What if that's just one part of how these things go: the other one believing for you. The other one believing when you can't.

I pull up my phone. I start to type.

"You really didn't have to come," Mere says. It's the fifth time she's said this to me since I knocked on her door this morning. The tenth time since I texted her last night. And like all the other times, I ignore her. I lead the way to her car instead.

I'm here. My presence feels almost like an accident. But still, I'm here.

Meredith puts the address into her GPS. It's a Center of Excellence, she tells me, as we pull onto the narrow Back Bay streets. A Center of

Excellence for HD. As if the name somehow makes the subject matter better. As if it changes anything at all.

We have an appointment with the genetic counselor, a woman named Annette Roper. Mere's met with her already, for the counseling required before getting the test.

I wonder what Annette is like, this woman who chose to work with death for a living. I wonder if all the conversations, the persistent press of death and dying, make the inevitable easier. If her own demise feels closer or further away.

Meredith is quiet as we drive, her attention on the road. It stormed last night, and the evidence litters the ground in front of us. Falling branches half hanging from trees, green and gray trash can lids scattered across the street and sidewalks, leaves, dark and dirty, everywhere.

The middle of November is ugly in Boston. The tourists who line the streets came here just in time for the worst part.

"Did you tell Dad about today?" I ask. "About anything else?"

Mere's snort is her only answer, but not for the first time, the question knocks around my brain: Would it change anything? If he knew, if he knew we were maybe dying, would it change anything at all?

I open my mouth, then close it. I sneak another peek at my sister—hands on ten and two, consistently checking her rearview mirror, never missing a turn signal—and I push the question away.

Last night, after I told Meredith I was coming, after she eventually agreed, Meredith told me how today would go. She told me how we'll be brought into a room with Annette, who has the results. Annette will tell Mere if she's positive. If she is, she'll help her navigate the next part: medications, counseling, navigating insurance.

"Are you okay?" Meredith has caught me staring. Her eyes tighten with concern. She looks tired, like I'm not the only one who didn't sleep well last night.

"I'm fine. I'm glad I'm here. No place else I'd rather be," I quip.

She raises her eyebrows, her gaze now fixed on the road again.

"Funny," she says, "because there's about ten million other places I'd choose."

Our laughter is forced, a photocopy of the real thing, but it helps. I can feel her relax an infinitesimal amount. And there's this moment of understanding, of something like relief, and then her blinker flicks on, and the car slows, and we are here. The so-called Center of Excellence.

We park and make our way from the garage to the clinic, weaving through a mix of medical staff in scrubs, students with backpacks, and passersby who I realize look the same as us. As if we all could be here for any harmless reason. Each of us, so easily blending in—never mind our tight chins, the stiffness in our shoulders, and the creases around our eyes.

A bright and loud lobby gives way to corridors that Meredith has memorized. Left, then right. Then right again. And then, without warning, we're in a small waiting room. Soft-yellow walls surround three chairs, two tables, and a neat display of gourds. They must be meant as seasonal, to remind you of Thanksgiving, but a choked laugh escapes me, and Meredith gives me a look.

A green sign with white letters catches my attention. It's a quote that's half familiar: HOPE BEGINS IN THE DARK.

I can't help myself. I nudge Mere, pointing to the sign. "A little on the nose, don't you think?"

"That depends on how you look at hope."

The voice comes from behind us, and we spin around. Or Meredith turns, and I spin; I spin too quickly, so I almost fall. So I am still righting myself when the owner of the clear voice reaches out to grasp my hand.

"I'm Annette," she says to me. She has a warm brown face and wears an encouraging smile. Her hold on my hand is stable. Steady. I find myself not wanting to let go. "And you must be Alex. I thought you might decide to come."

Annette nods at the quote again. "Have you read anything by Anne Lamott?"

"No," I say. I'm still trying to find my balance.

Annette only nods. "Well, she has some wonderful things to say about hope. Particularly how it's hardest to find when it matters most. How that's when we need to really look."

I flush. I can guess she knows what I was thinking about the gourds. But there's no judgment on her face, just that smile that I wish I could replicate. And it's immediately obvious that I was wrong about Annette. She is not a woman who is interested in death. She's interested in the living part, the part that calls for dignity. And when we sit down, with her desk and the results between us, I can tell she's not afraid. Annette has been here before. Annette will be here, with us, for whatever comes next.

"It's nice to see you again, Meredith."

"I wish I could say the same to you." Mere's voice is dry, but there's a softening around her eyes. I can tell she likes Annette. I can tell they like each other. I wonder if that makes any of this harder or easier.

Annette shifts in her chair, and the air around us shifts, too; it becomes sticky with implication. With what is coming, the part she still has to say. The part that will change everything. I hear voices wafting up from the street outside her window. Murmured conversations too far away to overhear.

"Alex," Annette says, and I half jump in my chair. "You understand that whatever happens today, it doesn't change anything for you. Your chances of inheriting the gene don't change, whether Meredith does or does not have it."

I nod my head, folding and then unfolding my arms. I wait, and Annette waits with me. I keep my eyes away from the window. I say my sister's name over and over again in my head.

A beat of silence and then Annette nods again. The slightest incline of her head. She reaches across the table to hand me her card; her fingers are warm when they brush against mine.

"I understand you have an appointment here, in December. But if you want to talk sooner."

When she turns her attention back to Mere, I'm relieved. For less than a second, I'm relieved because it feels like I passed some kind of test, but then I'm watching Annette turn back to Meredith. Because being done with me means we've made it to the next part.

Annette asks what I imagine are a standard set of questions. A script that Meredith must have memorized, because she answers each without hesitation. Back straight, voice steady, hands calmly folded in her lap. Just like I imagined. And my chest tightens, and something between pride and pain threatens to choke me. Because Meredith is calm and collected, and to anyone else, she looks like she is old enough, steady enough, to be here. In a room where life-and-death decisions are made. But to me . . . to me, she looks like the girl she was when we were kids.

She's the girl who used to wear her hair in two tight braids, right down her back. She would giggle as they smacked me in the face when she turned her head too sharply. She taught me how to ride her bike, holding the back of my seat with her thin arms, running along beside me. She pushed Robbie Holden in the dirt when he convinced me that red hair smelled like rotten tomatoes, and then she told me I was stupid for believing him. She's exacerbated sighs, and teenage eye rolls, and the face I've known the longest. She's lazy afternoons watching *Gilmore Girls* on our couch and screaming fights over the last piece of rhubarb pie. She's one of two little girls dipping their feet in icy ocean water, the one who goes in first, the one who the smaller one follows.

She's my big sister.

And I cannot lose her.

Annette opens the envelope. She opens the envelope and I open every cell in my body, everything I have, every bit of luck I get to call on, and I hope and I hope. I hope for her over me. I make the trade, in my mind, again and again. Easier every time. Easy in a way I never should have doubted.

Mere and Alex. Alex and Mere.

I reach out across the space between us, and I grasp my sister's hand.

Chapter 17

I think we often imagine terrible news like a thunderclap of pain. Agony coming to a head in an instant. Boom. The brutal wave washing over you, pushing down on you from every side, and you, just trying to stay standing.

There's something comforting in this image, I think. Something primal. Something that comes down to surviving, so that surviving is all there is. So that, in surviving, you somehow overcome what came first. You overcome what caused the pain. The terrible thing.

Except, that's never the way it goes. Not with truly terrible things.

When Tessa left, there was pain, yes, but I can't point to a climax. There wasn't one wave—there were hundreds, and then countless ripples extending outward, and even now, I can't say which part hurt worst: her leaving or the infinite moments that followed, all defined by her absence. I can't say what's worse: her leaving or what it said about me, how I was the one who had been left. How I cared, so much, about being left—by her. By a person who chose to leave me. Or how, later, I stopped caring, how I didn't even really care when my own mother died.

Terrible things. Terrible things that we survive but never really overcome. Terrible things that cannot be overcome because they never end. Survival in endurance, in adaptation, instead of resolution. That's the best we can do. The best we can strive for.

Chapter 18

Hope begins in the dark, the stubborn hope that if you just show up and try to do the right thing, the dawn will come. You wait and watch and work: You don't give up.

The rest of the quote from Annette's office. Sometime later that day, I'm not sure when exactly, I look it up.

I find the quote, and I read the words over and over again. I read them like I believe there's a chance, like there's any chance at all that I'll find something I keep missing.

But it's the agency that trips me up. The idea that we have a choice in what comes next. That in striving for more, we might get more. And I can almost believe that. I can almost take those words and hold them tightly to my chest and believe in what might be. Except, agency requires time. It requires the chance to see what happens after you strive. It requires the chance that the dark will break, that dawn will come.

So then, where does hope begin when there's only darkness left?

Meredith. Meredith. Why did you have to find out?

I don't sleep well that night. I toss and turn among dreams that might be memories: me and Meredith as children, playing manhunt in our neighborhood. Mere making me hide in the alley between our fence and our neighbor's while she keeps a look out.

Don't worry, I'll keep you safe.

I wake before sunrise. My eyes sting from unshed tears, and my legs and back stick to my sweaty sheets. Lying here is impossible. I shove a pillow under my stomach to try to dull the burning ball of anxiety. I should get up. Today is my last round of interviews at Kensington. My life is waiting for me outside.

Lying here is impossible, but getting up is inconceivable.

Positive. The test was positive. Meredith will get HD. My sister is going to die.

I picture a long colorful string, different colors and different weaves throughout. I picture it being cut. The later colors erased. Worse than erased. Never even existing.

I shove the pillow into my mouth to stop the scream.

I'm standing on her doorstep. I ran here from Somerville. I thought running would help . . . that it would somehow make me stronger . . . so, I crossed into Cambridge first, extending the route over the bridge to Boston and through the manicured lawns of the esplanade. I ran past busy Back Bay and the once-vibrant trees that reflect off the water in the pools of the public garden. I tacked on mile after mile, and at every step, I willed the tightness in my chest to loosen. I willed something to change.

I shouldn't be here. Meredith needs to focus on her family. On Syed. She would have told him by now. By now, he knows all of it. I shouldn't be here, not now.

Except. I need to see my sister. Flesh and bone. High cheekbones. Decided chin. I need to see her.

Meredith is my family. She's my whole family.

Cling, baby monkey, cling.

The door swings open, and then she's right in front of me. Wearing sweatpants. Eyes red rimmed.

"Couldn't help but notice you lurking," she says dryly. By some miracle, she still sounds like Mere. I jerk toward her and away in an awkward almost hug. I'm afraid of what I'll do if I touch her. I'm afraid of the well of unshed tears.

We walk into her kitchen, and I see Meredith's blue mug, her favorite mug, filled with half-drunk coffee, sitting on the table. The mug I am almost certain she was drinking from when she told me Tessa died. Meredith had known, even then, that something worse was coming. I wonder if she can sense now, how much more there is left.

The minutes tick by in silence. I can't decide where to start or what to say. "How are you" seems like the dumbest question in the world, but everything else feels less important. All I want is to know that she's okay.

Except, she's not. She's not okay. She's dying.

A gargling sound escapes my throat. Mere opens her mouth to say something, but I can't . . . I cannot be the one who's comforted.

"I'm sorry," I choke out. "I'm sorry this happened . . . that this is happening to you."

Meredith rubs her temples with her fingers. It's a familiar gesture. Mere used to get migraines when we were kids. She'd have to lie in her bed, in the dark, for hours. No noise. No little sister. I hated the migraines. They hurt my sister, and I couldn't help her. And worse, selfishly worse, they took her away from me. More than anything, I hated being alone.

She looks out the window, then back at me. Nothing but honesty between our eyes. "I just hope this isn't happening to you, too."

And there it is. The other part. The part only my sister can face head-on. Even after everything.

"Well, I think by now, at least, we've definitely fulfilled our crap quota." I'm trying to be flippant, to bring air back in the room, but the words come out wrong. They come out wrong because of the implication behind them: that if Mere has HD, then maybe I'll be safe. That bad luck must have a limit. That my life gets favored over hers.

The scream gathers in my throat again. I dig my nails into the palm of my hand, focusing on the angry red indents my fingers leave behind.

Mere has a husband and is planning for a baby. She has a job that makes a difference, that saves lives. And me . . . If it has to be one of us, it should be me. I have less to give. Less to lose.

A shuffling noise makes me glance up. Syed walks into the kitchen and stands behind my sister, resting his hands on her shoulders.

He looks at me over her head. "How are you doing?"

My line. It sounds better coming from him.

"I'm fine." I fiddle with the napkin in front of me. A green thread has come loose. "I just . . . I wanted to be here. With you guys."

"We're okay," he says, answering my unspoken question. His voice is firm, determined. He looks down at Mere, and she lifts her chin up toward him, and I see it there, between them: love. A force field built from it. The foundation of their own language, the words that pass unsaid between them. A thousand different words in that one look, that all add up to the same thing: I love you. I love you. I am here.

And I wonder . . . I *hope* that maybe that's enough.

But then Mere breaks her gaze, and I watch the next part—the moment before Syed raises his head. That moment when his eyes are still trained on Mere, even after she's looked away. I watch Syed's face turn in on itself, the lines of his jaw quivering with the effort that it takes to look at her. To look at her, to love her, and to know what's coming. He takes a breath, raises his head, and his eyes catch mine. For less than a second, they're on mine, and they are burning. Burning from the inside. Begging. Everything behind them, breaking.

For less than a second, I watch his world catch fire. And then, it's gone. His expression clears. But my heart races in my chest, too fast for my breath to catch up. I can't stand his agony. It's too close to mine.

I clear my throat. "What happens now?" As I say the words, it hits me: we never thought beyond the test. We never talked about what happens next.

But, of course, Meredith has. "Now, we know. Now, I make decisions. We sort out insurance; I get on lists for clinical trials. And we sort out our plans." She pauses, briefly glances at Syed. "The good news is that I only had forty-one CAG repeats."

My brain flounders, trying to grab hold of this news. Wet fingers sliding across slick rock.

"Forty-one sounds low," I say. "So that means a later onset, right?"

"It's not a perfect science. Generally, a lower score means later, but there can be massive variations." She hesitates. "A more accurate predictor would be knowing when our mom got sick."

We stare at each other for a beat, and then she puffs out a heavy breath. "But like I said, nothing is a perfect science. And at least I have the CAG score. I'm going to look into that more. See if it can help us plan." She gives me a tight smile. "You might not believe it, but I'm still glad I know."

You wouldn't admit it if you weren't.

My eyes flick to Syed, but he won't hold my gaze.

Logic. Facts. They're what bring Mere comfort. They let her move forward—the only direction she ever allows. But I'm still stuck on all the squishy questions that I cannot ask. How will this change their marriage? What have they talked about? What haven't they?

And then there are the other ones. The ones that I hope have never crossed her mind.

If she could go back, if she could stop Syed from loving her, would she?

And would he have stayed if he'd known from the beginning?

I picture Nathan's face. Wouldn't anyone . . . in the darkest recesses of their hearts, the parts they try to hide . . . wouldn't anyone want to run from this?

Chapter 19

I'm two hours late for work. On the train ride in, I aimlessly scroll through emails. An old *NYT* briefing. A bill from my last doctor's visit. A chain I'd missed between Nathan and Remy's behaviorist, Caroline. My thumb pauses in its scrolling. The words sinking in slowly, sharp claws pressing into my numb brain.

Caroline had done some digging on the council members and found out that one has a vendetta against dogs. He was bitten as a kid, and he consistently votes against off-leash dog parks.

How worried should we be? Nathan asks Caroline.

I stand outside the T station, and stare at the question, and fight back an urge to throw my phone. They have photos of Remy's bite, and a decision maker with a bias. We have a dog who still lunges at strangers and a trainer who gets nervous in front of crowds.

I lean my head against the brick wall of the station, my eyes closed tight against the sunshine. *We are going to lose.*

When I finally get to Kensington, Deena pounces, beating me to my desk.

"Where have you been? Your interview starts in twenty minutes. We were going to practice an hour ago."

I stare at her blankly. I don't know how to tell her that I don't care. How, a lifetime ago, I'd made a list on my phone because I thought I could choose what mattered.

The list is dead. An exercise in wishful thinking.

"I'm sorry," I say. "I had something come up."

I take my time turning on my laptop and plugging it into my monitor. Our company's logo flashes on the screen, casting a bright-yellow light across my keyboard. There are crumbs between the keys. The dirt, all of it, must have been building up for a while. I try blowing between the keys, but this makes the problem different instead of better—everything shifting, but still not where it's supposed to be.

Out of the corner of my eye, I can see Deena watching me, weighing my response. Deciding whether to be annoyed. Then, blessedly, she shrugs.

"As it happens, I also have news." Her wide eyes belie the forced casualness to her tone. "Bean and I are officially a couple. I'm using the word *girlfriend* now and everything. Can you imagine? Me."

My hand shakes on my keyboard, and I have to shove it in my pocket. I can't place this feeling . . . Jealousy, maybe? I watch her lips move as she talks about Bean. I notice how she seems to be bouncing on the balls of her feet, half a second and some fairy dust from taking flight.

It's a different world, the one she's in. A plane of space closer to Holly's, and one that feels utterly alien to my own. And maybe that explains the jealousy. Not of Deena, or not exactly, but of her journey. Maybe, I'm jealous of how far she's traveled . . . how far away she seems, not just from me, but from where she'd been. From where we'd been, together.

Her growth, her optimism . . . It should make me hopeful. I remember a night, not all that long ago, when it *did* make me hopeful. Now, I look at her, and I think of Holly. I think of both of them, moving on, and I feel inescapably alone.

"I don't know, though . . ." Deena's shaking her head. "Bean cooks. She gardens. She's a nurturer. One of those cozy people." Her next words come out like a question. "She's so much warmer than me."

The bouncing stills. I register the pause and the question behind it. I register it and I say nothing. For a breath, I say nothing, and then

I take another breath. I take another breath, and I drag myself toward my friend. I pull myself there with my fingertips. "Warmth doesn't have to be cozy. Warmth is caring. It's harassing a friend about an interview."

Deena looks away. She hides her smile. I cling to the ground I've gained. The smallest sliver.

Inevitably, the world goes on.

"So, tell us why you think you're the right candidate. Why should we choose you over somebody else who might seem equally qualified?"

It's a panel interview. Kensington's VP of Sales, Growth Director, and Delivery Lead stare back at me across the table. We've been at this for an hour. One question after another: provide your most successful client GTM strategies, share how you would manage crisis communications, describe your top priorities when launching a new brand.

And now this.

Why should we choose you? What makes you unique?

Only one in ten thousand people have Huntington's disease.

Meredith. Mere.

Bile burns the back of my throat.

Lauren, our VP of Sales, asked the question. She's watching me with an expectant smile and sharp eyes. Lauren's competitive and exacting. She uses phrases like *results-oriented* and is the kind of person who rubs her hands together with enthusiasm. She doesn't seem to care what people think, and I admire that. I admire her role in the company's leadership, too. I wonder what it feels like to wake up with all her energy, all her drive.

I pull my hair out of my ponytail and let it frame my face. I let myself remember the words Deena drilled into my head. About how I've worked my way up at Kensington, how I'm a proven entity. I'm supposed to talk about where I see myself in five years, without actually saying those words. I'm supposed to avoid clichés and generalizations, but everything I say should imply a certain future.

"I've worked at Kensington for almost two years," I begin. "I understand the client base and how our value prop speaks to their needs and goals. I understand how we differentiate ourselves in the market. Understanding all of that, who we are as a company . . . it takes time. With me, there won't be any lag time when I start."

They're Deena's words, and they feel alien in my mouth. But they're working; Lauren is nodding, and John from Growth and Jeff from Delivery seem to take their cues from her. I lean forward, gaining confidence. "More than that, though, I want to build something here. I want to grow my skills in a company I respect, a company that values my work and me as a human. I know what it takes to grow here—I've watched and learned from some amazing colleagues—and I'm ready to give Kensington what that growth requires."

I am amazed at how easy the words fall from my lips. It's like acting. I'm a million miles away watching a person who resembles someone I thought I wanted to be: successful young professional. Take two.

"What does it take, would you say?" Lauren asks. She's sharp; she's testing the meaning behind my words. "What do you think you need to do to reach your goals here? To help us reach our goals?"

Our eyes meet across the table.

"Some sacrifice," I say bluntly. Lauren steeples her fingers. "Exceptional work requires you to care. To make the work a priority. To care about it enough that it becomes a priority."

"So, passion," says Jeff unexpectedly.

"Yes."

"And you have passion for this work? You believe in it?" Lauren's eyes are silver gray. Clear, cool laser beams. I get the feeling they can see me fully. Like they can see both versions of me: the woman across the table and the woman watching from a million miles away.

Am I passionate about this work? About Kensington . . .

I think about how it feels when a scared dog chooses to trust me for the first time. How I'll try fifteen different things and none of them will work, and then, just when I'm inches from despair, something will happen. A wet nose against my hand. A fluffed-up tail bouncing around me with a ball in their mouth. A big retriever rolling on the ground in reckless joy, tummy exposed. Moments that look silly and seem small but are the foundation of possibility for these dogs. For these dogs and for me.

But with those images are the others: the dogs like Cliff, who will always be scared, who will never quite recover. The dogs like Remy, who recover but too late. Their fate already half decided. And the owners who have to make impossible calls. Their pain and regret and shame harnessed in countless emails, calls, and texts. The knowledge that I won't be able to do enough. All of it . . . the weight of all of that, all alone. No Holly. No partner. Just me. Just me, and all the things I cannot change.

No matter which way I look, left or right, up or down, all of it is hard. Not one bit of it is easy.

Except, maybe this job. Except, maybe this job, which will keep me busy and nothing else. This job that won't give me anything except what I'm happy to give back.

Mere's face looks at me from behind Lauren's head. My sister doesn't need another reason to worry. *I* don't need another reason to worry.

I need simple. I need this.

Passion . . . passion is a privilege.

I keep my eyes on Lauren. I keep them right there, and I lie.

Chapter 20

I get the job. Of course, I get the job.

They tell me the next day, and on Thursday, my work email pings with the official offer letter. I skim it, and then I forward the whole thing to Meredith. *Smiley face. Two thumbs-up.* I tap out the emojis, as if they are enough. For the past few days, since the appointment, our conversations have been stilted. We still talk as much as always, but I'm not sure what we say. Two animals, circling, trying not to spook the other.

I think she will be happy about the job. I am moving forward, just not in the way we'd thought. I imagine a celebratory lunch. Conversations about work trips and expense accounts. All the adult things that I took so long to do.

It's a dream job. *The* job. But as I close my laptop, I think of Holly—I think of the two of us on a couch in a tiny apartment. Talking about how we were going to live our lives differently. Live with a capital *L*. Passing a blue owl back and forth between us, asking the world for wisdom—I think of us, and I feel a sudden urge to cry.

It's Friday before I go see Nathan. I mean to go earlier, but I can't quite do it. There is comfort in the space between.

But now, I'm here, leaning against the door of his apartment, waiting for him to buzz me up. It's a warm day. Warmer than usual for November.

I remember reading somewhere that people with terminal illnesses and injuries sometimes get one last good day. One day when they feel like themselves, when they can enjoy the time with their family, when they can make one more good memory.

In that article I read, that last good day was described as a gift. But standing here, the sunshine on my face, feet away from Nathan, I wonder if it's the opposite. If, instead, the last good day only reminds you of what you stand to lose.

The buzzer sounds and I walk inside, foregoing the elevator for the stairs. With each step, I remind myself of my intentions. I build resolve as I climb. And I'm ready, I'm ready with my speech when he opens the door.

"Hey," he says, his eyes searching my face. I catch a whiff of cinnamon and take a half step back, crossing my arms across my chest.

"Can I come in?"

Nathan nods, stepping sideways so I can go around him. My right shoulder brushes up against the sleeve of his shirt when I walk by. My T-shirt against his T-shirt, nothing more. And still. My whole body stiffens.

I've had boyfriends. But I've never felt this—this need for physical contact. It's almost a compulsion, an irrational desire, a half-formed idea that I can breathe, I can be, if only we are touching. Deena once called this feeling chemistry. I wonder if she's right, and if that means it will fade. If that's what I should hope for.

I'm thinking about this, about not touching him, so I don't see it right away. I'm halfway down his hallway before I register what I'm seeing.

There are two sketches on the wall—both black and white, each with one pop of color. One has mountains and a bright-yellow sun, and I half recognize it; I've seen it poking out of a box.

I start to say something, but my throat closes over. I am silenced by what he's done.

I count to three, then try again.

"You unpacked." My voice sounds too high pitched, accusatory even, but Nathan doesn't falter.

"I did," he says.

I nod. I'm out of words again.

I walk slowly down the hall and into his kitchen. Green curtains. A framed Red Sox jersey. Mismatched dishes stacked in the cabinet. A photo of his family. Two different sized blue vases in the center of his table.

The cardboard boxes are all gone.

I stand there. I count my breaths. My face is smooth by the time I turn around.

"Why?"

"I got sick of living out of boxes."

He's being flippant. Trying to play this off.

"You might be leaving. You'll just have to pack everything back up again."

Nathan rolls one shoulder then the other, before reaching his left arm up to press the muscles beside his neck. I don't realize I'm holding my breath until he says what he says next.

"I've decided not to. Go back to DC."

No.

"Why?"

He quirks one eyebrow. "I would have thought that part was obvious."

"Don't be cute. Don't be funny."

"Now, see, that's going to be kind of hard . . ."

He's laughing. He's standing in his newly decorated kitchen laughing. As if he doesn't see it: the world I know, imploding. Nothing left but dust and debris. There's nothing to recover. Nothing, even, to make new.

"Your life is in DC."

His eyes get serious. "Maybe now it's here."

There is nothing here.

I sink down into a kitchen chair. It is a miracle that it does not collapse under my weight, under everything that sinks with me. When Nathan makes a move toward me, I hold up my hand. Stop. Stop. Stay back.

A frown plays at the corner of his mouth. "I had hoped you might be happy."

"I'm not," I say. "You can't stay here for me."

"Maybe I'm staying for the Sox."

I press my lips together. This is classic Nathan. Making light of grand gestures. Acting like the biggest things are easy. Forgetting that the small things still count.

He drags a chair over and sits down. Four feet of space between us. He can't touch me unless I reach out at the same time.

"I'm sorry about Meredith."

My head snaps up. "She texted me," he says. "I think she was worried about you."

Meredith. Meredith. Always worried about me. Always worried about the wrong person.

"When?" I choke out.

"Two days ago."

Two days ago. He's only texted me once since then, a link to a silly comic. He hasn't tried to help me. He hasn't tried to fix this.

I never imagined it could hurt this much. Letting someone know you.

"I'm sorry, Alex."

I shake my head. There is nothing to say.

"How is she?"

Making lists. Researching trials. Seeing patients. Protecting lives that are not hers.

"She's Meredith. She's marching forward."

"I admire her." His voice is low. I can't look up. I can't look at anything but my hands.

Meredith, building meticulous sandcastles at the beach. Meredith, braiding her own hair before doing mine. Meredith, picking me up when I was sixteen and sloppy drunk, her hands at ten and two behind the steering wheel. Meredith, Meredith. My whole life, hers and mine. One story.

"Me, too," I whisper.

He edges his chair toward mine. One hand covers my knee.

"Alex," he says.

He can't change anything. He can't make it better. But there is this. Sitting here together. It's not enough. There is nothing in the world that could ever be enough. But almost . . . it is almost something. And for one more minute, I take it. I take what I can get before the part that must come next. Before I do what I came here to do.

He shifts in his chair, his hand still on my knee. The pressure of his fingers keeping us connected. "I want to stay," he says. "I know it's the worst possible time to talk about the future, to talk about being happy . . ." His voice trails off. He must feel me stiffen. But then he keeps going.

Confident. Always so confident.

"We said we would see what we were, and then figure out the rest," he says. "Well, I'm ready for that part. The rest."

His eyes are fastened on mine. Wide gray-blue expanses, certain and sincere.

"I didn't choose you before," he continues. "I did take us for granted. I decided that love was an excuse not to worry rather than the biggest reason to fight. I'm not going to do that again."

I swallow. I straighten my shoulders.

"No," I say. "This is my fault."

I watch my words hit him. I watch the muscles in his jawline clench, his hand sliding off my knee. And then I make myself keep going.

"I let this happen. I let myself think what we've been doing was fair, to either one of us . . ." I can't look him in the eyes. "And the worst part is I knew better. I know you. I knew you wouldn't be able to help yourself."

"What are you talking about?"

My mouth is dry. My eyes are fixed on the hall behind Nathan's head, where the picture with the setting sun hangs. "Come on, Nathan. You doing this now? Unpacking now? It's who you are. It's in your DNA. You can't let me down. You can't let yourself down." I make myself look at him. It takes everything I have. "But it's not enough. Wanting to stay because you don't want to walk away isn't enough. It won't work. Not in the long run."

There's music playing in Nathan's apartment. I hadn't noticed before. It's the Beatles, a song I only recognize because of that movie, *Across the Universe*. The scene where the main guy and girl start to fall in love.

Nathan shakes his head. He looks stiff, his blue eyes cold and calculated. He looks the way he looks to other people.

I hate it.

"Well, it's good to find out what you think of me, I guess."

"I think you're wonderful." My voice is strangled. It makes both of us flinch. "I just don't think you've thought this through."

"Okay, help me then. Tell me what thinking it through looks like." He's leaning forward. His anger so easily forgotten. "Don't you think I deserve a chance to decide for myself?"

We stare at each other, the Beatles playing in the background. I listen to the song until it ends. Then, I stand up and walk over to his counter where his laptop sits. I push it open, wait until he gives me the password, then begin typing into the search bar.

We've avoided Huntington's. We've acted like the monster only exists if you poke your head under the bed. But lately, I've felt its hot breath sneaking up on us at the most innocuous times: when one of us catches the other one smiling at an older couple, the instant that follows the moment when I first wake up each morning, that time we joked about having a song that was ours.

And then Meredith got diagnosed, and the whole house of cards crumbled. But I knew he would put it back together. I know him. I never stopped knowing him. I don't think I ever will.

And so, I'm standing at Nathan's computer. My fingers hovering over the keyboard, poised to follow the advice from an article I read. About how to introduce someone to Huntington's disease. How to help them understand. To dig a little deeper beyond whatever googling he's already done.

I type *Huntington's disease* into the browser. I ignore the tightening in my chest. The fear or worse, the anticipation of an unspoken desire that maybe, just maybe, what comes up won't be as bad as I remember.

The screen fills with results—foundations, support groups, and first-person stories. Some of these are websites I saw on that day in Meredith's kitchen. The clinical sites with frightening descriptions about the deadly disease.

Progressive brain disorder.

Cognitive and psychiatric impairment.

Eventual loss of all motor function.

No cure.

It's just as bad. Maybe even worse.

My fingers stiffen against the keyboard. We read through each post line by line, link by link. We read first-person narratives—not the pretty ones from the major websites, but the dark, angry, and honest ones on chat rooms. About lost jobs and frightened relatives. About end-of-life care and advance directives. About suicide.

The content never gets any better. The end result is always the same: death and dying—the two impossible things paired one beside the other. Navy-blue typeface.

A few of the articles mention the importance of introducing loved ones to parents who are symptomatic. I read these with a note of bitterness that feels sick: wishing Tessa had stayed so I can use her illness as an illustration.

We stand in Nathan's kitchen as early evening slips to night. I watch the color follow the remaining daylight, slowly draining from his face. I watch it become real for him in a way it wasn't before. I watch him, and it's oddly comforting, because I'm so busy watching his horror, I almost forget to be horrified myself.

◆ ◆ ◆

It's Nathan who closes the laptop. He closes it, and with it, he closes his whole face. A shutter passes over the features that I know, leaving behind a man I don't. A person I've only been dating for a few months, as opposed to the man who was the boy I fell in love with as a teenager.

I knew. I knew this would be too much. Of course, I knew.

I saw Syed. I saw the burning man.

I knew. I knew. And still, I am undone. Looking at him, imagining him leaving, I am undone.

I am undone, and spinning backward. Twenty-one again, lying on a kitchen floor in an apartment he'd never seen but had held dreams of the two of us. Lying there, realizing that it's over. And then, it's three months later, and I'm calling him and saying the words, and hearing him agree. The pain, unbearable. Except, there was also the relief. Because being with Nathan had always felt like a trick. These two perfect years that could not possibly last.

I shiver. I'm back in his kitchen, those same eyes on mine. Those eyes waiting to remind me of what I've always known: that even among the best of us, there is a limit. There is a limit to how much pain anyone will willingly endure. We try to believe in the fairy tale, to believe that love is enough, but there are no guarantees. If we're honest, if we let ourselves be honest, self-preservation nearly always wins.

I knew better. I just let myself forget.

I steel myself. I look back at him, unflinching.

"Your health doesn't change how I feel about you," he says.

The right words, but they're hollow. It's as if he just rehearsed them in his head. Like they are the words you are supposed to say, and he's trying to convince himself he means them.

But he wants to mean them. He wants to. He does.

It's this that makes me cry.

"Alex," he says. His hand is on my wrist. He is so very tall.

"Don't," I say.

"Let's just . . . slow down, okay?" His voice is hoarse. "You might not even be sick."

"But I might be. I might be, and we should start with that assumption. I promised Meredith that I'd do the counseling, but I don't know if I'm going to get the test. I don't know if I will ever get the test."

His nostrils flare. We've never talked about this part. And I can tell he doesn't want to now. He'd rather avoid. Hope for the best. Believe the best.

"I never asked you to. I am just—just give me a minute to catch up."

"And then what?" I choke out. "Then, you tell me you will stay, when we both know you don't want to?"

He flinches, and I inhale, trying to ignore that my throat is on fire. And before he can respond, I push myself off his kitchen chair, swiping at my cheeks. Forcing in more painful breaths. Forcing my tears to stop.

Because I don't want to cry.

I don't want to be the girl who cries because someone might not want her. I don't want to be that girl: the one whose mother left. The girl who will take any scrap, from anyone. A long time ago, I promised myself I wouldn't be that girl. I would be better. I *will* be better.

I just can't be better when I'm with him. My love for him . . . it is too big. I think that's always been the problem. I was always going to need too much. I was always going to need proof.

Not just that he loved me.

But that it would last.

I tried to learn how to be different, but I couldn't do it. Not with him. All this time, I've been pretending.

The tears are hot against my cheeks. But I force myself to square my shoulders. To remember the lines I rehearsed this morning. The lines I should never have pretended I might not need.

"We should take some space. It's a lot. It's all been a lot."

The words are too steady, too cold; they slice through the air, making Nathan lean back. I imagine I can see the air rushing to fill the space where his body had been.

"You're doing this again?" he asks. His voice is hard. "You're deciding what we can and cannot handle."

"I'm doing this for both of us," I say.

"You think I haven't changed," he says. "Dammit, Alex. Seven years ago, I did take us for granted. I assumed too much, and I didn't step up when it mattered most. But I've changed. How can you not see that I've changed? I am not going to DC. I am choosing us. Do you really think I haven't grown up at all?"

"You're choosing us because Meredith got sick," I say. "Because you realized how much I will need you. Tell me that's not true?"

His jaw is clenched; his eyes are wild and tight on mine. "You're acting like I don't know what I want, and I do know. I want you."

"You want me as I am now." I wave my hand at the laptop. "You don't want all of this. You just don't want to admit it."

He glances at the computer, and I see his Adam's apple bob. "What exactly do you want me to admit, Alex?" The words ring of self-disgust. "That I'm terrified? That I wish I'd fallen for someone who is more likely to live until she's eighty? That I'm afraid I'll end up trapped." He falters on the last word, but his eyes are ice. "What terrible thing do you need me to admit so that you can believe that I know my own mind."

"I want you to think about it for more than fifteen whole minutes. I want you to admit that fifteen minutes isn't enough to have thought about it at all. I want you to admit that all the things we haven't talked about—the test, the future, kids . . . it means something that we haven't talked about any of it. And most of all, most of all—" My voice catches. I press my fingernails into my palms. I force myself to keep going. "I want you to admit that you have a habit of choosing obligations over yourself."

The silence stretches. His jaw is set tight enough to snap.

And I watch it happen. I watch him as he breaks.

"I don't want to think it through," he rasps. "I don't want to want to leave."

The truth.

The truth is brutal. Even when you see it coming.

"I'm sorry." His voice is ragged; his hand is in his hair. "Just give me—just give me a minute here. Please, Alex."

His stare is desperate. A well of anger that's not at all at me. I drag one of his hands into my lap, and hold it between both of mine. He will hate himself for this—for his doubts, for his honesty, for the things that he cannot promise. For the things he's not ready to look at. He will hate himself, and I don't want him to. It isn't fair. I'm the one who is asking for too much. For him to promise a future neither of us wants to face.

And isn't it awful? To know that what you need is wrong? To know and not be able to change it.

I would give anything not to need this much.

"It's not your fault," I say. "I'm the one who is ending this. I'm the one who needs to end it."

He doesn't answer right away. He just wraps his other hand around mine, automatic and tightly enough that I lose track. I lose track of who is holding on to who. And there's a moment, right then, where time seems to slow down, then jump ahead. A moment, lengthening, so that in it, I can see our whole future: the engagement in Colorado during a weekend visiting our old campus. The wedding at the inn in Ogunquit; us sipping champagne on that same balcony, this time for a very different reason. Two little boys with Nathan's gray-blue eyes and my red hair. A rental house near the water, watching our babies play in the sand. First grade and graduations. Anniversaries and birthdays. Every kind of kiss goodnight.

The hugs and scrapes. The beauty and bruises of a full life. Our life, just past my line of sight.

I see it. I see it all, just there. Close enough, I can almost feel it.

And then, I let go of his hand.

He nods, the coldest jerk of his head. And time restarts, and I can't see it anymore. There is just emptiness.

"If this is really what you want," he says.

I feel my chin move up and down. I watch myself stand and start to walk away.

I pause at the door. "We'll figure out Remy's training," I say. "We can . . . take turns or something."

"And the trial?" he asks.

"I will be there."

Another curt nod.

And that is it. Over. No need to even say goodbye.

Right before I leave, I look back at him, standing in his kitchen. And it hits me that I like his taste, I like his style. I like the way the colors in the room all line up together. I like the way he looks, standing by the table, his hands against the counter, the last bits of sunlight splattered across one side of his face. He reminds me of someone I used to know.

Chapter 21

One of my old clients, Alicia, bought a puppy from a breeder. She got the puppy when he was ten weeks old, and she did everything right. She socialized him with other dogs, scheduling controlled puppy playdates that guaranteed positive experiences. She had visits with her friends, so he'd get used to strangers and to children. She took him to breweries and Home Depot and rewarded him at every step. She followed every bit of advice in every book.

She did everything right.

But when her puppy was eight months old, he started having trouble. He'd bark and lunge at strangers; he started to fight with other dogs.

Alicia took him to the vet, who gave him a clean bill of health and recommended working with a trainer. And so, Alicia brought him to me. She brought him to me, and she told me everything she'd done. All the rules she'd followed. All the books she'd read.

She told me all of this, and I told her the truth. I told her she did everything right.

She did everything right. But, sometimes, it's not enough. The most important period of socialization happens before dogs even come to their new homes. It's those early weeks when they're still with their mothers, still with the breeder. The most important part of their development is the one period their new parents can't control.

And even if they could, it might not make a difference. There's genetics. There are the smallest of experiences that you can't predict and can't undo.

There is life. There is no way to do everything right.

You get the dog you get. And then you do your best.

I am numb. By the time I walk from Nathan's to Downtown Crossing and ride six stops on the orange line and walk up through Sullivan Square and past the man living in the tent under the bridge, I am numb. And wet. I am wet, because at some point, it started raining.

I should have checked the weather. I should have worn a raincoat. As I push open the door to our apartment, I think about the man under the bridge. I try to remember if his tent had a tarp.

Holly's home. I notice her shoes before I notice her: gold, glittery flats, impractical for this late in the year, kicked off by the door. She's always leaving her shoes everywhere. I can't count the number of times I've tripped over them or kicked them or bent down to put them away.

James must know this about her. She must leave her shoes scattered around his place, too. Their place, now. Or almost. Less than six weeks until she moves.

I told Holly I was going to find a new apartment, a one bedroom if I can swing it, but I haven't even started looking. There have been people traipsing in and out of here, though. They come by when we're at work. Strangers looking at our walls and running the water in our sink. Do they laugh at Holly's owls? Do they imagine they know something about the two girls who live here, who've spent four years calling it home?

Holly's sitting on our couch—the blue couch we bought together—her feet tucked up beneath her. She's reading one of the Harry Potters, which she's read a thousand times before. I can picture her in our college dorm room, reading it in just the same way. Feet in exactly that position. We've barely seen each other since my birthday, and right now, here, I miss her in a way that makes my chest ache, so I need to stretch my shoulders back—away from the tightness gathered there.

"Have you talked to Deena lately?"

I tense at something in her tone.

"I saw her at work. Why?"

"You missed drinks tonight," she says. "Where were you?"

Unexpected anger—swift and hungry—replaces the ache in my chest. Where was I? She hadn't been home in four days. In, arguably, six months.

"I was with Nathan. I went over after work."

"I mentioned you got the job. To Deena. And I guess . . . you hadn't told her."

My brain whirls. "Shit," I say, remembering. Remembering I'd forgotten. Remembering every hour Deena has put into my career. All the time I never even had to ask her to give. "Shit," I say again, pulling out my phone. "Maybe they're still there. I can go explain—"

"I think she went out to dinner, but it's okay. I think she'll get over it." She hesitates. "She's really happy, you know. With Bean."

I can't tell if I imagine the defensiveness, the double meaning in the words. I grab a bottle of vodka from the freezer, mixing a splash with soda water in the only tumbler I can find. Holly has already started packing, items disappearing in the hours when I'm asleep or somewhere else.

I take a sip. Bitter. Bracing.

"Are you okay?" she asks.

Do you even care?

I bite back the question. I'm being petty, childish. I can feel the erratic currents of my anger converging all at once. But still, her question feels like an obligation, like a cardboard cutout, meant to disguise her absence: from our apartment, from the training company. From the spaces in between.

"I've just been busy." The excuse hangs between us, its flimsiness mixing with the vodka, making me say what I say next: "And we haven't exactly been keeping each other up to date."

The air sharpens, and, already, I wish I could pull the words back in. Stop this conversation before it starts. But Holly sits up straighter. It happens slowly: the straightening of her spine, the lifting of her chin. She studies me. She doesn't look away.

"And that's my fault? It's my fault that you don't tell me about your life."

"You're not exactly around to tell." I'm speaking quietly, but my heart is pounding in my throat.

"That's not fair," she says.

"Come on, you're hardly here." I press my lips together. "It's different now."

"Because of James? Because I'm leaving? You stopped telling me things ages ago."

"Because you stopped showing up." My voice is high and fast, each syllable slapped together. The words I've tried not to think for months are tripping over my tongue and piling between us. "You quit DogKind without even really telling me. We started it together. And when I talked about restarting it, you didn't even offer—you didn't offer anything at all."

The silence is angry, the air shivering. I open my mouth to course-correct, to apologize, to stop. To stop all of it. But I'm already too late.

"I wondered if we'd ever do this," says Holly. "I wondered if you'd ever tell me that you were mad at me. If you'd ever admit that you were mad at me."

As if it's my job. As if it's all on me, when she's the one who changed the rules.

"If you thought I was mad, why didn't you ask me?" I ask.

"Why didn't you tell me?" Her face is splotchy, her voice uneven. "Fine, maybe I messed up with DogKind. But then, you shut down on me. You don't tell me about your mom. You barely talk about Nathan. You don't even tell me when you're mad. And that's not how this works." Somehow, she's ended up standing. "It can't always be my responsibility to figure out what's going on with you."

Her words burrow beneath my skin. Tiny, persistent needles.

I still haven't told her about HD. I'd convinced myself it was because she was pulling away and I didn't want this to be the thing that stopped her. I'd told myself telling her wasn't fair. But I wonder now if it was also something else: if I was trying to prove that she wasn't the only one who could create distance.

My anger is gone, and my bones feel sloppy. Through my open bedroom door, I can see my soft blue bedspread.

"You should have been honest," says Holly. Her voice is quiet now. "You should tell me how you feel."

Tell me how you feel. As if that is easy. As if that's fair to either party.

I glance down at my glass then up at her.

"You're right," I say. "You're right." I put the glass down on the coffee table. I try to say the next words gently, how I mean them. "But, Holls . . . I don't think you really wanted me to tell you. I think that's why you didn't ask."

She looks at me. And the denial is on her lips, her mouth opening, her head shaking. But then, she stops. Her eyes find mine, and she stops, her chin still jutting to the left. She exhales, long and slow and sad. She sits down on the couch beside me. The weight of her body is so familiar. The way she bends one leg beneath her.

"Yeah," she says. "Okay."

We sit together. For a long time, we don't speak. But when she presses her knee against mine, I press back.

We bought this couch four years ago. We were too cheap to pay for the assembly, so it came in a cardboard box, and neither one of us knew how to put it together. We drank two bottles of wine and fought over the directions, and in the morning, we woke up curled on top of it. Entirely assembled.

It was a cheap couch. Pretty but cheap. I've always suspected we put the screws in the wrong places, but still, somehow, it's standing.

"I am sorry about the business," she says at last. It's not what's most important, but it is something. A place to start. "I should have said that a long time ago."

"It's okay," I say. "We aren't twenty-four anymore. You were allowed to move on. I didn't want to stop you."

"I should have talked to you about it, though," she says softly. "Admitted when I wanted to step back. I didn't want to hurt your feelings . . . so I decided to let it play out. I convinced myself it would be easier for both of us."

It wasn't, though. I'd become so insecure when she'd suddenly stopped showing up. My mind had gone into overdrive with all these different explanations. Most about me. About whatever I'd done wrong.

And then I'd done the same thing to her.

She pulls a piece of hair out of her ponytail, twisting it around her finger. "I'll always love the company. I still believe in it. But I—I learned I like stability. I like working on a large team. I want things like maternity leave"—she blushes—"and predictable hours . . . I . . ." Her voice trails off.

"You changed," I finish. "What you wanted changed." It's not an accusation. But what does it say about us that she couldn't tell me what she wanted? And I wonder, then, if this is the downside of long friendships: their tendency to lock each of us in place. Taking away the potential for evolution. For choosing what comes next.

A neighbor slams the door down the hall. His heavy steps pound against the thin walls of our apartment. I wonder if we will decorate it for Christmas. A few years ago, I found these tiny Santa hats we could put on Holly's owls. I wonder where the decorations are. I wonder if I can find them among the other boxes.

"I am sorry," she says, again. "For all of it."

I miss you.

The words balance on the tip of my tongue, but I don't say them, because we are back to where we started. Where I am afraid of inertia and what it means. Of what happens if I say the words, and nothing changes.

Tell me how you feel.

It's too much. It's asking too much to be the one to admit to that much need. To put one more set of blocks on my side of the scale.

Especially right now.

I uncross my arms. I let my shoulders relax. I say the one thing I know I won't regret.

"I'm sorry, too."

Chapter 22

We leave it there: at almost enough. A tough conversation, a step toward honesty. The door of our friendship opening the smallest crack. One good wind away from the end or a beginning.

I tell myself it's something, and I leave it at that.

I miss Nathan. All weekend, I miss him. On Saturday, I wake up in the middle of the night and there's a moment before I remember that he is gone. This one moment. But rather than relief, I just feel sadness. My legs are heavy, and it feels like someone is sitting on my chest, and instinctually I'm sure that I don't want to leave my bed. Something terrible has happened, but I don't remember what.

And then I do. I remember. And then, every ache expands.

By Sunday, I am sick of myself. I am sick of sitting in my bed. I am sick of eating takeout. The world begins to yell at me from outside my window: the screech of tires and men swearing, laughter coming from a neighboring stoop at dusk, a dog barking a boisterous greeting.

I get up and wash my face and stare at my pale reflection peeking out from beneath my tangled red hair.

Back in August, I had an idea. I had this idea that I could be a different kind of person. The kind who knows how to go after what they want. Who knows how to choose what makes them happy. I was going to help Remy. I was going to figure out my career. I was going to be with Nathan. To trust him without asking for quite so much.

Tougher. Stronger. Alex 2.0.

But I made other choices. I chose the safer job. I chose to be on my own, to accept what I can't handle.

And that other person? I'm not sure that she ever existed.

I press two fingers into my forehead, just as the dog barks again. I look back at the mirror.

Remy. There is still Remy.

◆ ◆ ◆

I spend the rest of Sunday morning trying to figure out a plan. I look into the city council member that Nathan's behaviorist emailed about—the one who supposedly hates dogs—and it's as bad as she described. It won't matter what Nathan, Caroline, and I say. He's going to need proof, and something more than us talking about Remy walking through a crowded park.

By the afternoon, I have sketched out a rough strategy. I don't know if it will work; I don't know if anything will work . . . but it is something. I send Meredith a few memes about the perils of being a GP (I've been sending her stupid stuff every day, my own poorly articulated love language). And then I drag myself outside, wearing ratty sweats and an orange windbreaker that clashes horribly with my hair, and I point my feet toward Cambridge, toward the other thing that I can fix.

Deena's apartment is the first floor of a triplex with peeling gray paint and a newly renovated deck—the common East Cambridge combination of dilapidated and redone. She opens the door before my hand has even left the doorbell. The surprise on her face, the surprise before anything else, tells me what I already knew: It's weird, me being here. We've known each other for years, and I've never been to her apartment. And now, I am here, on a Saturday morning.

"I'm sorry," I say into the silence. "I'm sorry about the job."

There's a rustling behind Deena, and then Bean's face appears. They're both wearing coats. A bright-red scarf hangs from Deena's hand.

"I'm sorry," I say again, backing away. "You guys are on your way out."

"Don't be silly." This, from Bean. She's pushed her way around Deena and is smiling at me with warmth I don't deserve. A pair of sweet dimples tugs at the corners of her cheeks. "We were just going to do a quick walk, around the block or so. You should come with."

Deena's watching Bean with a mixture of exacerbation and amusement. And something sweeter, something that flushes her face with color. She makes a show of winding the scarf around her neck. One, two, three turns.

"Let's go," she says, stepping around me and onto the small stone walkway to the street. Bean gives me an encouraging nod, and then we're walking, down the neat sidewalks of East Cambridge toward the dark water of the Charles. It's one of New England's nasty November days—damp without rain, so you feel the cold on the inside, seeping right into your bones. The wind quickly rubs my cheeks raw, blowing dead leaves around our feet. I'm jealous of Bean's wool coat, of Deena's scarf.

We pass a playground, and I'm surprised at the number of children, the number of parents, braving the day. High-pitched shrieks and laughter echo across the concrete. A patch of sunlight breaks through the clouds and glints against the yellow plastic slide.

I cough. I move my hands from my pockets to my sides. "I'm sorry," I say for the third time. "Really. It was shitty not to call you immediately. You were the biggest help with the interviews. You're the whole reason I got the job."

Deena glances at me out of the corner of her eye. She glances at me, and then she looks at Bean. Those dimples.

"I may have bitched about you a bit," says Deena. Bean shoots her a warning look, but Deena just grins. "Only a bit," she says.

She sighs then, and stretches her hands above her head. "But, Alex, hey, what's going on with you? It's whatever about the job. But come on. You're off these days."

I stiffen. A cold breeze nips against my fingers. I can't feel the tips at all.

"I'm fine," I say. "Really. I've just been distracted."

Deena shakes her head. She lifts her hand and begins to count off on her fingers. "You show up late for work, or these days, not at all." Her voice is quieter now. "You stopped going out for drinks. You don't seem to care that you got offered the job that you supposedly needed to have. You text me that you split with Nathan, and then you tell me it's not a big deal . . ."

"Because it's not a big deal," I say, automatically.

"Then what is?"

A young mother walks by pushing a stroller. A pink pom-pom from her baby's hat is just visible over the rim of the basket. At first, I think the mom is singing, but then I realize she's having a quiet conversation. She's carrying on a whole conversation with her baby: She's telling her baby that she is special, that she is loved. She's telling her that she is safe. I watch them—this mother and her baby—in their own private world, in the middle of Cambridge.

I watch them and I think of Mere, and tears smart against my eyes.

By the time my throat clears, we've reached the river. Runners jog past us, their long slim legs pumping under bright-colored spandex. Muscles flexing, sweat tingeing their brows. I count them as they go by. I get to ten before I speak.

"I didn't mean to take what you were doing for granted. It was a shitty thing to do."

Deena shrugs, her voice uncharacteristically gentle. "We all have our moments." She hesitates. "Do you even want the job, though?"

"I don't know," I answer honestly. I picture my desk at Kensington, the way I'd catch my own reflection in the dark screen of my monitor just before it turned on. I put this image alongside another: the energy from my coworkers, the vacuum pulling them together and forward at the same time. "I want to want something that is possible."

I jut my chin toward Deena. "What about you. Are you happy?" I mean to clarify, to qualify my meaning within the confines of Kensington, but I let the question hang between us. I notice how her eyes flick to Bean's face and then back to the water.

"It depends on the day, but honestly?" She shrugs. "It's all harder than I expected. I had the same ideas as everyone. You get the job, the cute apartment, the cute girl"—she winks at Bean—"but the thing is, even with all that, it's still hard. It's all still really fucking hard."

"But you keep doing it," I point out. "You keep showing up."

"Showing up. Not showing up. I can't say for sure which one is better."

"Showing up," says Bean, her voice firmer than I've ever heard it. She gives me a small smile. "It took me a long time to figure that one out," she says. "But choosing nothing won't keep you where you are. You'll still end up somewhere else."

My gaze travels from the dark water back to the steady stream of runners to the cars rushing down Memorial Drive. Something wiggles in my mind, like a loose tooth. I imagine touching my tongue against it. The pain first. The pain and then whatever comes after.

When we get back to Deena's apartment, Bean kisses my cheek, then leans into my ear. Her breath tickles against it. "Sometimes, I think we forget that we can give it to ourselves." She leans back, and her eyes crinkle at my unasked question.

"Grace," she says. "Even just a little."

One more squeeze, and then she's retreating, up the path and through their door. I register that she has a key. That in these months, they've gotten from there to here. That I missed it.

"She's kind of unbelievable," I say.

Deena's smile is automatic. Full and wide across her face. "I know."

"I'm happy for you." I reach out and squeeze her hand. "I'm really happy for you both."

Deena's smile widens farther, then shifts, her expression thoughtful, like she's trying to decide something. She rocks back on her heels, then lets out a puff of air. She keeps her eyes on her front door. It's painted a bright blue. I hadn't noticed before.

"I never thought I'd meet someone like her," she says. "I never even let myself want to meet someone like her. My parents . . ." Her jaw tightens. "They're good people, and they tried to support me, in their way, but I don't think they ever saw me. And the more I started to understand myself, the less I think they wanted to. The less I think they want to." She shifts her shoulders back and takes a breath. "Then I met Bean. And she sees me all the way through. She sees me and she stays."

Her words sketch a picture I'd always missed, and the shame pricks me in the gut. A string of responses trickles through my mind, each more inadequate than the last. Each claiming an intimacy I don't deserve.

I lick my lips. I try for honesty.

"Five years," I say. "We've known each other for five years. But . . . we don't know each other that well, do we?"

She sighs. It's heavy. It settles across my shoulders. "No, no, I guess we don't."

"I should have asked more questions."

"I'm not sure I wanted you to."

"I wish it wasn't so hard," I say into the silence. "Getting to know each other. It used to be easier, I think."

"I said that to Bean, once. Want me to tell you what she told me?"

I incline my head; a damp piece of hair slaps against my cheek.

"That we make it harder than it has to be."

We stand in front of her triplex, and the cold wind bites my nose, and I count the questions I've never asked. The answers I've never given. And then, I do the thing I should have done months ago.

"I might be sick," I say. I take a breath. "My mom. She had a pretty nasty condition, it turns out. The kind that kills you in the worst way. And I might have it, too."

Deena looks at me. Her eyes are fierce. "Dammit, Alex."

"I know."

"Do you want to—"

"No." I shake my head. "I haven't told many people. I haven't even told Holly, and I don't think I'm ready to get into it just now. And it's not an excuse for how I was this past week. Okay? But, Deena, I'm glad I told you."

She won't hug me—Deena is not a hugger—but she pulls herself up to her full height, and presses her hands together in front of her.

"I think you know better than most how crap life can get," she says. "And I think you're a badass. I think you will be okay." She grabs my hand and gives it one quick squeeze, the gesture utterly out of character. "You are thoughtful, and you are loyal, and you make allowances for everyone but yourself, Alex Bailey. I'm very, very glad to know you."

A warmth spreads from her hand to mine and then right into my chest. It's different, telling her. It's different than telling Nathan or talking to Meredith. Because there are no implications here. No one to protect or guard against. It's just me. And Deena. And her certainty in me.

Here is the truth: I cannot do this with Nathan. I cannot handle being the person who might be sick. Being the person who might be a burden.

I cannot do that with Nathan.

But maybe, it turns out, I can do it by myself.

Chapter 23

The week leading up to Remy's trial, Nathan and I start texting back and forth about her schedule and final training prep. For Remy's sake, we revert to polite acquaintances again. But every time I see his name pop up on my screen, my stomach lands somewhere near my feet. Every text I send, I imagine sending him another one: one that says I changed my mind. That I want to try. I imagine that maybe, if I live with this long enough on my own, I'll eventually wake up as a person who can live with this with him.

I imagine all of this, but I say nothing. I've never been one to confuse dreams with reality.

Nathan keeps me updated on his own training sessions, and twice, he drops Remy at Lois's to work with me. It's better this way—not just for the two of us, but for Remy. It's better for her to get trained by different people in different places. And it's better that Nathan learns to handle her by himself; she's his dog, after all. (His dog. *His dog*. Not mine. Never mine. I tell myself this again and again. I try to make it stick.)

Once, when they drive away, I can feel Lois watching me watch them, and I wish I'd worn more layers.

"Do you know what you're doing?" she asks me.

"I'm training a dog that needs my help," I say. "That's what I am doing."

The day of the trial dawns gray and misty. I can feel my hair frizzing as soon as I step outside. I consider going back upstairs for hair spray, but I can't bring myself to care. All the energy I have is focused on Remy. On what will happen today. Or more to the point, what might happen tomorrow. Euthanasia.

(Such a word: *euthanasia.* I looked up its origins the other day. It's Greek for *good* and *death.* A "good death" as opposed to one that drags out. One that's more painful. I can't decide what I think about that idea, whether death can ever be good. But then again, I think I conflate good with something else—with not dying at all.)

Nathan and I get to city hall at almost the exact same time. I see him before he sees me: his long legs, his purposeful way of walking. All of it familiar. All of it, almost mine.

And then, he's right in front of me. We are in front of each other. His eyes hold mine, and I lose track of the pavement. I have to stop walking altogether.

I can feel my eyes falling into his. I can feel everything, at once.

"Alex," he says. And my name in his mouth seems to act like a reminder. He draws back into himself, his features transforming into how they are for other people: his eyes, calculated and assessing; his face, handsome and almost haughty. He's wearing a suit and tie. Tailored and crisp. He reminds me of how he looked when he came to my house three months ago.

Under my winter coat, I'm in dated dress pants and a blousy shirt that keeps coming untucked. Our mismatch is as apparent now as it was then.

"How are you?" I ask. I'm trying for friendly, but I immediately regret the question. I don't blame him when he raises his eyebrows. When he doesn't bother to answer.

"How's Meredith?" he asks instead.

I bite the inside of my cheek. "Good. I saw her at Thanksgiving; she made her usual feast. So, you know, still being Mere."

This is half a lie. Mere is Mere, and the food was delicious, but the atmosphere was thick with forced cheer and carefully constructed phrases. It was the worst Thanksgiving I could recall. Even worse than the first one without Tessa, when Meredith made cold-cut turkey sandwiches, and our dad passed out in front of the TV before the parade even ended. At least at that one, I remember laughing. Meredith tried to bake a chocolate pie from scratch, and we ended up with cups of gooey brown sludge. Our spoons dipped back into it almost as soon as we got them out. We ate it all, every sludgy bite, while watching *Romy and Michele's High School Reunion*. I remember laughing around the chocolate mess in our mouths.

"How's your mother?" I ask Nathan.

His jaw softens. "She's—recovering. They think the chemo is working. She might get her fourth miracle."

His eyes trace my face with something like an apology, and I think I know why. I shake my head. I reach my hand out and then let it drop. "That's good, Nathan. That's really good."

He's looking at my hand. I almost think he's going to grab it. But then, he shifts, and the cool mask slides back over his features.

"You ready to go in?" he asks.

I nod, and we pass through the heavy doors into the entrance hall. We're scanned through a set of metal detectors by two security guards with a soberness that makes me ache.

My mother left us and left Boston and moved to Maine. Was it simpler there? Safer? Less potential for pain?

Or was it just easier to pretend not to see it?

The behaviorist, Caroline, is waiting for us in the lobby. She has short, dark hair and clear brown eyes and a voice that brooks no argument. She and Nathan met months ago, and she re-evaluated Remy with him earlier this week, but this is our first time meeting. I watch how she smiles up at Nathan when she shakes his hand—there's respect in her eyes, and something more. And I realize, then, that she is pretty.

He is handsome and she is pretty. And their confidences seem to match. And they just . . . fit together: a veterinarian and a lawyer who loves dogs. It sounds like one of the cheesy movies that Holly used to make me watch. The kind where you know how it will end before it starts.

I put my hands behind my back, grab my wrists, and squeeze. I picture Remy. Remy with her rust-brown fur, and half-bent ears and steady eyes. Remy, who loves to toss her head in the wind, and who likes to put that same head in my lap so that I can rub her ears. Remy, who believes it's her job to keep all of us together.

Remy is why I'm here.

The three of us go inside the main room, and all automatically sit together. We listen to the charges: a history of bites, the last, a level three. There are photos. Detailed photos. And I watch how the council members cringe. I watch them start to make up their minds before she's even been defended.

One by one, we're called to speak. Nathan goes first, followed by Caroline. They both are eloquent and clear. Caroline, especially, is persuasive, though I notice she chooses her words carefully. She never speaks in absolutes, because she knows she can't make promises. And despite her confident assurances, when I look at the faces of the council, I can tell they are not convinced. Caroline notices, too, and she tries to give me a reassuring smile, but she knows. We both know how this is going.

"There's a trainer here, right?" says Wilkins, the Council Chair, a graying man with glasses and sharp eyes. "The one who's been working with her since the start."

I nod and push myself up on shaky legs. "Um, yes. I'm her. I mean, I'm Alex Bailey, the trainer."

When I get to the front, I hold my hands together to keep them from shaking.

"Alex Bailey, previous owner of DogKind. Certified professional trainer, correct?"

I nod. "Yes, sir."

He asks me a few basic questions. About whether I've witnessed Remy in crowds. Whether she can be controlled on leash, and how she acts in certain situations. I answer honestly. I talk about her progress. I talk about the walk I did in Cambridge with her last Tuesday, weaving through a crowd of strangers without incident. I am not as articulate as Nathan and Caroline, but I do the best I can.

Wilkins peers at me over his glasses. "Do you have experience with aggressive dogs?"

"Yes," I say. "I mean, I have experience with dogs who have a bite history. Dogs bite for a lot of reasons."

He shuffles the papers, and then holds up a photo. "You don't think dogs who bite like this are aggressive?"

I feel my spine straighten, annoyance burning away my nerves. "If pushed hard enough, any dog will bite like that. Dogs are dogs. They don't get to use their words." There's an uncomfortable beat of silence, and when no one responds, I keep going. My voice is softer but no less clear. "The world can be scary," I say. "And some dogs are more afraid than others. And they react poorly. Training dogs isn't about forcing them not to react; it's about helping them know they don't need to. It's about helping them feel safe."

Wilkins looks at the picture, then at me. His expression is impossible to read.

"You call yourself a dog whisperer, don't you?" asks another member of the council. I don't remember his name.

"I'm sorry?" I ask.

"My daughter showed me a video of you and some dog. She said you're a dog whisperer. A dog miracle worker. Which, I'm sorry, miss, but sounds a bit like baloney."

I glance to my left, toward the onlookers, and I find Nathan's gaze and I have to catch my breath. His face is dark and his posture rigid. He looks like he might leap out of his chair.

I look away from him and back to the council. I square my shoulders.

"You're right," I say. "It is baloney."

Out of the corner of my eye, I see Nathan lean back.

"I'm not a dog whisperer. I don't perform miracles. That dog in the video?" I squeeze the podium for Cliff. For the ways that I had failed. "I didn't save him, not in the end. So I'm not here to tell you that all dogs can be saved. I know better than anyone here—certainly better than you—that that's not true. Not everything can be fixed." I bite my lip. "But that's not Remy. If I thought it was, I'd tell you so. I'm not particularly good at spinning the truth."

There's a pause.

"One more question, please, Miss Bailey," says Wilkins. "And please keep in mind, these meeting minutes are public." Nathan shifts, but I just nod. Wilkins isn't trying to threaten me, he's trying to protect me. To remind me that this is my reputation.

He holds up another photo. One of the ones with blood. "Do you think the dog who did this might still be a risk to others?"

Of course, she might be.

But isn't it unfair that animals are killed for being scared?

We didn't euthanize Cliff because he might have harmed someone. We did it because he was deeply unhappy. Because he could not recover. Because his life became the size of his crate. I blink. *A good death. As opposed to one that's drawn out.*

I feel tears sting my eyes. Something like relief, not sadness.

And then, I look back up at Wilkins. I take the biggest breath I can, so my chest expands. I feel larger entirely. Remy is not Cliff. Her world is full of possibility with some very important guardrails.

Would she hurt someone again? That's what this man is asking. And the truth is this: I can't say for sure. No one can. Caroline didn't. Because you can't be certain about a dog.

But I am certain of Nathan. When he showed up on my doorstep, I was surprised he had Remy—I was surprised he had the time—but now I can't imagine him without her. I've watched him choose her again and again. I am sure of everything he's learned and everything he will do for her. I am sure that Nathan loves her, too. Nathan will keep her safe.

And as it turns out: I don't really give a shit about my reputation. There are some positives when you have very little left to lose.

I take out my phone. I ask Wilkins if I can show him something, and he nods. I plug my phone into the monitor at the front of the room, and the video pops up.

It's a video I made this week. The first video I've made since Cliff.

It's filled with clips of Remy from the past month—walking through crowds with strangers, sitting quietly in a busy park, relaxing in Nathan's apartment. The council watches impassively, and then we get to the last clip. The one I took this week. Remy is lying on her back, her jowls falling back to reveal her long, sharp canines. The teeth some people call fangs. They are nearly a half an inch in length, tucked inside her long jaw. I walk over to her while she sleeps, and she lazily opens her eyes. Her tail thumps against the wall. One. Two. Three. I place the tip of my finger against one long tooth. And then, I kiss where my finger was. My lips, my whole face—exposed.

She opens her mouth and licks my cheek.

"Remy is not a risk; I'd gamble my career on it," I say. "Remy knows how to learn to love a stranger. She did that with me."

I see them as soon as we walk out of the courthouse. Lois, with her gray hair neatly curled and pinned back, her bright-blue eyes anxiously searching my face, searching for an answer. And Remy—my Remy queen—sitting quietly beside her. And before I can stop myself, before I can consider that Nathan orchestrated this, them being here, I'm running toward them. Sprinting like a madwoman, like I'm worried something might change before I reach them. I fling my arms around Remy's neck and bury my nose in her soft fur. There's no fear left between us now. There's only understanding.

"You're going to be okay," I tell her. "You're going to be okay."

I keep whispering this into her coat, until she shifts under my too-tight grip. Reluctantly, I lean back, until we can see each other's faces, and I swear she lifts an eyebrow. Haughty. *Get a hold of yourself, Alex.*

I let out a snort of laughter.

"You're going to be okay."

She stands up, shaking her red-and-white coat out with great dignity before swiping her tongue across my cheek. Licking away the salty tracks that my tears have left behind.

Enough of that.

A second lick.

But also: *I love you, too.*

I blink back another set of tears. People who say that dogs can't talk simply don't know how to pay attention.

Remy looks over my shoulder, and I follow her gaze to him. To Nathan, standing maybe three feet behind me, leaning against a tree. Arms crossed, a casualness that's ruined by his eyes. By a stare that threatens to consume me.

Nathan, who believed in Remy first. Who believed in me. Who believed in me enough to bring her here today.

His jaw is tight with emotion, his sharp features softened by his relief. Neither of us says a word. We don't need them. All we need is this. Us, being here. This moment. This one thing that we did together.

Right now, it is enough. This one brilliant thing that we got right.

Chapter 24

"Can I walk with you?"

That voice. I'm half a block from the courthouse. Nathan falls in line beside me before I have a chance to answer.

Lois left; she's dropping Remy at Nathan's place and then heading back home herself. It's just the two of us now, walking side by side toward Broadway. We go another two blocks before he speaks again.

"Did you mean it? What you said in there?"

I glance at him, and I notice that his suit jacket is unbuttoned. The quiet joy from the courthouse has morphed into something else. He's flustered in a way I've never seen. Nathan's honesty is how he stays in control. He never lets himself get caught out.

"Gamble your career?" He grabs my arm, pulling both of us up short. He's worried. He's worried about me. "Jesus, Alex, Wilkins was right: These meeting minutes are public. That will get out. If something happens with Remy . . ."

"Nothing is going to happen with Remy," I say. "She has you."

"So you trust me to take care of her, just not you."

I flinch. I start walking again, my head bent against the wind. I don't understand how Nathan is not cold. I'm bundled up like it's mid-February—blue down coat, light-gray scarf, and an oversize winter hat. All the protective gear I own.

"When did you make that video?" He catches up to me easily. One of his strides is worth two of mine.

"After you told me about the new council member. I knew we were going to lose."

"What if she had hurt you?"

"She wouldn't have," I say. "I trust her."

He makes a noise in the back of his throat. We've stopped again, this time next to a bank on the other side of Broadway. My back is pressed against the building. The jacket looks warm, but it's old. I can feel the cold bricks against my back. I look down, and there's a penny under my shoe. Something stings the back of my throat, but I catch it before it rises to my eyes.

Nathan sees the penny, too, and our eyes connect, and then, wordlessly, we both start walking again. One block after another, until we get to the path down by the Mystic River. Dark, slowly flowing water. It's quieter here, making room for all the things I need to say. The truths I suddenly know I need to tell him.

Nathan is the one who breaks the silence.

"You trust Remy, but you don't trust me," he says. "And Alex, I understand. I hesitated. But I *will* get there. I know myself. And you're not even giving me a chance."

An aching heaviness. I blink it back.

"It's not about you, Nathan," I say softly.

"Then . . . what."

"Then, *me*," I say. "You're putting this on yourself, but we won't work because of me. It will be like last time. Me, breaking us apart because I can't handle it. It's too much. All of this; it is too much for me."

"It won't be like last time," he says. "That wasn't all on you. And I'm staying now. I'm choosing you. And yes, I said that I couldn't think it through—but that was because I was scared and I didn't want to risk screwing this up. And all you heard was scared. Not the other part. About how I need you."

He grabs my hand with his. "I need you, too, Alex. Just as badly."

My heart feels swollen. Battered. I imagine I can feel it bumping up between the ribs in my chest. *I need you, too.*

I pull my hand away. I cannot do this if I'm touching him.

"It comes back to the same thing," I say. "You're staying, at least in part, because of this disease, because of what I might be facing. Not only because you want to stay."

"Why can't it be both?"

"Because I can't handle it being both. That's what I am trying to tell you. This isn't about you." My hands have ended up fists at my side. "*I* cannot wake up every day wondering if you are here out of guilt. I can't live my life wondering if this will be the day you decide to leave. I can't catch you frowning and think: *He wishes he hadn't stayed. He wishes he was in DC. He wishes I hadn't derailed his life.* Even if you never think those things, I will think you are. I know myself. And *I* cannot do it."

"You won't even try."

"And watch you give more away while I do? No. I won't."

"And it doesn't matter," he says softly, "that I love you."

My feet stop moving. My scarf is too heavy around my neck. I'm staring at the water. Mud-brown ripples.

Love. He says it now. The biggest word we have. Thrown out now, at the tail end of November, like a last resort.

I love you.

He never understood. He never understood that love is not always enough.

I don't know how long we stand there, together beside the water. Three ducks swim near the bank, poking their heads in and out among the reeds. I wonder when they will fly south. It must be too cold for them to stay here.

I love you.

In a way, I'm glad he said it now. Not because it changes anything, but because it helps with my resolve. Because I am not as certain as I am pretending. Because he is still Nathan. And if he pushed hard enough . . . I think that I would still take the pieces. With Nathan, I will always accept the pieces.

But he loves me. And the simple truth is this: It is better for him to leave. Even if he loves me. Maybe especially if he loves me. Because more than ever, his confidence—his beautiful, insufferable assurance in what he can withstand—feels like it's worth preserving. And I can't do that. I am not the one to do it. I am still the girl left behind, in the silent kitchen, in the yellow house. Left behind with my father. With myself.

And so, where Nathan sees possibility, all I can see is Syed. I see the burning man, and call it weak or silly, call it whatever you want, but I know, in my very core, that I am not capable. I am woefully unprepared for the responsibility of someone else's pain. Because it is a responsibility: wanting him to stay.

Isn't it better? To know your limits? To know what you cannot handle? Isn't that one kind of strength?

"Alex."

My name. It still sounds different when he says it. It sounds like the name of a person who I'd one day like to be.

"Take the test, then, Alex. At least give us that chance."

I stumble, but right myself quickly. I think I knew that this was coming.

"Most people at risk never get tested," I say into the cold, dead air. "Less than twenty percent. That is my reality. I can't take the test for you, Nathan." I pause; I wrap my arms around my middle. "And even if I could . . . whether it's negative or positive, I'd always wonder if the result is the reason that you stayed. Getting tested won't let me put any of this back in the box."

I let my arms drop back down. I square my shoulders and take a breath. I picture the other future waiting for him. The one I want for him. The one that I cannot . . . I cannot give him.

Love, unburdened.

Love that's unattached to having anything to prove.

"You have someone in DC, don't you?" I ask.

"What?" His body gives him away. His shoulders pulling back just the smallest amount, the skin around his eyes tightening. All of it subtle. All of it enough to tell me I was right.

"The girl in the photo." Blond hair. Wide blue eyes. A smile that looks genuinely sweet. Her face poking out of an unpacked box in his living room. "The girl waiting for you back in DC."

I count the ducks who filter past us. Four more on top of the original three. Two are smaller than the others.

"Annie." The name leaves his mouth like a gust of air. "Her name is Annie."

"Girlfriend?"

"We're not together."

"But you were."

"Yes." He pauses. "She was my fiancée."

An ice-cold fist to my chest. Worse than I imagined. Even though this should be good. Even though this is what I thought I wanted.

We didn't talk about our exes. We skipped over pieces. We got to choose what mattered.

Annie. Her name is Annie.

"Was. She was my fiancée," he says. "When I left DC, we decided to take some space. We decided to use the space to see if what we had . . . to see if it was right."

Is that what space does? Has anyone ever found that that's the way it works?

"So, you leaving . . . you thought it would help you decide. If you wanted to get her back."

"Yes."

"And then you found me."

"And then I found you."

He reaches his hand forward, and I pull both of mine behind my back. I clasp them there. A breeze kicks up the grass between us. "If you'd never seen the video—if Remy had never gotten in trouble . . ."

"But she did get in trouble. And I did watch the video." His voice is urgent. And I see what he is seeing. Fate. Capital *F*. The unbridled force that tugs along the biggest love story. The thing that makes you think you don't have to make a choice. But that isn't right . . . I am almost sure that isn't love. I am almost sure that love is all about choices. The ones you make and the ones you don't.

"It's over with Annie," he says. "It was over a long time ago. I realize it's bad . . . me not telling you. But you have to understand that Annie . . . my life with Annie, it felt entirely separate from us. A world away. Too far away to matter—"

"The real world, Nathan. It was the real world."

He sets his jaw. "As opposed to us."

"Yes." Our voices have both gotten louder. But I welcome the release. I want to scream. To stampede. To rend the grayness with my pain. "We've been in a bubble, Nathan. And that's why it worked. That's why it was so easy."

"Then, we step out of the bubble."

"I don't want to."

The pain on his face knocks me back. And I have to look away . . . at the deserted pathway, at the swimming ducks, at the patches of dead leaves left behind. I look around, as if I will find what I need. Something sturdy to hold on to.

"It's better this way," I say. "It's better if we stop now."

"What? Before anyone gets hurt?"

I swallow. I pull my hands up into my coat; my fingers are like ice.

"I know you're scared," he says, earnest again. Not giving up. Never giving up. "But this is what we do for each other. You let me be every version of myself, even the parts that I struggle to like. You show me that it's okay to be every version. And I believe in us, even when you can't. Alex, when you can't, I believe for both of us."

I want to sit down. I want to drop onto this damp and dirty path and pull my legs into my chest and press my face into my knees and wrap my arms around my ears. So I won't see him. So I won't hear him.

So I can convince myself that even if everything he said is true, that doesn't make it right.

I don't want him to have to believe for me. I want him to have more. I want him to have everything.

A soft place to land.

And still: I start to reach out to grab his hand.

It's at this moment—this moment just before I start to move toward him—that a jogger runs around the bend. She's the first person we've seen today. Her head is down, bent low against the wind, and she doesn't see us standing there. She doesn't see how we move apart to let her through. How it's only in our separating that she is able to keep running. Her path uninterrupted.

I exhale through my nose.

"There's not one person for you, Nathan," I say. I say this from where I'm standing. From where I've ended up on the opposite side of the path. "That's all I am trying to say. I'm not your one person. You've already had another. You've already had someone you wanted to marry. That's the truth. That's the part you're refusing to see." I wave my hand around us, at the wet and dirt and gray. "This doesn't have to be your story. I don't want it to be."

"Why do you think you get to choose?"

Because I do. Because in all the things I can't control, this is one thing I can. Because him leaving now is better than him wanting to leave later—better for both of us. Because it's my fault for letting it get this far in the first place.

But I don't say any of that. I can't find any words that won't start another argument. That won't make him think he can still win.

So instead, I'm moving. One leg following the other, my knees stiff and creaky, until I'm rounding the bend where the runner first appeared. Until going becomes gone. I'm gone, but it hurts. The pain in my chest is expanding so quickly I'm afraid I will explode. Little pieces of me left along the water's edge. *Go, walk, go,* I chant to myself. And I'm focusing on this chant, on matching it to my breaths, and I don't know if I imagine what I hear, the words that drift up from the water, from where I'd left him standing. I don't know . . . because we imagine things sometimes, don't we? I honestly don't know if he says them one more time. Those three words.

◆ ◆ ◆

Two opposing things can be true at the same time.

The truth is, I left for both of us. So that neither of us would ever wonder if he'd regret his choice to stay. That part is true. But I also left for me. For me alone.

I left because, for one instant, I could see it. For one instant, right after that instant when he told me I was loved, I could see it: me. Alex, the way I want to be.

And in leaving, I could keep her. I could keep the bitterness at bay and remember this instead: his hand and how it felt in mine; two years, growing up together; learning to be adults together. And then, three months, remembering and remaking; three months with a person who understood me. Who loved me. Who saw me, all the way through. Gray-blue eyes. Stormy afternoons.

I left so I could keep remembering that person. Not him, but me. The person who he loved.

Chapter 25

When I get home, I sit on my couch. I stare at Holly's half-packed boxes. For the longest time, I do not move. I just sit there and I look at it: my life. Such as it is. So much smaller than I once expected.

But there are things that I am grateful for. I am almost sure of that.

I stand up and grab the change jar off the counter, and I sit back down, this time at the kitchen table. I start to pile pennies, one on top of the other. I pile pennies, and I count.

My sister. Deena. Holly—not here, but somewhere always. Syed and Lois—both chosen members of my family in different ways. A new job, one that is comfortable and pays well. Memories of a man who I got to love not once, but twice. And Remy. Queen Remy. Not mine, but alive. Out in the world, cocked ears and graceful gait and sweeping tail. In part, because of me.

These are not small things. These are things that are worth more than pennies.

I wanted to be braver. Tougher. I thought that if I became those things, I could have a different kind of life. Colorful. Bolder. Hunger and sustenance, intertwined.

But maybe I don't need that kind of life. Maybe I did not ever really want it. I have this one—this one that is a bit more muted, and certainly not what I'd imagined when I was twenty, when the world was still so very much unknown and untapped—but, maybe, it is enough. It is, at the very least, real.

Maybe there is a difference between settling and seeing what is here. Between standing still and staying.

◆ ◆ ◆

On December 3, I go to my first counseling appointment with Annette. If I choose to get tested, this will be the first of multiple: two to three counseling sessions, followed by a physical exam, followed by the blood draw, followed by the results. It's odd, finding myself back in that awful room—everything the same, except that the gourds have been exchanged for candy canes. There's even a sprig of mistletoe. The bright-green leaves read as defiant, a sign that love gets to be here, too. And I am, again, reminded that however much I hate this room, I very much like Annette.

She talks to me about the testing process. The blood draw. The CAG repeats, and how to interpret the results. She asks me tough questions: About what I would do if I were positive. About how I would feel if I were negative, especially given that Meredith is not. She asks me if I have a partner, and I tell her that I do not, even as I picture Nathan's face. I don't mention him to Annette, not because he doesn't matter, but because I know in my bones that I have to make this choice for me alone. Nathan cannot be the reason I find out.

At the end of that first appointment, she asks how I'm feeling, and I tell her the truth. I tell her that I am glad that I am here. That I want to choose my path, one way or the other. To get out of this place—the one where I am in the middle, waiting for someone else to decide how it will go.

Outside of the visits with Annette, I stay busy at Kensington. I go out for drinks with Deena and Bean. I help Holly pack while I move my stuff from one room in the apartment to the other. And I worry about Meredith. I keep picturing her. Sitting in her perfect, polished home, with the empty room that is supposed to be a nursery. With every fear and every hope condensed into a shorter timeline. Tetris blocks flipping over and over again, until she finds it: a way to make them all still fit.

The thing about Meredith and me is that we don't have major fights. Oh, we have our small and snappy blowups; we bicker. Sometimes, when she's being particularly controlling, I feel a very strong urge to pull her hair. But that's about it. There are positives to not winning the parenting lottery, and one of them is how well we got to know each other. Bone deep. Knowledge that lives in every matching expression, in the way we can read each other's face, in the sound of the other's voice, eerily familiar, the closest we will ever come to hearing how we sound to someone else. She is very nearly me, and so not me at all.

But now or later, angry or sad, on that list of things I'm grateful for? Meredith always comes first.

Which is why, when I don't hear from her, when days go by without a text, I know something is wrong. Something more. I know it without her saying it. So, I go. On a Friday after work. I show up on her doorstep unannounced, for the second time in a month, and she answers in yoga pants and a hoodie rather than jeans and a linen shirt, which, more than anything, confirms what I already knew.

"What's wrong?" I ask. I am not even in her house yet. "I mean, besides the obvious."

She gives me a look. Her big-sister look. Her *don't try to manage me* look.

"Nothing is wrong," she says.

I feel a flash of irritation, because she never will admit when she needs help. She always has to prove that she can handle things. That she is stronger than the rest of us. But my annoyance doesn't last, because already, she is moving us into the next part. All while not looking at me. She's looking at the street when she says what she says next.

She did the egg retrieval. Yesterday.

She did the egg retrieval, and it worked, and she and Syed can have a baby. A baby who will not get sick.

She tells me all of this, but not in celebration. She never stops looking at the street.

"We got the test results already," she says. We are still standing on her porch. It feels deliberate: her keeping us outside. "Three eggs were fine. They don't have the gene. It was a really good round. As good as someone who was healthy."

As good as someone who was healthy. As in, someone other than Meredith.

Tears prick the back of my eyes, and I can't speak. I need a moment, just one moment. I can't imagine how she doesn't need more, because it's all happening too quickly. I want to tell her to slow down, but how do you say that to someone who is already preoccupied by every passing minute?

But maybe it doesn't matter. Looking at her outfit, maybe I don't need to tell her anything. Maybe she has finally realized that for herself.

"Can we go inside?" I ask.

She looks around, like she is surprised we are outside. Like I was wrong, and it is not deliberate, but instead, automatic: her not wanting this conversation in her house. I think that might be worse.

When we pass through the kitchen door, I realize she hasn't bothered to turn the lights on. It's five thirty at night in December. We are nearing the shortest day of the year, which means Meredith has been sitting in the dark for over an hour.

I'm the one who flicks the light switch. And when I do, I see it. Sitting on her table. An announcement that matches the one I have tucked in my desk drawer.

I look at it, and then I look at Meredith. She purses her lips, then nods.

"I'm going," she says. "To the memorial."

"Why?"

"Because I need answers," she says. "Because I don't know if I can do it. Have a baby. And my husband doesn't understand, and so I need to figure this out. I need to know more. I need to know more about how I will die."

She says this in a way that is not at all dramatic. That is matter-of-fact. But that doesn't change how she's spinning her watch round and round her wrist. That doesn't change the fact that she is scared.

"I need to know how it will go," she says. "I need to understand the timeline. If I know how many CAG repeats Tessa had. If I know how quickly her symptoms progressed . . . it will help. It will help me decide."

"If you want to be a mother?"

"If I am able to be a mother."

"You are," I say firmly. And she glares at me. We glare at each other. Because it's understandable that she wants more facts, that she wants to be as informed as possible. But the thing that trips me up is that there are no real answers here. She has done the research. She told me last week that she spoke with other people who knew people with the same number as her. Most didn't develop significant symptoms until their late forties. But some were sooner and others later.

No matter how many questions we ask, we always return with the same answer: There is no crystal ball.

Mere's looking for more than facts and figures. And I don't know how Maine will help. How Tessa will help, this woman we've never needed and who Meredith is nothing like.

I don't know. I'm not sure what Meredith will find, but I can see now that I was wrong before. About her needing to slow down. I can see it: how, if she stops, if she pauses now, she might not restart. More than anyone, I understand how that can happen. For Meredith, I think, movement of any kind is enough, even movement in the wrong direction. Because movement is how she figures out how to do it. Get at what she wants.

Maine. *Tessa.* The person we've never allowed ourselves to need.

I look at my sister. I shift my shoulders back, mirroring her body language.

I don't know. I don't think there is anything there to find. But Meredith is out of her mind if she thinks I'm not going with her.

Chapter 26

Before I accepted the job at Kensington, Lois referred me to a new client. A woman named Jodie. I don't want to go—I'm putting this chapter behind me—but by the time I get the reminder on my phone, it's too late to cancel. Too late to disappoint someone who needs answers about someone she loves. So the day before we leave for Maine, I go and I try to do it once more. I try to help.

Jodie's apartment is an artist loft, with brightly painted rooms and rows and rows of hanging plants. She has a big, booming laugh that bursts out of her at inappropriate moments, and, for some inexplicable reason, it makes me want to laugh with her. Her dog, Pepper, is a herding breed who has been barking at everything and everyone: neighbors getting their mail, small children playing in the park around the corner, bikes and bikers, plastic bags. Barking and now lunging, too, Jodie says, laughing and wringing her hands at the same time. "She's really very sweet at home," she says. "She's like a different dog."

We talk about Pepper's routine and the importance of work and stimulation. We discuss walkers and scent-work classes and interactive toys—different options to help Pepper work off her energy and use her brain. We talk about the danger of boredom with this kind of breed. Then, we dive into training specifics—basics, like sit and stay, and then deeper strategies based in counterconditioning and positive reinforcement. I give her straightforward tips for getting Pepper to look at Jodie before she reacts. I suggest a program where Pepper will get most of her calories from training: dinner and breakfast fed over the course of her walks—scary bike, look to Jodie, get a treat; running child, look to Jodie, get a treat. Repeat, repeat, repeat.

Jodie writes down everything I say. She sits across from me at her kitchen table, while Pepper plays at her feet, and she writes and writes in a red notebook. She asks me smart questions and pushes me for more ideas. She shows me videos she has of Pepper, then asks more questions. I am glad I brought my water bottle; my mouth is dry from all the talking. I imagine Jodie's hand must be cramping. And still, she asks more questions.

I like Jodie. I'm impressed by her dedication, but it's more than that. There's something familiar about her, something I can't immediately place because I'm thrown off by the whimsical apartment and the laugh, and so, it's not until nearly the end of the ninety-minute session, when she taps her pen against her list, touching each item one by one, that I see it. I see her. Meredith.

"Will it work?" Jodie taps the list, again, with her pen. "If I do all these things, will Pepper be okay? Will she be able to go back to how she was?"

I want to say yes. I want to tell her that if she sticks to her plan then, yes, everything will work out the way it should. Pepper's progress will follow the path she wants. But one of the worst parts of dog training is that there are no guarantees.

"I don't know," I say, honestly. "Training takes a lot of time, and it's different for every dog. We'll try different things, and some will work, and some won't. Some will work for a while and then stop."

Jodie scans the list again, then laughs. "But we'll narrow down what works, right? And then we'll focus on those strategies."

"It's not always easy to see what's having an impact. Sometimes, you just have to keep trying."

"Even if you aren't sure that it is helping?"

There's a smudge of blue paint on Jodie's cheek. I look at this and then at her. This time she doesn't laugh.

"Especially then," I say. "That's when she'll need you most."

The morning we drive to Maine, the weather is perfect. Sun shining, a light breeze. I'm tempted to forget that it's December and roll the windows down. It feels good to start the day this way: moving, going somewhere. We drive up 93 and then 95, and the highway is empty. It's too late in the year for leaf peepers and too early for good skiing.

Syed's sister's birthday is this weekend, and Mere convinced him not to cancel, so it's just the two of us. We talk a little bit more about how the IVF process has gone. They froze the tested embryos, and Meredith can start the implantation process whenever she wants. If everything goes well, she could be pregnant in a month. If that's what she chooses.

"How was the visit with Annette?" she asks me. We're thirty minutes into the drive.

The question throws me off balance. We haven't talked about it yet, and I thought that was by design—because I'm the only one who still has hope. I wish I'd thought to bring a cup of coffee. I want to have something else to do with my hands.

"How did you know I went?"

She rolls her eyes. "You've never been one to break a promise. At least not one you made to someone else."

"Talking to Annette was good . . ." My voice trails off, then restarts. "It helps, not burying my head in the sand. I feel like I have some control, not over the results, but of myself. Of how I am going to handle it. You were right to push me."

Mere gives me a sideways smile. "Well, I'm rarely wrong."

"Noted," I say with a snort.

We settle back into comfortable silence. The sounds of Adele and John Legend fill the car. The road rises and falls gently beneath our feet. Sometime after we cross into Maine, Meredith clears her throat. "Can I ask you another question?"

I almost laugh. "As if you've ever needed permission."

"How's Nathan?"

Just his name. And there's his face behind my eyelids when I blink. A rush of warmth replaced by something less inviting. He's gone. Gone. The word flips over on itself. Boxes probably repacked, sitting in an apartment in another city with another girl.

I roll my shoulders. "He's moving back to DC. What we had . . . it was fun, but it was always temporary, him staying here."

"It didn't seem temporary," says Mere.

"Boston?"

"The way he looked at you."

I turn my face to the passenger window. We've just pulled off the highway and are winding our way down a curvy road that dips and falls away into shadowed woods, bare gray trees with branches that stretch up and around their evergreen companions. It's beautiful here, in a stark way. A raw honesty sketched out in deep greens and grays and tans.

"Did you tell him to leave?" Mere asks.

"He wanted to go."

"That's not an answer."

But isn't it?

My voice sticks to the bottom of my throat. I struggle to push it out as something even. "Nathan doesn't need to be involved in all of this. He still has a choice."

Meredith sears me with a look. "It's always a choice. No one gets to guarantee forever, Alex."

"I'm trying to make this easier."

"For him? Or for you?"

I love you.

My breath catches below my rib cage. A swelling with no place to go.

"You're not giving Nathan a chance." She drums her fingers against the wheel. "I remember when you two got together. You were just kids, really, but it was real. It terrified me, how much you loved him. How young you were. But you did it anyway."

I rub my temples with my fingertips. "What does that have to do with anything at all?"

"You used to *believe*. You used to *want*. Even after everything that happened to us. And now . . ." She lets one hand slip on the steering wheel. Ten and four. "I'm worried you are going to let this be the thing that defines you."

I almost laugh. It catches in my throat, leaving behind the taste of something dirty. "Come on, Mere," I spit out. "Huntington's will define us. One way or the other."

"I'm not talking about HD."

"Then what?"

"Pain. And whatever you can do to avoid it."

I blink, and we're at a kitchen table. Sitting side by side, just like we are now. The table's faded and covered with old water stains and the black-and-blue remnants of markers. Bright-yellow place mats try and fail to hide the damage. To hide the history. The table is in our dad's house. Only, it's not his house yet . . . It's still ours. My parents are here, too. My dad shuffles a deck of cards; my mom elbows him and tells him not to cheat. She keeps calling him bucko. She always used to do that. "Ruby princess, you're up first."

I blink again. I swear I can smell the markers. It makes my head ache.

"If you got tested," says Mere. "If you got tested, and you were negative, you'd try with Nathan?"

"I can't get tested for him."

"I agree. But that wasn't my question." She shakes her head when I don't respond. "You act like it's HD that keeps you two apart, and I am not really sure that is true."

For thirty miles, it's silent. Thirty miles and nearly twice as many minutes, as we wind through the woods of western Maine, turning left and then right, on roads that can barely be called pavement. We're trundling across potholes that have me bracing one hand against the ceiling, the effort of staying straight capturing all of my attention, one jostle after another, so that I almost don't notice them. The white flakes sprinkling through the air.

Snow. It's starting to snow, the second week of December. Two hours ago, we were in sunshine. Fifty-five degrees.

I lick my lips, then clear my throat—the noise making both of us flinch.

"It's easier," I say into the broken silence. "To fall in love at eighteen and believe that it will last. Because real life hasn't started. Because you still get to believe in magic."

Mere's quiet for another minute. "And now?"

I open my mouth to tell her no. To tell her not to be silly. But the words stick to my tongue as the flakes melt against the road. Sprinkles of stardust. There one instant, and then gone the next. I watch them, and then I turn back to my sister, hands back on ten and two. Eyes on the road ahead. Trying. Striving. Hoping.

A month ago, she told me that love will always end up being an obligation. And she's right. I can see that now. But it doesn't matter with us. Because in the end, we will always choose each other. With Mere, I may have been an obligation, but I never once doubted that I was also something more.

And that's the difference, I think. Love should always be more than an obligation. It has to be more. I need to know it's more. Because Tessa left. Our own mother left. And if the obligation of motherhood wasn't enough to keep her, then obligations are not something I can trust.

But I can trust my sister.

And now, Nathan, Holly, Deena—my whole life—are suddenly a million miles away. Suddenly, they are the least of what matters, of what is worthy of the magic we might get.

It's just us, me and Mere. Surrounded by white, watery flakes that someone could call stardust.

"I want to believe," I say. I say this to Meredith. I say it like a promise.

My sister flexes her fingers. "Me, too," she says. "I want to believe, too."

And maybe that's enough.

Chapter 27

When I hear someone say, "That dog tried to bite me," it always makes me sigh. Because the thing is, generally speaking, if a dog tried to bite you, it would have bitten you. Dogs are fast. Scary fast, really. Their reflexes put ours to shame.

All I'm saying is that if a dog "tried to bite" you, it probably would have bitten you. It's pretty hard to dodge a dog.

More likely, the dog was warning you. Because long before a dog bites, they give off warnings. They bark and growl; they run away; they lunge and even smack you with their nose; they nip and snap their jaw. They do all these things to tell us to stay away. Use caution. Give them space.

So, when my clients would come to me and say—Can you teach my dog not to bark and lunge? Can you teach them to not do these behaviors that I don't like?—I had to tell them, it's not that simple. I had to explain that what they really want is to teach their dog not to be afraid. It's the fear, not the behavior, that's the problem.

In fact, the behavior is a weird kind of blessing. It's the warning that dogs are honest enough to give us. If we take away the behavior without fixing the fear, we are forcing them to lie. We are forcing them to hide their feelings, and that's where the real danger starts. Because without the warning? Well, then, we've backed them into a corner. And when things get bad enough, when their fear gets bad enough, they have no choice but to bite.

The closer we get to Bancroft, the more nervous I expect to feel. But the nerves never hit. I am oddly detached. Calm, even.

I think it is because we're here for Meredith, not for me. And maybe more accurately because I am finally okay with where I've landed.

And so, when we drive into Bancroft, I don't flinch. I look out my window at the small New England town, and my primary emotion is curiosity. Because Bancroft *is* small. Quaint, really. A sweet green parkway with a classic white gazebo; colorful office fronts marching up main street; big colonials with window boxes jauntily positioned, pretty even absent of summer flowers; cozy restaurants and a coffee shop with "open" flags snapping in the breeze.

When I think of my mother, she's decidedly cosmopolitan. She was a cellist; she spent her career with one of the greatest orchestras in the country. When she traveled, it was to cities: to Barcelona, to Rome, to Paris. And then, to Bancroft? The Tessa who I remember lived so large . . . the smallness of Bancroft doesn't add up.

The cemetery is a few minutes past the main town area, and my first impression is that it's surprisingly large. We park, and then Meredith winds her way confidently through the headstones marching row after row. All of them, varying shapes and sizes, a rainbow of muted colors—white marble, glossy black, polished silver, and dusky gray. Bouquets of flowers and balloons stand out against the backdrop, sparks of color made all the brighter by the surrounding leafless trees.

I wonder how Meredith knows where she is going. I watch her purposeful steps, and I wonder, again, why we are here. Why we're really here. What answers she hopes to find for the questions she won't say out loud.

We're almost twenty minutes early, the first people to arrive. Mere stops by a small clump of trees, and I fall in beside her. To the left of us, a funeral, a real funeral, is starting all the way on the other side of the cemetery. I see the cars pull in, the strange slow procession, a crowd to pay respects.

"I wonder who will come," says Meredith beside me.

I shrug. "People who knew her, I would guess."

She makes a noncommittal noise, and then we lapse back into silence. I'm staring at the gray-fingered branches overhead, wondering how much time has passed, when she says what she says next.

"I think about it sometimes," she says softly. So softly, I almost don't hear her. I almost miss it entirely.

"I think about leaving. Even though my number is low, as good as I could have hoped for, really. I think that if we have a baby, I might leave when they get older. I might do exactly what she did."

It takes a moment for what she's said to hit me. And I am not ready for its impact. The violence of it. A hammer slamming against my chest.

"No," I say.

Nothing else. Just no. It is the only word I can get out.

Meredith acts as if I haven't spoken. Her next words leave her mouth almost of their own volition. Like she's been waiting to say this until she got here. Until she was standing next to the one person who will understand.

Not me. But Tessa.

Something sludgy rises in my throat. Black tar pooling on a hot summer day.

"It's not even just about the baby," she says. "It's about Syed. It's about you. It's about having to be sick like that in front of you. I keep thinking that leaving . . . leaving might be better."

"For us or for you?" I snap.

Her head jerks, like I've slapped her. Her eyes are too wide in her face, her complexion draining of color.

And I want to pull the words back. I want to apologize. To tell her I understand.

But I don't. I don't understand at all. Every time I think I understand something, it seems to slip away.

"Alex—" she starts.

"No," I say. "You stay. You stay because your kid deserves to know you will not leave. Your kid deserves to know that you will stay until you can't."

"But who decides what that means? *Until you can't.* Who decides?"

She's angry now, too. Her voice is jagged, her eyes cutting into mine. But I just shake my head.

"This is why you wanted to come," I say dully. "Not because of her CAG score or whatever else you told me. You wanted to know why she left. You wanted to know if she made the right choice in leaving, so you could feel better about yourself. About your own choices."

A pause. The length of a heartbeat. So infinitesimal I only notice because I'm holding my breath.

"Maybe," says Meredith softly. "Maybe that's true."

And now, I'm looking at Meredith, but I'm seeing Tessa. They're not the same—*they're not the same*—but I'm losing all perspective. My hands are in fists at my side. I imagine I can feel the slow shifting of the earth beneath my feet. Isn't that true? That we are always moving?

"I don't want you to leave," I say. "Your kid won't want you to leave."

"But what if I can't stay?"

She's looking at me, those too-wide eyes. And she needs me to understand. But I cannot find my way there. Not while standing in this place, where the lines have gotten too blurry: between the past and the present, between Meredith and my mother.

I duck my head. I look away from her completely.

And it's at this moment that people start arriving. The people who Meredith came here to meet. Who knew who Tessa became when she stopped being our mother. When she started belonging to them instead of us.

When she chose another life.

I thought I was ready. I thought I was okay. But I'm not prepared for it. For any of it. And it is an effort not to simply turn around. To go back, even quicker than we came in.

The first arrivals are a pair: a black-haired man next to a woman with iron-gray hair and a frame that looks too frail against this wind. They pad across the grass and stand next to us. It's early, though. Still too early. And now, the woman's talking to Meredith. Talking about her friend, Tessa. Her friend, who was strong and brave.

I shove my hands deeper into the pockets of my coat.

Strong and brave. And kind. The gray-haired women starts telling a story, and I look away. I try not to hear the words, and then I am looking at it: the gravestone, the gray-brown grass underneath. I expect fresh-turned earth, but, of course, it's settled by now. Tessa was buried months ago. Her name a line in a paper already thrown away.

Dead. She is dead.

My fingers twitch. I'm biting the inside of my cheek so hard I can taste blood.

I've known she was dead for months. I stopped saying goodbye to her a decade ago. And still. I cannot breathe. My heartbeat picks up speed. I imagine if I look down, I will see it beating. The press and push of blood and organ rippling against my sweater.

I never wanted to come here. I didn't want to feel this.

Strong and brave and kind.

The truth is this: Sometimes, I remember Tessa, and she's exactly like the person this woman's describing. I remember her, and I don't understand how that person gets from my memories to here.

A small man walks up then, and he says hello to the couple beside us. He looks official, like he's the reverend or the priest, but he reminds me of my homeroom teacher sophomore year of high school. Mr. Collins, I think.

He puts one hand on the gray-haired woman's arm. I think she might be crying.

After Tessa left, I used to lie in bed at night and try to understand—not how she could leave her children but the more important part. How I had missed it, her being the kind of person who would leave her children. A person I shouldn't have trusted. I lay in bed at night, and I tried to find the clues, because there had to be clues. There had to be signs—a trail of breadcrumbs that led to that moment when she walked out the door. She was my mother for fifteen years, and I never doubted her. Somehow, I must have missed the breadcrumbs.

Another gust of wind. It leaves my lips chapped, but I can't be bothered to wet them. I'm too busy with these memories. Memories that I don't want.

In the cemetery, Mr. Collins is starting to speak. But it's early. It's still too early. Except, I check my phone, and it's not. We are already five minutes late.

And it hits me, then, that no one else is coming. That there is no one else but us.

I don't know what I expected, but it wasn't this. Three people, one of them required.

I expected more. Wanted more, for her. For anyone, really.

My gaze travels back to the gravestone. The words etched on plain gray marble.

Not this life, but the next.

I read the words once, and then again. Three times. And then, it's hard to swallow. Hard to make myself breathe around the lump in my throat.

I don't want to feel this.

Pity. For everything she lost.

For everything she gave away.

I love you, Ally Cat. It's bigger than the world, bigger than the universe, all my love.

The blue-coated back. Her back. I can still see it. And yet.

Fifteen years. Hundreds of goodnight kisses and storybooks before bed and hot cocoa in our pajamas on snowy mornings. Her voice, loud, singing to the radio. Her cool hands on my too-warm cheeks.

I love you. I love you.

Fifteen years. And then everything that happened after.

Which is the part that matters more?

I look back at the gravestone in the ground. On the markings that say her name and his. Her name and ours. Still our name.

Now, and always: Tessa Bailey.

I don't want to feel this.

It is clear to me that I should not be here. Not in this cemetery, this pretty town, these places that are all hers . . . these are not places that I should be. Not now. Not just as I was starting to get it together. Just as I was coming to terms with all of it: my life and what it is.

I should not be here. In this place that makes it very clear that I have not come to terms with much.

The ceremony is over, and I can feel Meredith turning toward me. Preparing to restart the conversation we just ended. My whole body is prickly. Uncomfortable.

"Did you hear what she was saying earlier?" Mere asks, gesturing at the gray-haired woman who is now standing next to Tessa's grave. "Did you hear how she was describing Tessa?"

"Oh." She's shifting the conversation. Coming at it from another angle. I pull my vest in tighter around me. "You mean how she didn't really know her."

Mere wrinkles her nose. "What?"

"I mean the person she described. Not exactly the same person who leaves behind two kids and never looks back."

"That might not be true."

"That she left?"

"That she never looked back."

I bite my lip. I look at the gravestone. I spend the space of two breaths trying to figure out what to say next. How to get us out of here and back to Boston. Back to a place where we can find perspective.

And I'm two breaths in, two breaths of silence, when Meredith's expression changes. Determination slices to pain. And then to fear. Her left hand flutters and lands on her lower abdomen; the diamonds on her engagement ring catch the light, a flurry of tiny rainbows dancing across the gray tombstones.

"Meredith?"

Warm brown eyes. The eyes I've known the longest. Three blinks. And then my sister falls.

Chapter 28

Time plays tricks on me. One minute we are in the cemetery. Meredith on the ground, me holding her head between my hands. She has always seemed so big to me, not just in height but in depth—like even the smallest parts of her body carried more weight than mine. Now, I notice how her collarbone juts out against her sweater. How her eyelashes lie in delicate clumps across her cheekbones. I notice the fine lines around her mouth and eyes, and the hints at the thinning of her hair. Her fingers are icy cold and no bigger than mine. Delicate, even, on her taller frame.

In the slow blur of those first seconds, I notice all of this—all the things I've always missed—and then everything speeds up. I am frozen, holding her, and then I am moving. My fingers fast across my cell phone, my lips against Mere's ear as we wait.

Hold on hold on hold on.

I stroke her hair. We are children, except our roles reversed. Everything backward, kneeling beside our mother's grave.

Time starts and stops. Rewinds, then jumps ahead.

We're in an ambulance. And it's so loud. The roaring of the sirens slams against my brain. I want to cover Meredith's ears. I want to drive the ambulance. I have never been sure of anything, and yet I am sure that I can do this: I can get us there faster.

She's too pale. Chalky white.

Hold on hold on hold on.

Thirty-two-year-old female. No known allergies. No medications. I tell the doctors at the hospital what I know. I don't mention Huntington's disease. I'm not sure if I can. I remember snippets from the websites, about insurance, about what to disclose when. I should have read the pamphlets. I should have clicked on the articles Meredith sent.

I say nothing. I tell myself it doesn't matter. She is too young for it to matter.

I call Syed. I hear him moving toward the car before the words are halfway through my lips. I tell him everything I know, which is really very little. He swears into the phone. There's been an accident on 95. It will be more than four hours until he gets here. More than four hours that she will be here, sick, without him.

"I'm here," I tell him. "I'm with her."

I hear his breathing slow. And in the blankness of this hospital, under the stark fluorescent lights, it hits me in the chest: that my words matter. That they make a difference. To him. The only other person who might love her as much as I do.

When they let me in to see her, I ignore the chair beside her bed. I ignore it and, instead, lie down next to her. My arm against her arm. Our heads almost touching, red and brown. I listen to her breathing. I count her breaths.

Hold on hold on hold on.

The hospital smells like nothing. Not clean, not dirty. It's nondescript. This is what strikes me later, after I've spoken with the doctors. When all that's left to do is wait. People always say hospitals smell like disinfectant, like too-strong cleaners, all the things they use to mask the smell of sickness, of death. But I can't smell any of that. I can't smell anything at all, just a distinct smell of nothingness, and somehow that—the sensory loss—is worse than I imagine any other smell could be.

It's loud, though. I can't avoid the noise. The constant beeping of monitors coming from every room. The noise is overwhelming. Alarming, even. Which is, perhaps, because these actually are alarms. The beeping becoming urgent every few seconds. Urgent beeping but not enough people running, or at least that's how it seems.

Ovarian torsion. A complication from IVF. That's what they told me. Impossible to prevent.

She lost blood. A lot of blood. It had been a dangerous complication, and she was okay, but she had lost the ovary. That's what they said.

Potential infertility. I sound the words out in my head. So many syllables, so much there, and still: I can't quite grasp their meaning.

Syed is here now, and I am no longer on her bed. We sit in the two navy, straight-backed chairs, side by side, both of our hands balanced on our knees, our bodies angled forward. We sit and watch my sister breathe. We sit and wait for her to wake because that is what we need. We need her to open her eyes and tell us she is okay. It doesn't escape me that what we most need is the thing that will bring her pain.

"She'll blame herself." His voice is soft, and still, I flinch. "She'll think she caused it."

"No," I say, but he's right. I swallow. I look at Meredith, sleeping. "She's a doctor," I say. "She knows the science. She knows she didn't make this happen."

Potential infertility.

Meredith said they had three embryos. Now, maybe their only three chances, if they still want to get pregnant. Three chances and then what?

I peek at Syed, then let my hair cover my face. A red curtain that smells like my conditioner, floral, vaguely soapy, and familiar.

"We argued." Syed's voice is hoarse, rough against the smooth plastic all around us. "About her getting pregnant. I didn't want to hear her fears. I didn't understand why she couldn't let us be happy. I wanted . . ." His voice trails off. I fight around the smell of my hair.

"You wanted her to have something good."

Lemonade from lemons. Stupid. Just stupid. And yet, there's a sharp pain when I swallow, and I have to blink twice.

Three times.

"I ignored her, too," I say, before I can think better of it. "She tried to talk to me, before the ceremony, and even before that. She tried." I push my hair out of my eyes. It's true. It's all true. Her condo, three days ago. And then her living room, back in October.

"I didn't listen," I continue. "I never listened. I told her she was worrying for nothing. I didn't want to hear it, either."

Syed's eyes search my face, and I watch the question forming, the one Meredith wouldn't ask. The beeping dulls to pinpricks against my ears.

"Why not?" he asks.

Because, like you, I wanted her to be happy. Because she'd be a great mother. Because I don't want this disease to ruin something she's always wanted. All the answers, all the whys that make sense, they sit on the tip of my tongue. But I can't open my mouth.

I stand up and walk across the room to the window. I open the blinds and blink against the sunshine. We're higher up than I realized. Only three stories, but the cars below somehow seem small. There's a blue one that reminds me of Nathan's.

"I think she's starting to forgive our mother," I say, still looking out the window. Still looking at the blue car. "I think she's starting to understand her."

"And you don't?"

I shrug. "I just know they're not the same." A picture book plays, page by page, in my mind: Meredith cheering at my soccer games; Meredith wrapping our Christmas presents after she thought I'd gone to sleep; Meredith in front of me, yelling at our father; Meredith, the first person to stand at my college graduation. The smile on her face. The only one that mattered. "Meredith can raise a child and be a mom and have HD. Meredith can do this."

When I turn back to Syed, there's too much understanding on his face. He hesitates, and I lift my chin, daring him to continue. Daring him to assume that he could possibly know something about us—about me and Meredith—that I don't.

He looks at my sister. He looks at me. He shifts in his chair.

"You want her to be better than Tessa."

I let out a breath. This is not a revelation. My mother left; Mere stepped in. Of course, I don't like the comparison.

"I don't need to want it. She is better than Tessa."

"Okay," he says. And then, "But what does that mean, exactly?"

I look at him blankly.

He sighs. "How do you know? That she's better than Tessa, I mean. What does she have to do?"

"She doesn't—She just is. She's Meredith. She doesn't have to do anything."

"Does she know that?"

There's a steadiness to Syed's waiting. A gentle but immovable expectation.

I look away from him and back down at my sister. My sister, who just this morning was standing in the cemetery, deep panic on her face at what she'd said out loud. I remember the way her hands clenched around air like she was trying to find pieces to hold on to. To hold together.

Alex and Mere. Mere and Alex. *I love you.* We don't say it enough, but only because we don't need to. Only because it's inevitable, absolute. Even when I can't stand her. Pulled hair, smug smiles, her maddening condescension. And always this.

Alex and Mere. Mere and Alex.

Inevitable. Absolute.

How many memories do I have that prove that?

And then: How many do I need?

A nurse pokes her head in the room and says something to Syed. I can't make out the words, but when she leaves, he turns back to me. He's still wearing that awful expression. Something like pity on his face.

"You think it's my fault," I say. "You think it's on me, the high expectations that she has for herself. You think I need her to be perfect, so she is?"

"No." He leans forward. "No, I don't think that at all. I think with or without you, Meredith would hate to disappoint people. Would hate to fail. I don't think that is on you. I'm not saying this for her; I'm saying it for you."

"And what are you saying?"

"I don't know exactly." He rubs his forehead with the back of his hand. "Except, you are the one person who tries not to put people in a box. And yet, you've done exactly that with Tessa. You've made sure she is the villain."

"And she is."

"But what happens if she's not?"

I think of the expression *silence is deafening*. Whoever said that got it wrong. Silence is a vacuum, pulling in every thought you've tried to hide. And now, it's all bundled together: Tessa and how sure I was she loved me and then the silence after she left. The woman in the cemetery, who knew who Tessa became when she stopped being my mother, who thought that person was good and kind and brave. Meredith and the strength I've always counted on, stacked up beside her fear.

All the things that don't compute. The actions that don't add up to what I thought I understood: how to choose the people you can trust.

Syed is still watching me, his hands splayed across his knees, his kindness magnified on his features. The beeping fully recedes, and I'm stuck here in the silence. Because I know what he is saying, and I can see how he is right, but also . . . isn't it okay, to want to draw some kind of line? To ask for assurances before giving everything away?

Isn't it okay to need that? To acknowledge that I need that. Isn't that the lesson I thought I'd finally learned?

I think of Holly. I think of Nathan. Of Tessa buried in the ground. I press one hand against my own chest.

I can feel the answers on the tip of my tongue, but I can't quite find a way to turn the feeling into words. Into an explanation that is concrete, about what I should do differently. About what I should do next.

And then, I realize that the beeping has come back. I hear it, like a song on repeat, the word *love* in high staccato, the only sound between us three. Syed raises his hands over his head in mock defense, and the gesture is so ludicrous that I can't help but smile. It's creaky and awkward, but it's there. And then it's bigger, wider, spreading from somewhere in my chest . . .

Meredith is awake.

Chapter 29

When I think of all the dogs I've known, I always come back to Rosie. She was a forty-pound mix of indeterminate breeds with a black spot over her left eye and a tail that twisted like a bent wire. Her eyes were the lightest brown I'd ever seen, and, like so many dogs, she could fix you with a stare that squeezed your heart. Rosie lived with an elderly woman in an isolated home until she was eight years old. Eight years alone with this woman who loved her, who made Rosie her whole world. And then the woman died. And there was no one to take Rosie.

You hear these stories all the time. The dogs whose owners die, whose owners lose their housing, who for one reason or another, cannot keep their dogs. Sometimes the dogs find new homes. And sometimes, the dogs are like Rosie.

She wouldn't let anyone near her. I'd see her, huddled in the back corner of her pen at the shelter where I volunteered, growling at anyone who walked by. The shelter staff were remarkable. They tried everything they could: slow, repetitive exposure; bringing in trainers far more qualified than me; even expensive medication. But Rosie stayed in that corner. The whites of her eyes were now the thing that made them noteworthy.

Sometimes, you cannot fix what's broken. Some damage cannot be reversed. Sometimes, the kindest outcome looks the cruelest.

These statements are all true. Undeniably so. And it's their truth that makes Rosie's story so extraordinary. Because six months later, the shelter sent me a photo of her playing with her new owner. Rosie ended up okay.

Sometimes, you cannot change. And then, sometimes, you can.

Meredith is dozing now, her face turned toward the window, and a beam of light tracks across her cheekbones, hiding the new shadows under her eyes. Earlier, I stood in the corner while Syed told Meredith what happened. What she may have lost. I heard the guttural sound she made; I saw how she grabbed her abdomen. I stood there and I watched my sister's face, as everything before simply fell away. I watched as all three of us realized we are living in yet another after.

And there is that: that sadness and devastation and the thumping questions of what more can go wrong and how much more are we expected to stand. There are all these reasons I should feel devastated and overwhelmed—and I do, of course, I do—but then . . . besides all of that, there is also this: the expression on Syed's face when Meredith took his hand and whispered something in his ear. The two of them, together, murmuring promises about what might come next. The faintest outline of a future hovering just above them. Getting stronger every moment.

Under these stupid lights and amid this manic beeping, they are still here. Holding on to each other. Holding tightly so that they can still move forward.

The gray-haired woman from the ceremony is Dr. Martha Gates. Our mother's doctor. The woman Meredith wanted to come see.

She seemed frail in the cemetery, but now I realize she's simply thin. She's unremarkable looking, really, except in her hands. I can't stop staring at those hands: long fingers, broad palms, calloused skin. Strong and capable. They remind me of the women in the prairie stories I read as a child: *Sarah, Plain and Tall* and Laura Ingalls Wilder. Stories about adventure and hardship, alongside supposedly simpler times. I remember reading them after Tessa left.

On another floor, down a different hall, Meredith and Syed sit crouched together. They're talking about moving forward with the implantation. With the three chances they have left. They're talking about a baby—a baby!—with bright eyes and trembling fingers. They're talking about the future, about hope, instead of about something else: how hard it is to realize what you want only after you've almost lost it.

I don't know what they will do, but it's this—this switching, their choice—that's gotten me here: sitting in front of Dr. Gates's desk. Straight instead of slouching. Ready for the answers Meredith came here to find. The ones she admitted in Boston and then the ones she admitted here.

When was she diagnosed? How long do we have?

The first answer surprises me: Tessa was already forty-nine years old; nine years before she died. But she was symptomatic for longer.

The second one is even murkier, good mixed with more questions. The good: Tessa's CAG score is one higher than Meredith's, so Meredith's progression should be even slower. But Dr. Gates emphasizes the *should.* And she reminds me, Tessa's diagnosis came after her symptoms. Nothing is black and white.

But still. Answers. More than we had before. More than I ever wanted.

And still. I don't leave the chair. Because among all the answers I didn't want, I now have the biggest one.

Did she leave to protect us?

There. Right there.

"We thought that HD . . . We thought maybe that was why she left." As soon as the words leave my mouth, I feel stupid. "But that wasn't it," I continue. "She didn't even know yet."

Dr Gates just lifts her chin, considering me. And again, I'm reminded of pioneers. Of women who have seen and lost too much. "Your mother was sick before she was diagnosed." She steeples her fingers, one pressed against the next. "The earliest noticeable signs of HD are generally physical; things that look like restlessness or muscle spasms or odd changes in facial expressions. But for your mother, it was the psychological symptoms that became apparent first. Depression most of all."

She stops there. She looks at me. I look back at her. A fly buzzes somewhere in the back of the room, near the ceiling. I wonder if Dr. Gates can hear the buzzing.

"She was depressed? She left because she was depressed?"

"I can't say for certain. But, yes, I think so. She saw a therapist. She tried medicine. And when it was not working, when she was scared enough, she left."

Prescription bags on the counter. Skipped soccer games. A blue-coated back. Breadcrumbs, just not the kind I was looking for.

I turn my eyes to the small window. The last bit of sunlight visible through the graying pane. *She left because she was sick.* Something warm burrows beneath my ribs. And I think about getting up right now. Getting up and leaving with this: a story that makes sense. Everything, finally, neatly tied up in a bow. Her leaving because she had to. Because she maybe did not have a choice.

But I can't move. Because that's just a story. And Dr. Gates and I both know that it's not where the story ends.

"She got help, though," I say. And Dr. Gates straightens in her chair. "I mean I know it's not a perfect science, but she got help. For a while there, she was okay?"

Dr. Gates nods. "Yes, she got help. And yes, for a while, she was okay."

"And she still didn't come back."

The words puncture the air. A period after each. Dr. Gates does not flinch. She doesn't even blink. Instead, she leans forward across her desk, not like she is trying to tell me something, but the opposite. Like she wants me to know she hears me.

"After we got her on the right medications, she was doing well," she says. "But Tessa wanted to wait. To make sure it would stick. To make sure she was well enough to go home and stay with you—the people she loved. And then, eventually, she found out she had HD. And that complicated her decision."

I nod, slowly, but I'm doing the math in my head. "It would have been four years before she found out about Huntington's. You're telling me that she spent four years waiting? Four years trying to prove that she was well enough? Four years waiting, that she could have spent with us."

She holds my gaze across her desk. "I'm telling you that the longer you wait, the easier it is to keep waiting."

There's a truth to her words that stings. But it's a bug bite. The smallest pang beside a bigger pain. One that is gathering in my chest and spreading everywhere too quickly. I wrap my hair elastic around my finger, tightly enough that it cuts off the blood supply.

"That's it?" I say. "She got used to waiting? That's supposed to be enough for not coming back. For taking four good years from us. She could have watched Mere graduate from college. Start med school. She could have explained what happened. She could have—there was a lot."

Dr. Gates doesn't respond, but her eyes stay on mine. Clear, gray steel. Something to hold on to.

"It's not enough," I say. My voice is louder now. "I'm sorry that it was hard for her. I really am. I'm sorry for everything she went through, but she was our mother. And she left us. She left her daughters, and she could have come back. She could have at the very least told us when she was diagnosed. She could have been there."

I am shaking; I can hear my voice echoing around us, gaining speed as well as sound. "We could have inherited it. Meredith did inherit it. She could have been there for us. But instead, she dropped a bombshell with a letter. With a goddamn fucking letter." I never swear, but the harshness of the words feels good against my tongue. Against the avalanche of anger spilling not just from my mouth but somewhere deeper.

"It's not enough," I say. "Her being sick. Her being scared. I'm sorry, but it's not enough. It doesn't make up for enough of it."

"No, I don't suppose it does."

Dr. Gates's voice is calm, so matter-of-fact, that I am silenced. I sit back in my chair, my fingers still pulling against the elastic, the anger already fading, so I can recognize it for what it was: its final gasp.

For a long time, no one speaks. We just sit there—two people who do not even know each other, who both only knew her—waiting for the next part.

"I never needed to forgive her," I say at last. I'm calmer now. My whole body is settling into the plastic.

Dr. Gates watches me from across her desk.

"I didn't need to forgive her. I didn't need her to be better than she was. I'd made my peace with it," I say. "In a way, it would be easier to hate her. But for a minute there . . . I thought, it would have been nice if she could have just been a good person who hurt us because she had to. Because she was sick or because she was protecting us. Who did a bad thing for a good reason. It would have been really nice if those choices had ended up being our story."

Choices. Choices that Meredith is considering. Choices that I think I can find a way to understand. They are not Tessa's choices. Not really. And there's an argument that this is a good thing: proof of just how different they both are. My world order restored.

But I can't find any comfort in that argument. It's too flimsy now; all the old lines have already been erased, and it's too late to recreate them.

I take a breath, and I think that it's time to stand. That this has been enough, and the next part can come later. But then Dr. Gates clears her throat.

"You know, your mother came to me because I work with patients with chronic conditions," she says. "Not just Huntington's, but mental health conditions. Conditions that my patients will have until they die. I've learned a lot from them. A lot of lessons. The biggest one being that when you are sick like that, when you are sick and your loved ones are not, you have to learn how to do it faster."

She waits until I meet her gaze. And when I do, she nods as if in answer. "You have to decide that you are enough all on your own. You have to decide that first."

The words hang in the air between us. Big and bright and hard to look at. And so I look away. I search the walls of the small room, but really, all I can see is Tessa. Tessa and Dr. Gates's words hovering behind her.

You have to decide that you are enough all on your own.

And for the first time, I don't think about forgiveness. I think about regret, instead. About apologies. About the enormous weight of having to apologize for all the things you cannot change. I think of all of the apologies that Tessa must have thought that we were owed: for her every fear and for her every misstep. For all the ways she'd let us down, beginning at the very beginning: with the genes that made her who she was. Our mother.

She was our mother.

My eyes drop to my pants, and I realize I am crying. There are tears dripping off my cheeks, hitting the fabric of my leggings. I watch the water gather there.

She'd been scared.

I can understand fear.

I can understand waiting.

I almost miss the anger. Anger would be easier than this. This strange unraveling.

"Was it all bad for her?" I'm trying to swallow my tears, so the words are sticky, garbled together. "I mean, after she left, was she—did she at least get to be happy?"

For the first time, the steady look on Dr. Gates's face flickers. "I don't know," she says. Her crisp voice is soft now. "I like to think she was happy enough. At least, for a while. I like to think she found some peace here." She pauses. "What I do know is that she kept tabs on you girls. She used a fake Facebook account to follow your lives. She had photos of you in her wallet. Photos from when you were little and then grainy printouts from after she left. I'm not telling you that because I think it is enough. But I do know that she loved you."

Love. I swipe my hand across my cheek. I can still hear the fly buzzing from somewhere behind my head.

"She loved you, and she left and didn't come back," says Dr. Gates. "She loved you, and arguably, she did everything wrong. Those are the things that happened. And I don't think anyone can tell you what sits in between them. I don't think anyone can tell you what is or is not enough."

Love. That word again.

I've always thought of love as something powerful. Something primary. The thing that comes before everything else.

Tessa isn't what I thought love looked like. She isn't what I would have chosen.

She loved you.

She loved you. And she didn't come back.

Love. That word. The mess of it. Messy because of us: the subject, not the verb.

I can see people walking in the halls outside Dr. Gates's office. I picture Meredith in a place like this when she gets sick. I blink, and I picture her in a place like this with a baby. I hold on to that, and I let go of the elastic. I feel the blood rush back into my finger. I let the rushing carry me along.

I still have more questions. About what she regretted. About whether she ever came close to coming back. All of these questions with answers I'll probably never get, sealed away by Tessa's death. And that's awful and unfair and also . . . also, maybe, okay. Because sitting here, with all these questions, I can't find one answer that really matters. Not one answer that will change what's taken me so long to see.

The gray space. The potential there.

The sunlight shifts from yellow to dusky red. Purple hints in the corner. It's beautiful, and fleeting, and right now, it's right here.

I look back at Dr. Gates, at this woman I cannot help but trust. "At the ceremony, you said she was brave."

"I did."

"Did you mean it?"

Dr. Gates puts her hands flat in front of her. Open, palms down. "Your mother lived with the knowledge of what was happening to her for nine years. Nine years: That's over three thousand days. Three thousand mornings she woke up waiting to watch little pieces of herself get chipped away. Three thousand days spent watching the people who knew her prepare to lose her and the people who didn't know her begin to fear her." She presses her palms into the desk. I watch the whitening around the knuckles. "Yes, Alex, I would call your mother brave."

They keep Meredith overnight. A precaution, they say. Syed claims the chair beside her bed, and I end up at a motel that smells like cigarettes and cheap detergent. A far cry from the cheerful inns on Bancroft's main street, but real in a way they weren't. Real in a way that makes what's happened more believable. Like the tendrils of understanding that I stumbled upon will turn into something that will last.

The next morning, I tell Meredith about Dr. Gates. I tell her what I learned about our mother. We talk about the dates and timeline and what they may or may not mean for Meredith. Or what they could one day mean for me. When I describe Tessa's depression, when I tell her about her choices, Meredith closes her eyes, then opens them. She studies my face, her tired expression clearing.

"Thank you," she says. "For getting me here. For finding out what happened with Tessa. I can't imagine that was easy."

"Does it help?" I ask. "She didn't leave because she found out about Huntington's. But it was, in part, why she didn't come back. Does that help you know what you want to do?"

"I want to have a baby," says Meredith simply. "And I'm not Tessa." She shifts against her pillows. "You asked me if I came here to learn how to leave. But I think, really, I came here because I wanted to learn how to stay."

"And did you?"

She glances at a photo that Syed put on the small table by her bed. The three of us, sitting on the beach, squinting up at the sun. Sand stuck everywhere.

"Yes," she says. "Yes, I think I did."

She looks away from the photo and starts adjusting the blankets on her bed. Pale-blue hospital sheets that match the veins running across the back of her hand. She's wearing makeup and a soft gray turtleneck. Diamond stud earrings. I didn't pack for the extra day, and I'm in the clothes I slept in: old spandex, a faded flannel that may or may not have once belonged to a pajama set.

"Do you think people ever change?" I ask.

"Loaded question." Mere gives me a look. "But sure. Of course, they can."

Can. It's such an easy word to throw around. Far easier than *will.*

"I wanted to change," I say. "That was really why I had the whole three-things idea. I was sick of myself and sick of feeling stuck, so I thought I'd go after what would make me stronger. Make me happy. I never showed you my list." I toss my phone to Meredith, barking out a laugh. "Silly, right?"

Meredith looks down at the screen. She shakes her head, slowly, like she's not even aware she's doing it. She looks back up and right at me. "You've got Kensington on here? And no Nathan?"

I blink, and she shakes her head again. This time with more intention. "Is this really what you wanted?"

"I wanted to move forward. I wanted to be more independent."

Mere considers this. "I think that being more independent starts by making the right list."

A nurse comes into the room then, and the rest of the world restarts. He bustles around Meredith's bed, grabbing empty cups and glancing at the monitors. He's young and smiling, with reddish brown curls that remind me of Nathan. (I see him everywhere, it seems. I keep wondering how long that will last.) The nurse calls Meredith ma'am, which makes me grin and makes her roll her eyes. He pushes the chair closer to the window, and, after he leaves, when I pull it back toward Mere's bed, it makes a scraping sound. A harsh screech that lets me focus on the noise instead of what I say next.

"What about us?"

Mere's brow wrinkles. "Us?"

I swallow. "Are we really any different than we were when we were kids? With each other, I mean. You, always trying to protect me. Me, always expecting it. Resenting it."

She looks toward the door, and I imagine she's looking for Syed. I wonder what he told her about our conversation yesterday. "I think it's the same thing. I think to change, you have to want to change. You have to know what you want to change."

"And we don't?"

"What do you think?"

Alex and Mere. Mere and Alex. The two of us, and all the reasons I've never questioned what I always thought worked.

I lick my lips. Dry from the motel. From the raw wind, and the overly filtered hospital air.

"You are always there for me," I say. "And I've relied on it; I'm not going to pretend I haven't. But the thing is, Mere, when it feels like someone is always trying to fix you . . ." My voice trails off.

"You start to believe you might be broken," she finishes calmly.

I nod. I look down at my hands. I am uncomfortable; my clothes are hot and itchy, like I can feel every seam.

"If you change your mind. If you decide to leave one day. If that is what you need . . . I will be okay," I say. "I think we both need to know that I will be okay. I need you to stop assuming that I won't be. *I* need to stop assuming that I won't be."

Meredith's head tilts back, and her chest expands. Her eyes catch mine, then hold, and the hospital narrows down to just us two. I wait. I clench my fingers around the bottom of my chair.

She exhales. She smiles.

"Okay," she says. "Okay."

And then out of nowhere. Or maybe, out of this conversation, she says one other thing. One more thing I don't expect in this place I never thought we'd be.

"I'll respect whatever choice you make about the test."

I blink. "Thank you."

She nods, slowly. She licks her lips. "There's an argument, you know," she says. "About the test. Not finding out, moving forward without a map . . . There's an argument that that is harder."

Her brown eyes latch on to mine, serious and soft and every bit my sister. "I should have told you that before."

The conversation ends as gently as it began. And maybe it's my imagination, the byproduct of too much time in a hospital or cemetery, but I can almost believe it worked. I can almost feel it: a shifting between us. The smallest step.

I hold on to this feeling. I hold on to it while Meredith goes back to sleep, her chest moving up and down in equal rhythm. My eyelids grow heavy under the gentle warmth of the sun streaming through the window. And I must fall asleep myself, because when I open my eyes, the rays are stronger, and Mere's eyes are open, too, staring at the ceiling.

She must sense that I'm awake, but she doesn't move.

"I wonder if he knew," she says, like we're continuing a conversation. "I wonder if he knew she was depressed when she left."

Him. She means our father.

I see him on a sunny day, years ago. A memory I didn't realize I had. My mother in a pale-blue dress with yellow buttons down the front. I remember her staring out the window, expression closed, while my dad stood over her, his voice raised. I remember he reached down to shake the table with both his hands, and the saltshaker tipped over. Little white specks like sand scattered across the faded wood.

It's an ugly memory. Which maybe explains why I forgot about it until now. It's an ugly memory, but it's more than yelling. It's more than anger and spilled salt. It's the way his voice broke, and the way his hands ripped at his hair. It's the look in his eyes when he saw Mere and me watching. Not us watching him, but us watching her. It's the gentleness of his hands when he pushed us out into the backyard.

And it's the minutes leading up to this memory, the ones where he touched the back of her palm, when he asked her to look him in the eye, to tell him anything at all.

I blink the memory away. Meredith's still looking at the ceiling.

"It was clinical," I say. "There was nothing he could have done."

"Yes, that's true."

"Do you think it would matter to him now? Knowing there was a reason. At least a reason that she left."

At this, she looks at me. And I see the words gather—the warnings, the reminders, the list of all the reasons to stay back—I see the outlines of them between us, as familiar as the sound of my sister's voice. I wait for her to say them, for their outline to solidify into the real. And then she looks back up at the ceiling. She looks away and she closes her eyes.

"Maybe," she says. "Maybe. I don't know."

Chapter 30

I stopped at the cemetery on my way out of Bancroft. I parked Meredith's car, and I wove my way through headstones until I was back in front of Tessa's. I pressed two fingers to the gray stone and was struck by its surprising warmth.

I went there because I had this idea of the things that I might say. I had this ridiculous idea of closure. Of telling her I understood. Or not that, exactly. More like the opposite: like I didn't understand but that was okay.

I had this idea of the things that I might say.

But once I was there, I couldn't find the words. Every sentence felt silly—somehow make-believe. Like I was ten years old, again, trying on Meredith's clothes and pretending that they fit.

So, I didn't say anything. I stood there and felt the sun pass from me into the stone under my fingers, and then I knelt down and let my hands rest on the ground, cold and damp and full, green, spiky grass mixed with brown beneath my fingers. I thought about an article I read once, maybe back in college. About how grass doesn't actually die in the winter. It looks the same as dead, but really, it's just sleeping, waiting to wake back up in the spring.

I knelt there for a minute, and then I pressed down—hard, with all my weight—so that when I pulled away, I could see the smallest indent. I looked at this, the gentle outline in the grass that was not really dead. I looked at my handprint, and then my mother's name, and then I walked away.

Chapter 31

I'm still here.

The text is waiting on my phone when I get home on Sunday night. No name, just a number I'd tried to forget.

Nathan.

Still here for me? Still here in Boston?

In the hospital, I asked Meredith whether people can change. I asked because, already, I was afraid of what would happen when I got home. I was afraid of how easily we forget what once felt momentous. How easily we overlook the realizations we knew, absolutely knew, would change everything.

We are creatures of habit. And the truth is, change is hard.

I had an idea in Maine. A half-formed intention driven by an unfamiliar feeling.

And now I am back home. In an apartment that won't be mine for much longer, with an almost ex-roommate whose friendship I miss. I'm home, two miles from another apartment where I spent months with a man feeling like a bigger and bolder version of myself. I'm home. And on Monday, my promotion at Kensington becomes official, and I get one step closer to getting what I thought I could decide to want: stability, safety.

I remember reading somewhere that saying two words that mean the same thing implies something, something not so great, about whatever point you're trying to make.

I had an idea. I had a feeling.

I'm still here.

I stare at the text. I hold the phone in my hand until I fall asleep.

I sleep through my alarm on Monday, and I'm late leaving the apartment. I'm late, but it feels early. The sun is just peeking out over the gray and brown roofs of Somerville. By the time I get home tonight, the sun will already have set.

New job. But same commute. Same stifling T ride, same thunking of the train's brakes as it slows down through the tunnels. Same walk across the channel, the cold, salty wind hitting my cheeks, throwing my carefully brushed hair into messy tendrils around my face. Same building, the same click-clacking of heels under the same fluorescent lights.

New job. Different desk. Next to a window, so I can see the mix of tourists and Bostonians streaming on the streets below. Out of the corner of my eye, I catch a flash of movement that's familiar, and when I crane my neck, I find myself choking back a laugh. They've opened a dog park almost directly across the street.

"Well, glad to see you're smiling on the first day."

I swivel my chair away from the window and toward Deena's scratchy voice. She's in red again, this time a crimson blazer over tailored blue jeans tucked into knee-high boots. Are boots back in style again? I open my mouth—maybe to ask this, maybe to explain about the dogs—and then I stop. I catch the expression on her face.

"How's Bean?" I ask.

"She's moving in." The words rush out of her mouth in one breath. And then, before I can respond. "I know. I know it's fast."

"Fast doesn't have to be a bad thing."

"Still." She fiddles with the pens on my desk. I've never seen her look this nervous. I think about our conversation on the Charles and then at her doorstep. About what does and doesn't have to be so hard.

"Are you happy?"

"Yes."

"Well, then." I pull the pens away from her. "I think this is one of those times when you should leave things at that. At being happy. Don't borrow trouble, or something like that."

Her eyes crinkle; her shoulders drop back down to their normal level. She scans my desk and then my outfit, and then, finally, my face.

"First day," she says.

"Yep."

"So far, so good?"

"So far, so good."

Two women from PR round the corner, flagging down Deena as they pass. I can barely follow the words—something about a client and an ad and a series of problematic tweets—but Deena nods along, and then the women are gone, disappearing around the other corner as quickly as they came. They leave behind a trail of perfume, sticky sweet, and I wrinkle my nose. I wrinkle my nose, and I think about how I always mean to wear perfume.

Deena's eyes flick from where they went back to me. She chews her lower lip; red lipstick grazes her tooth but doesn't stick.

"Go on, I'm good." I gesture at my desk, the emails in my inbox. "Plenty to keep me busy."

She pushes herself away from the wall, and I turn back to my computer. Seventy-three emails. I scroll down to the beginning. *Congratulations*, the first one reads.

"It's okay, you know."

I look up. She's still standing by the corner of my desk.

"If you decide you don't want this, it's okay."

I stare. Her words rattle around in my head, trying to find a home. Trying to land somewhere, so I can respond with something that makes sense. I bite my lips. I focus on her words but can't get them to stick.

And then it doesn't matter because she's gone. She's gone, and I'm here, with my emails, looking down the hallway where she disappeared.

I wore a new dress today. It's the same jade green as my eyes. I bought it at a store that Deena recommended. When I looked in the mirror this morning, I barely recognized myself. And Maine . . . well, that felt like someone else's story.

But oh, I think I *liked* the story.

I draft responses to the emails; I go to meeting after meeting; I studiously avoid the view from my window. I look at my reflection until I've memorized what I'll see.

And still. There's a burning, a jingling, like unspent coins in my pocket when I was a little girl. Deena's words, pounding and insistent, and finally, finally settling. But they settle as a question: *What do I want, what do I want?*

The list. *The right list.*

I'm not stupid. I know something needs to change. But I can't define the something. There's just this manic unfed energy, entirely unfamiliar but not unwelcome. My tongue pressing harder against the loose tooth.

This goes on for three days. Three days at Kensington. Three days, each in a new outfit, trying to decide what fits. On Wednesday afternoon, I find myself driving by Lois's after work, as if by accident. Her Christmas decorations are abundant—white and gold lights drape across the roof and trees; red poinsettias crowd her doorstep; an almost audacious candy-cane wreath hangs from her red-paneled door. The girls are coming home for Christmas, she tells me. She's bought thirteen different types of frosting for the gingerbread.

She squeezes my hand. She talks about the gingerbread and the farm where they can cut down their own tree. I wonder, aloud, if she'll need help cleaning up the decorations when they're gone—when she's alone again—but she laughs at this. She shakes her head, her eyes bright in her face. She pats my cheek with one warm hand.

"Sweet, silly girl," she says, "you're worrying about the least important part."

She gives me a tight hug before I leave, an extra squeeze tacked on at the end. I watch her wave as I walk to my car, my work phone a weight in my back pocket.

But a work phone? What a thing. What a luxury. Proof of something, I'm almost sure.

I'm drained by the time I get to the apartment, by the time I've opened the door and registered the new piles of boxes. All Holly's, none mine. I keep meaning to pack. Three blocks down, a tiny sublet waits for me, the only thing in the vicinity that I could afford on my old salary. The new job is still too new to depend on.

My work phone pings with another email. I shut my eyes and open them. The world is topsy-turvy, made worse still by all the boxes.

Bean and Deena. James and Holly. Meredith and Syed and a baby. Lois and her grandchildren and a house filled with memories she will always get to keep.

Nathan, always, Nathan.

Deena under those awful lights reminding me to remember what I want. Except, I'm still not sure. I still can't see it. And I cannot understand how anyone decides. How anyone can be here, in this world where nothing is certain, nothing is permanent, and choose to want what they don't have.

Especially when what I have is good. Objectively, it's fine.

And I'm thinking about this, about how to get at what I want—*What do I want? Honestly want?*—when I see Holly standing in the doorframe of my room. I see her standing there, and, before she opens her mouth, before my eyes travel down to her hand and find the blue-and-white pamphlet clenched inevitably in her fist, I know that she knows. Because

I see it, all over her face: the questions. The fear. The resolute denial. I see all of it. I see myself. I see every part of this that I still don't want to face.

What do I want? What do I want?

I don't want to die.

No. Not enough.

Coins, unspent coins.

I don't want to die like this.

"Alex," she whispers.

I tell her. I tell her everything.

Chapter 32

The summer I spent at the lake with Nathan, there was one morning when we both woke up extra early. The house was quiet, and he grabbed my hand, and we walked out to the dock. And while everyone else was sleeping, we slipped into a canoe, him paddling, me leaning back and listening to the thrusting noise his paddle made when the tip drove into the water.

I remember holding my hand up above my head, watching the sun make patterns against my skin. I remember feeling his eyes on the back of my hand, the tops of my shoulders. The warmth of his gaze mingling with the sunshine and the absolute certainty that, in that moment, I understood what mattered.

I am there and everywhere. I see all of it. Each second taking the time an hour takes today.

Is it enough to want that? To want a feeling?

Holly. Standing in the doorway. A pamphlet in her hand.

If this were a movie, it's obvious what would happen next. All the things that bring death closer—a cancer diagnosis, a freak accident, the death of a loved one—all these terrible things, they trump everything else. They give you perspective. They make you see the world differently. Fresh start, fresh perspective. All that jazz. Our friendship, immediately reset.

And for a minute, when I tell Holly, it does exactly what you'd expect. It cuts through the crap. *Of course* it cuts through the crap. It's Huntington's disease. It is, arguably, one of the most terrible things.

And even after everything that's changed between us, Holly is still my best friend. And she is still Holly. She rallies quickly. She remains hopeful in a way that doesn't feel forced. She leans into the muck with me. She doesn't shy away.

"I hate that this is happening to you."

"Me, too."

"It's unfair. That doesn't even seem like the right word."

"It's bullshit. That's the word for it. Meredith and I decided."

Holly's fingers dig into her wrists. "Meredith. God, Meredith. How is she? God, that seems like a dumb question to ask."

I remember Meredith's face as she got in the car with Syed. How she softened when his hand pressed against hers, one leg on the ground and one in the car. How they stayed right there, for just a moment. How I saw it pass between them: some silent understanding that had everything to do with them. That had nothing and maybe everything to do with HD.

I kept watching Syed, even after Mere had looked away. I was waiting, I think, to see if the look would hold. If any of it would last as long as she would need. And it hit me that before, when I saw the burning man, I might not have kept watching long enough. I hadn't given them enough time to get here, to get to the next part.

"You know, I think she's going to be okay. She's strong."

"You are, too, Alex," says Holly. She shakes her head when I snort. "You are. You'd have to be, to deal with any of this."

"Who says I'm dealing with it?" I quip.

Another headshake, this one quicker. She holds up her left hand, counting off on her fingers. "You've been there for Meredith. You've learned more about your mother. You saved Remy. And now you're talking to me."

"And that's enough?"

"It's more than most people could do. More than I could do. I wish you'd give yourself more credit." She hesitates. My stomach flips. "Have you decided yet? If you're going to get tested, I mean?"

There. Always there. Get tested. Do or don't.

Decide decide decide.

"I'm figuring that out right now."

She looks down at her hands. I imagine she wishes she had an owl, but they're all packed away. "Are you scared?"

"Out of my mind with it sometimes."

"Sorry, another stupid question."

"Not really," I say with a shrug. "It's funny, the things you can get used to. Sometimes, I can almost forget about it. Almost. Sometimes, there are other things that feel bigger."

Holly bites her lip. "Maybe because they are."

I open my mouth, and then I shut it. Because she might have a point.

"I wish I'd known," she says. "About Huntington's. About what you were dealing with."

"It was me who didn't tell you. That's on me, not you . . ."

"Still." She sits up, waves her hands at the boxes. "I wish I wasn't moving out."

"So do I." I pause. "But I'm starting to think you had to. I'm starting to think . . ." I fiddle with my hair elastic. I pick the next words out carefully. "I think that maybe our proximity—the job, the apartment—fooled us a bit. I think it made us believe it would always be easy."

"Staying friends?"

"Staying close."

She leans back, so our shoulders are pressed together, and I look at the pictures scattered around our apartment: College graduation, hugging each other in ugly nylon robes, our arms overlapping. Nashville, a spur-of-the-moment trip when we were twenty-five, our tongues out and eyes wide. The two of us, big grins, standing in front of this apartment on the day we first moved in.

I still don't know. I still don't know how we got from there to here. To this place where this is still love, still all this love, but there is also something else: the truth that, at some point, we stopped trying to grow together and we let ourselves grow apart. We did that—the both of us. We cannot take it back. And then, there's this: that maybe we shouldn't want to. Maybe that wanting is where resentment wins.

I don't know. I really don't. But this isn't a movie. And I think that wherever we go next, whatever all this means, we still have to start from here. From the people we've become instead of the girls in those photos. And I think that just might be okay. Starting here might be how we figure out how to be honest—about what we mean to each other, about what we want and why. About where we want to go.

I feel her glossy hair against my cheek. It's longer than it's ever been since I've known her. I squeeze my eyes shut, and I make myself picture us in five years and then ten. I picture us if the worst were to happen. And I can still see it: I can still see us, not here, somewhere else, but still leaning against each other. The image is a little fuzzy, but it's there. I hold on to it. I tell myself that we will be okay.

Sometime later, Holly leaves. She leaves, and I stay there, on the couch, watching the last of the afternoon's light trickle into the window. I remember that we are very close to the shortest day of the year.

Holly didn't press me about getting tested. But she asked me about Nathan. In the pamphlets on my desk, she found the piece of paper with his number. She asked me if I missed him. She asked me if I wished that he had stayed.

"I think about him," I said, honestly. "I think about him a lot. But the thing is, I'm not sure if they were real."

"Your feelings?"

"Yes."

"How come?"

I'd pulled a blanket up and over my knees. The fleece was soft against my bare skin. "Look at the timing of all of it. There was life-or-death nonsense everywhere I looked, and then this boy, this man, my first love, for God's sake. Showing up just when I wanted to think of anything else."

"Fate."

"Nostalgia," I countered. "Heady nostalgia just when the present seems most unbearable. It doesn't take a shrink to see how that could confuse anyone. Trick anyone into making the imaginary real. Creating a story out of nothing."

"Okay," said Holly. "I hear what you're saying. I do. And you could be right. It could be nothing." She paused.

"But?"

"But isn't it just as likely that it was real? And this—you telling yourself that it's not—is the story?"

She didn't wait for me to answer. She didn't need to. She just reached her hand into a box and grabbed an owl. Fluorescent colored, one of our favorites. She placed it on the coffee table in front of us.

"There's always a reason not to try."

She left the owl there, next to the paper with Nathan's number. The one he gave me months ago. I'm looking at it now. I'm looking at it and the card I placed beside it: the one belonging to Annette, the genetic counselor. I've finished the counseling sessions and the physical. The only step left is scheduling the blood test.

I stare at the papers, these papers, both choices I need to make. The unfed energy drives me toward them, ever closer. Whispering in my ear the things I understand. The things that I didn't understand before. About my mother. About why someone might leave. About what it means to need something from someone who cannot give it. About how to survive anyway. About how to need again.

I know this. I think I know this. And still. Even with all this knowing, I am frozen. I am stuck, here, on this couch with these decisions that I am still not ready to make. All the knowing in the world isn't enough to make me do what's needed: Decide. Jump. Reach.

I get up and walk away from the table and the cards that sit on it. I grab an empty cardboard box and begin to pack my things, haphazardly.

A candle, a decorative plate. I tell myself maybe this is enough. Maybe this is a start.

A book. A photo of me and Holly. Then another of me with Mere. One step forward. A stupidly small one.

I stop. I pull the last photo back out of the box. It's from when we were kids, back before Tessa left. It was taken on Halloween. I'm dressed as a lion; Mere is a ballerina. I'm roaring at the camera, my mouth wide open, my eyes fierce.

I stare, mesmerized, at the Alex that existed in that photo. Strong, brave, and unafraid.

I shut my eyes. I remember every choice that came after. And then all the ones I refused to make.

Decide. Jump. Reach.

Maybe here is harder than there. Maybe brave looks different from this vantage point.

I walk back over to the table. I pick up the paper.

Chapter 33

I've been standing outside the door for ten minutes. I know this because I've checked the time on my phone four times. Four times, I've reached into the back pocket of my jeans and pressed the little plastic button on the side of my case and watched the screen light up the darkness between my face and hand. Four times, I've been newly surprised by how few minutes have passed.

I've been standing here for hours. If it weren't for my phone, I'd be almost sure of that.

Under my old poofy coat, I'm wearing my rattiest jeans and an ancient thermal with holes I can stick my thumbs through, snug and secure. I didn't put on makeup or fix my hair. I didn't wear the heeled boots that give me height—some semblance of stature. I didn't do any of the things I would usually do.

Where do we start? How do we jump? How much starts with pretending?

I fish my hand into my pocket for the fifth time. I touch my thumb to the screen. I look at the photo on the background: a group shot from my birthday dinner. Holly and Deena. Bean, James, and Syed. Meredith. Nathan. Me, right in the middle. Right before the cake arrived.

One wish, right now. Don't think.

I put the phone back in my pocket. I press the buzzer.

◆ ◆ ◆

These are the things I remember about my father. These are the things I know.

He used to hold me high over his head, his strong hands keeping me steady, so steady, while I placed the star on the top of our Christmas tree. When I was nine, he built a soccer net in the back of our house, just for me. He is half of Meredith, biologically responsible for one of the people I love most. He stayed after Tessa left. Every day, he went to work, his money keeping us fed and clothed and comfortable, even after everything inside him fell apart. He is my dad. My father.

All truths. All true.

My dad. My father. In the years after she left, he told me that he loved me exactly four times. Each time, he was drunk. Each time, I would tell myself the words weren't real—a product of whiskey and nostalgia and the red hair I resented. But still. Four times. Four times, and I remember each one. Sixteen, eighteen, twenty-one, and twenty-five. I love you. I love you. I love you. I love you.

My dad. My father. He never hit me. Never yelled. But once, the tumbler shaking in his hand, he told me I needed to be careful, or I would end up just like her.

And still. I liked it when he drank. I liked it when he saw me.

All truths. All true.

◆ ◆ ◆

"What are you doing here?" His face is tired, more lined than it was those months ago when I stood on this same stoop with Mere. I register that he's sober, that I can't smell anything on his breath.

"Can I come in?"

I ease by him without waiting for an answer. It's me who leads us to the kitchen, and I'm the first one to sit down. My eyes skitter over the framed photos on the sidecar table: me and Meredith, maybe six and nine years old; Meredith at her wedding; a holiday photo Syed took four years ago. All trappings of a family. How many times have I wondered, who printed them? Who framed them and laid them out?

"We went to Bancroft. We went to the ceremony."

He's silent, his face blank. There's something awkward about the way his sweater tugs at his left shoulder. Almost as if he yanked it on in a rush.

A tightness gathers in my throat, and I force myself to swallow. "I think you might want to go there someday," I say. "It might help. To say goodbye."

Something flickers behind his eyes, gone before I can place it.

"What are you doing here?" he asks again.

"I'm trying something new."

A gust of wind rattles the glass panes, so they screech against the wooden frames.

"Do you remember how much that noise would scare me as a kid? I used to think someone outside was crying."

I might imagine how his eyes flick to the cabinet to the left of the counter. "You should go home," he says.

"You used to tell me I had a big imagination. You used to tell me that made me special."

He looks down at his hands.

"She was sick already," I say. "When she left, she was already sick."

I'm watching him so closely my eyes are stinging. I have to remind myself to blink.

"The condition she had . . . it could lead to depression. Paranoia. It did for her. But she couldn't have known what was happening to her. No one could."

I can hear the cuckoo clock ticking from the hallway. I can hear the wind rustling the bare branches of the trees. I can hear the engine, from a neighbor's car, grumbling to life. I imagine, if I listen hard enough, I could hear two hearts beating in this room. The even thumping of life, of blood being pushed through veins. Of bodies that get to go on living.

"Dad?" He looks at me. He lifts his head up from his chest, a millimeter at a time, and looks at me. And it takes everything in me not to hide it, to let him see my need. The aching shape of it, pooling across the table between us. Dripping right up to his fingers, so that he leans back. He leans back and away.

"Alex." Perfunctory and dull, the voice I've heard a thousand times but has never become familiar. "I have a work dinner tonight. You need to leave."

Right here, in this kitchen where she used to sit, my heart scrunches and expands too quickly, and then cracks. He and I have the same eyebrows. I always forget. I always see so much of her in me, I forget all about him.

But he loved her. He loved my mother for more than thirty years. He loved her after she was gone. After he tried to hate her. And more than anything, I want that love to be the full story. I want it to be enough. To make up for everything else.

"You don't have a work dinner." He doesn't have anything. The sweater was for me. "You just don't want to talk to me."

"Don't be difficult."

"Her leaving wasn't your fault. And I don't think it means she didn't love you."

He gets up. He gets up and walks out of the room.

I can hear the clock ticking in the hallway.

I could follow him and tell him about HD: how it's killing Meredith; how it might be killing me. I could tell him and see if the truth makes a difference. If all of it adds up to a world where saying the right things makes him love me, too. A world where we get to choose, where there is a formula of things we do and say that makes us lovable.

I never tried to find out before. Not with him.

There is Meredith: always pushing, always proving she is worthy. And there is me. Never trying to find out. Or if I did, I was selective. Sticking with the examples I thought could prove me right. The ones I never had to test.

When I swallow, I think I taste blood. Or metal. Something elemental. I stand up and push my chair under the table. I walk over to the photos. I find the one of me as a baby, and I touch my finger to the frame.

He's sitting in the living room, the TV casting a faintly bluish tint to the otherwise dark space. He's eating chips straight from the bag, the pretense of the work dinner forgotten. But this small honesty feels less like a victory and more like an ending. The façade that's sat between us for years is gone, and all that's left is emptiness, stale and stagnant and almost, already, forgotten.

I stand in the space between the front door and the living room's entrance. I cross my arms over my chest. I think, again, about all the things that I could say. About what I want in return. I hold all of it to my chest, and I wait until he looks up at my face.

"I love you," I say.

I wait. I wait and watch my father's face, and for a second or less, in that instant in a blink right before my lashes close, I think I see something. I think I see him seeing me. But then, the moment is over, and he's turned back to the television, and there is nothing but the sound of Sunday football, and I am gone, again.

And I feel all the things I'm holding to my chest. And I imagine leaving them here. And I think that maybe I am okay.

Chapter 34

I've never liked New Year's Day. It's always struck me as an overrated holiday, a combination of the worst parts of endings and beginnings. The holiday season winding down, lights coming off trees, the return-to-work date looming. The longest, coldest month of the year stretched in front of you, alongside the pressure of supposed fresh starts, of resolutions that won't be kept.

The first of January: the calendar's biggest Sunday scary.

And so, when I wake up on the first, and the sun is still sleeping, and my bare toes brush against the icy pane of my sister's guest-room window, I brace for the inevitable: the persistent sense of shrinking.

And then, it doesn't come. I sit up straighter in my bed, dragging the quilts with me, up and around my shoulders, and settle right by that window. I place my hand an inch or two from the glass and feel the cold air radiating from outside. I move my hand closer, bit by bit, noting how the air gets colder and colder. And still, even with this knowledge, it's a shock when I actually touch the icy glass.

I hear my gasp, my unreasonably startled disbelief, but I don't move my hand. I wait and watch the early morning sunshine get up and play games across the cobblestones. I watch an older man ride by on his bicycle, and a young family laden with luggage totter to their car. I see a dog escape its owner and chase a cat down a side alley. I wait, and I watch, and when I finally move my hand, the pane is warm.

Later today, Meredith will drive me and my belongings to my new apartment. She will shake hands with Mazie, my new roommate, who is four years younger than me, and whose soft, hopeful smile reminds me of a young woman I once saw in a restaurant. When we met, Mazie told me this was her first time living in a city. "I've always wanted to try it," she'd half whispered, as if afraid of her own daring.

Later, I'll text Deena and explain that I'm going to resign from Kensington. I've lined up a part-time job as a dog walker, and I have started reaching out to my past clients for training, and for now, thanks to my tiny new apartment with the woman whose life is four years behind mine, that is enough. Deena will help me strategize the best way to cut ties at Kensington while telling me I'm crazy, and Bean will shush her and tell me I am brave, and I will know they are both a little bit right.

These are all the things that will happen later. But for now, for now, I pull the blanket tighter around my shoulders and tuck my feet under a pillow and grab my laptop from my bag propped beside the bed. I pull up the website I found more than a month ago. The one with messages from strangers sharing their experience with HD—both those who did and did not get tested. The posts I shied away from because their strength filled me with a kind of shame. I scroll through all these posts until I find the one that I want. From a woman named Jackie. I find her post and read it again. I read it twice.

> Being at risk never gets easy. It's never okay. But one day, you wake up, and it's just part of your life. You breathe in and out, and the risk is there, and that is simply (and not so simply) your life. And maybe you'll live differently and maybe you won't, and either way, that's cool. That's up to you. It's your life. You get to choose. Just like anybody else.

When I read her words the first time, I was jarred by her candor. By how quickly I was inclined to trust her, and then, in knee-jerk fashion, how quickly I decided that I couldn't. How I decided she must not be telling the whole story. She must be oversimplifying because that made it easier to pretend to be okay.

Because how could this ever be normal? How could I ever wake up and call this feeling—this pressure, this pounding question, this naked fear—normal? And if I ever could . . . why would that ever be okay?

But now, sitting in my sister's bed, watching the world trickle awake around me on this morning that, despite all my expectations, does not feel like the worst morning of the year, Jackie's words sit differently in my stomach. Because the thing is, the thing I missed before is this: She never said it was okay. Waking up and knowing what could happen and still finding a way to breathe—she didn't say that was okay.

She said that it was life.

I wait two days. I wait two days because I tell myself there is no rush, that nothing can change that quickly. I wait two days because regardless of what I've learned and what I've decided, it's all still easier in theory than in practice. So, I wait and try not to worry, and then I wake up in the middle of the night with an almost violent certainty that there is, in fact, a rush. I wake up and remember that everything can, in fact, change that quickly. A phone call; a little bit of blood captured in a vial by a stranger; three one-syllable words and who does or does not hear them; whether and how we choose to say goodbye; the thoughts that wake us in the middle of the night—all of these things, these tiny and giant things, that can change everything in an instant.

I wake up, and I wait until the sun finally joins me, until it is acceptable to send this text, until I send it and then have to wait some more.

And then my phone pings, and I read the words, and this time, this one time, I don't hesitate. I put my phone in my pocket, and I get up and walk right out the door.

◆ ◆ ◆

His parents' home is in Winchester. It's adjacent to a well-known nature preserve, which I know from my clients is filled with dog-friendly walking trails. A couple of years ago, a guy I was kind of seeing described how he liked to go mountain biking there. I told him that I didn't realize there were mountains at the preserve. I didn't mean anything by this—I didn't know anything about mountain biking—but he got a bit huffy, and I found myself not caring that it would be our last date. Not because he was unkind or uninteresting but because it seemed essential that he date someone different, someone who could see the potential in making flat trails into something else.

I sit in my car for seven minutes before getting out. And then, I don't go to his door. I go onto the trails instead because I am too good at avoidance, yes, but also because I smell the dark, wet earth, and I see the gray-green trees, and it all reminds me of Maine, and I think I need that memory first. I walk down a path that wraps around a reservoir, and it's surprisingly quiet, maybe because it is quite cold, but it's also beautiful, both in sight and sound: dark water that laps up against the banks, a white sprinkling of ripples; my breath, the faintest shadow in the air between me and everything else; the evergreen trees somehow greener than they are in summer, a pop of color coming to life in a sea of gray; the careless crunching of sticks and needles under my feet; the sun—so infrequent this time of year—making the darkness of the water less foreboding, a translation from cold to calm. To clarity.

I walk along the trail, and I think about dying. I am less afraid of it here, in the woods. It feels somehow less important, both smaller and even more inevitable. Unchangeable, but also just short of okay. Because look at all of this. Look at all the things that will stay.

I think maybe Tessa knew this feeling. I think it's why she went to Maine, why she stayed as long as she did. I think this feeling, in the woods, is what let her breathe again. I think she chose that instead of coming home. And I don't think I have it in me anymore to begrudge her that. To begrudge her breathing.

A stick crunches behind me and I jump and turn, my heart catching somewhere below my throat. Catching just in time to almost stop entirely. Because he is here. Of course he is here. Tall and lean and solid. Wearing a green knit sweater that I can't imagine is keeping him warm and an expression that is half wary and half hopeful. The second part comes naturally. The first is undeniably an effort. A thing I forced him to try to feel.

He lifts one hand in half a wave. He stopped walking when I turned around, and he's staying put now. Maybe fifteen feet down the trail.

But still, he came to me. He followed me out here. Which isn't right. Him coming to me is not the way I wanted this to go.

I ignore the wave. I shake my head, instead. I'm fighting off an unreasonable and embarrassing urge to stamp my foot.

"I wanted to be the one to come to you."

"Well, you're the one who drove here."

"Still. I wanted to come all the way. I think that mattered."

He shrugs. His shoulders are bigger than I remember. "Maybe not so much."

I want to touch him. Will I ever, ever see him and not want to touch him? Such a thing feels impossible right now.

"I think you make it too easy for me," I say.

"Maybe you just make it too hard."

A cloud shifts, and the sun catches my eye so that I have to shield my face. So that I almost miss it. The half smile. The beginning of a smirk. "You can come the rest of the way, if you want," he says. He half salutes me. "I won't move a muscle. Scout's honor."

"You weren't a Boy Scout." I'm maybe two steps away.

"Caught me," he whispers. And his breath is against my hair. And his hands are on my shoulders, down my back, the heat of them somehow sinking through my coat as he pulls me in, pulling me in as quickly as I can push my body forward, until my head lies secure, against his chest. *Here, right here,* I think. I think this again and again, my nose breathing in his smell, my body breathing in the feel of him. *Here, right here.*

It's another minute or an hour before I realize that I want to see his face. That I need to see his face. There's so much more to say—the explanations he deserves and should demand—but right now, I just want to see his face. So, I pull back my head and tilt my chin until his eyes are on my eyes. Until I can see myself reflected in the blue and gray. Until I can see all of it. All of us. All the things we get to choose.

"You waited," I say.

"You came."

Chapter 35

Sue hugs me tightly when she sees me, and my whole body falls into hers. I forgot this part: how it felt to let her hold me. Of all the things I missed, I let myself forget that she was one of them.

She pulls back and looks at me, a warm smile on her face. She is Sue, but she is smaller than I remember. Her sickness catches up to me in glimpses: in the careful way she holds her cup, in the looseness of her skin, and in the lilting laugh that fades too quickly. In the way her eyes linger on her son, Nathan, and his sister, a heavy softness in the once familiar green eyes that forces me to look away.

Remy gets to me after Sue—a fluffy torpedo barreling at me as soon as Nathan opens her crate. I kneel down, burrowing my nose in her thick coat. Nathan tells me how well she's done with his family. How much more progress she has made. *Remy queen, you did it.* I pull back and look into her topaz eyes. I swear she lifts an eyebrow.

Nathan's house looks older inside than out, and almost exactly how I remember it: cherry cabinets that need updating and paint that's peeled in places. It's a cozy kind of oldness, rich with history and handprints, and when Nathan sits on the counter, I can see him there as a little boy. As a teenager. As all the versions of himself that came in between.

His father is on a shift, but Kit is home for the holidays, just as sweet and snarky as I remember, with Nathan's same quick tongue. And I can tell that she and Nathan have gotten closer. That she knows him. Really knows him. And unlike Sue, she's still unsure of me. And I find myself thinking she is right to be unsure, and then thinking, no, she's not. Kit teases Nathan while Sue makes dinner, and I am mesmerized by the three of them. By how easy they are together. And watching them, I see it: how much more Nathan will someday lose because he has all this. But also, also, I see the other part: how much more he already got because he had all this.

Sometime later, I feel Nathan's gaze growing more intense. I feel the urgency of the questions he must have, and the answers that I owe him. I squeeze his hand and let him lead me upstairs to his childhood bedroom. And I'm ready—to talk, to explain—but then I step in all the way, and I stop. I give my breath time to catch up to what I'm seeing.

His bedroom is a time capsule in red and blue. Early 2000s Red Sox paraphernalia adorns the walls. Pedro Martínez, Jason Varitek, Johnny Damon—names I forgot I still remembered—their faces pressed up next to photos of high school boys in soccer jerseys; I catch a glimpse of Nathan's dark, red-brown hair, already inches above the rest. There's the beginning of his book collection, shoving aside old soccer trophies, and a faded college flag, half dangling from the antique writing desk. I take a step in farther, feeling his body behind me. Feeling his own hesitation, the slightest stiffening. The last time we were in this room, neither of us knew it would be the last time.

I turn around. I wrap my arms around his neck. I have to stand on tiptoe.

"I'm really glad I came."

His body relaxes against mine. "Me, too," he says. "Me, too."

Some amount of time passes—my head resting against his chest, the steady thrum of his heartbeat beneath my ear, the gentle weight of his chin against my hair—and then, inevitably, it happens. The next part.

"Why did you?"

I close my eyes.

"Come back, I mean?" The arms below my rib cage loosen, letting a breath of air in between us. A breath of hesitation. "What changed?"

I'd known this was coming. I know I need to explain, to help him understand that I am here, for real, this time. That, this time, I will not bolt.

And there are words for that. Words I mapped out on the drive over. Words about what I'd discovered in the hospital and in the minutes and days that came after. Words that explain how close I came to learning the wrong lesson, or at least, learning only half of the right one. About how it can change everything or nothing: what we decide we need from others to be brave. Lowering the bar or raising it . . . it's irrelevant without the part that comes first. The part that has nothing to do with others and everything to do with me. With deciding that—regardless of everyone else, regardless of what they can or cannot give, regardless of what the world will inevitably take—I am brave enough to do it. To need. To want. To reach.

And knowing that is how I came back. It's how I hope to stay.

I want to tell him all of this. But the words feel inadequate, silly even, because they are just words. And so, what can they really prove? I left him. I didn't believe in him. And so, the words feel silly, especially here. In this room with all this history, in this house with even more. Here and now, where all the timelines have condensed into one simple, pressing sentiment: Try. Try now. Try as hard as you can.

I open my eyes. I say the only words that count. I say them first.

"I love you."

Two seconds. Two seconds of silence. The same amount of time it took him to return my kiss on that first night outside my apartment. And remembering that, it comes to me that, maybe, I am better at jumping than I realized.

Two seconds. And then I feel the rise of his chest, the breath before he'll speak. But there's more I need to say. More from me first.

"I love you," I say, again. Both harder and easier the second time. "But that's not what changed. Because I think I knew that already. Deep down, I think I've known for a while."

"But you didn't trust me," he says.

It's my turn to shrug. "Maybe not. I wrapped it up like I was doing you a favor, but I got a lot of things wrong." I pause. I riffle around for the words that will make sense. "You are the most confident person I know."

"And that's a bad thing?"

"No. I love it about you. I love that you always show up for everyone. That your instinct is to protect." I press my hands together, then put them back on him. "But sometimes you can't. Sometimes, you make promises that you might not want to keep. And with us, I thought there were really only two ways this could go. Either you stayed, and eventually, you'd leave. Or you'd want to leave but wouldn't. And the crappiest part? I couldn't decide which one was worse."

He nods, slowly. His eyes are locked on mine. "And now?"

I think of Sue, of the easy way she hugged me after everything that's happened. I think about compassion. About what Bean called grace.

It's all nuance, really. Ignorance or optimism. Weakness or compassion. Expecting less or being more generous in our expectations. All these pairs of words, each belonging on different sides of the same coin. The difference between them, whisper thin. The difference being whether you can accept that this closeness is okay. That sometimes the coin will flip one way, and sometimes it will flip the other. Knowing this and choosing to stay. Choosing to stay before you see what side comes out on top. Choosing, every time.

"I think that maybe you will leave," I say. "Or maybe on the days you want to leave, somehow, you won't, and the next day will be different. And maybe that will be enough. Or not. I think that I don't know." I push my hands against his chest. Not to push him away, but the opposite. To feel the weight of him pressing back against me. "But I think I am okay with the not knowing. I think I am tired of assuming the worst. Of you or of me."

I pause, watching his face. I want to be sure that he hears what I am saying. Every bit of it.

"That's how I feel," I say. "That's why I came here. But this, us . . . it will only work if you are honest, too. If you tell me how you feel. If you're not always trying to protect me. I wasn't upset that you were scared; I was upset that you wouldn't look at it. I need you to look at it, come what may. Just like I need you to understand that if you told me to leave right now, I'd still be happy I came today. I'd still be happy for the last few months and every moment that came earlier. I'd be happy for every single penny."

His eyes rove across my face, and my chest hitches at what he's doing. At the emotion he's letting spread across his.

"I am terrified," he says. The words come out hoarse. Desperate and honest. "I am terrified of loving you and losing you. I won't pretend I'm not. I won't do that to you again." He touches my hair, smoothing a piece behind my ear, the gesture reminiscent of a decade ago, the moment when I realized that the rarest thing can happen in the most ordinary setting. You meet someone, you sit in a canoe, you have just one conversation . . . and finally, you get to feel it: what it is to fit.

"I'm terrified," he continues. "But I'm not even a little bit worried that I will regret staying. I don't want to downplay love. I don't want to act like what we have isn't extraordinary. Like it hasn't already changed my life. I'd choose this feeling for three months or fifty years. No matter how much it hurts."

I blink.

Love. *The mess of it.*

"I never wanted to be the thing that caused you pain," I say. "I wanted you to find someone who made your life easier, not harder. There's a part of me that still wants that for you."

"You *do* make my life easier. You don't flinch at the worst parts—of who we are and what we'll face." One of his hands catches my cheek, his eyes glittering. "I don't want someone who takes away my pain; I want someone who helps me navigate it. There's going to be shit no matter what, Alex."

We stare at each other, and white-hot heat suddenly flares between us. And I am desperate to kiss him. To do more than kiss him. But, also,

I want to be fair. I want to start this next part right. To have the first of the conversations that we've ignored. It won't be everything; it won't be enough. But it will be a start.

Sometimes, you simply have to start.

I lick my lips. I lean back the smallest amount. "I've done all of the required steps. To get tested . . . to find out."

"Does that mean you're going to . . . ?" His voice trails off as he scans my face. When I smile, it's easier than I expect.

"I am almost sure I know the answer to that question." I touch my fingers to his chest. "Do you need me to? Get the test, I mean."

His palm is still on my cheek. My fingers are balanced on his chest. This most delicate of holding.

He looks away and then back at me.

"I don't know," he says. He exhales a release, his eyes never leaving mine. "I don't think so. Not right now, at least. If we decide to have kids, or if something happened with my own health . . . I think there are reasons I might want to talk about it one day. I can't guarantee that I won't change my mind." He drops his hands, squeezes my shoulders. "Is that okay?"

"Yes." I pull my shoulders back. "I think that is okay."

"And if we end up wanting different things?"

"Then we try to work through it. We try as hard as we can."

"And that's really all you need to know?"

I hear his mom laughing downstairs. I can feel his breaths rising under my fingers. I can feel both of us, standing here. On the edge of what comes next.

"I was wrong about one other thing," I say. "About not making promises that you can't guarantee. I think that you are supposed to make the promise anyways. I think the promise itself might be the whole point."

I wait then. I take in his room again. I find the poster of Pedro Martínez. I can still remember the game where I saw him pitch; it was one of his record no-hitters. I didn't even care about baseball, but I loved that game. The feeling of watching something magic. Of history being made.

I'm looking at this, at Pedro, when Nathan finally speaks.

"So, what you're saying is . . ." He pulls my hands away from his chest so that he can step in closer. "What you're saying is that you want to try?"

"Yes, if you do." And then. "Strike that. Even if you don't."

He leans down. He bundles me against him, my whole body enveloped. He whispers three words in my ear.

Chapter 36

Summer

His name is Caz. Another shepherd—the classic black and tan. One of his ears is slightly floppy, almost like a puppy's. It keeps dropping over the top of his left eye.

He was rescued from a fighting ring. One of three dogs who survived. He's only eight months old.

Nathan coughs from behind me. I glance over my shoulder, and our conversation from last night rushes back to me. His words against my ear. One truth: I think we should live together.

Here's a truth: I fell in love when I was eighteen years old. I didn't have to try. It was immediate, like tasting chocolate. And then there was everything that came next. Everything that was hard. Joy so sharp it hurts.

I give Nathan a small thumbs-up, and he raises his phone in his hand. The ball I'm holding is soft and orange, and I toss it up to grab Caz's attention. Every breath I take smells like summer: damp earth and fresh-cut grass. The fizzy taste of sunshine.

Four months ago, I applied for a grant for DogKind. For money to house and train dogs that no one wants. The ones that shelters cannot take. Dogs like Cliff, and dogs like Remy. Dogs like Caz.

I got the grant. Or, at least, part of it. Not enough to pay for everything, but enough to make me think that I can make up the rest.

Which is why I'm doing this today. This thing I thought I'd never do again. Creating another video. This one to post online. Another video, with another supposedly broken dog. But this time, it's different. It's not about a magic fix. It's about a string of never-ending steps. A time-lapse of hours upon hours of training. The slippery movement of change. Nothing linear about it.

Live.

I throw the ball, and Caz sprints for it. A blur of fur against green grass. He drops it a few yards away from me, and I toss treats in his direction. Other than the light scars around his muzzle, he looks like any other dog. Barely more than a puppy.

But still, he's never brought me back the ball.

"One more try," says Nathan. "I think this next one is it."

That confidence. Endless optimism.

"I'm not sure," I say. "He's already done a lot today."

"One more try. I think he'll go the rest of the way."

I reach into my fanny pack for treats, and my thumb bumps up against something hard. A small wooden owl. Sweet and inconspicuous. Holly gave it to me after my last counseling session with Annette. There's a note stuck to its foot. *Owl you need is love.*

Last month, Meredith sent me an article about a clinical trial focused on a cure. The article talked about "when," not "if." Smart people in white coats in the corner photo. They wore a look I recognized from my sister: unbridled determination. I printed out the article. I stuck it in my nightstand drawer.

I read all of Meredith's articles now. I'm not hiding, not anymore.

One more truth: I got the test done. Three months ago, I walked down a hallway to a lab, and I sat in a hard plastic chair and watched a stranger take my blood. It was arguably the bravest thing I've ever done.

I am prouder of the part that followed, though. Where I didn't look at the results. Where I didn't need to look at the results. Because there's nothing a piece of paper will tell me that's going to change how I want to live my life. And that's what I want to do: I want to live it.

I have the results. I have the answers.

But I don't need them. And there's a difference there.

Because, yes, being at risk changes everything. It is the worry that sits behind all the other worries. Constant and pervasive. That part is true.

But the bigger truth is this: When I talk to my friends . . . when Deena talks about having kids with Bean, her face tight with worry because she doesn't know if she has it in her to be the parent that her parents weren't. Or when, on a Sunday afternoon, Holly tells me that she feels guilty all the time—*all the time*—because she knows her life is good and lucky, and yet, and yet, there is a sadness she cannot shake . . .

When I talk to them, when I see all the other things that are real, I think: It would be there, anyway, the worry behind the worry. I think: It is always hard.

And then I look at my sister, with her list of clinical trials and her ever-rounding belly. I look at my friends, and Remy and Nathan. At love that holds me like a hug. At the dogs and their parents and the things we will and will not be able to fix. I look at all of this, at my life, and I think something else, something more important. I think: It is worth it. Every time.

I squeeze the ball between my fingers. Nathan raises the camera.

I throw the ball and I wait.

Acknowledgments

It is not an overstatement to say that writing this book changed my life. I start with that to explain: I mean each "thank you" with my whole heart. I wrote the second draft of *WCN* while pregnant, and I edited it postpartum, and the people who helped me through it are the reason it exists.

And so, while *acknowledgments* seems like too small of a word . . .

To my lovely Brittany Riley, thank you for reading the various versions of this story. You were with it through its every evolution and always my biggest cheerleader. This book wouldn't breathe without you.

Meghan Brown, you gave me the courage to send *WCN* to agents. Those 2:00 a.m. conversations while I was feeding my newborn son . . . you'll never know quite what they did for me. The hope they instilled.

The biggest kiss and cuddle to my fluffy princess, Lucca, for inspiring Remy.

To the beautiful people who believed in me: my parents, my siblings (the ones I was born with and the ones I gained), my Monica, and so many other incredible friends . . . thank you. There are words that have always mattered most to me—*friend, sister, daughter* . . . I doubt I did them justice while trying to balance work, new motherhood, and writing. Thank you to those who gave me grace.

To my incredible agent, Ann Leslie Tuttle, who believed in this book even when I didn't. Writing is a vulnerable affair, and your encouragement held me up.

Thank you to the team at Lake Union Publishing—Chantelle Aimée Osman for seeing the potential in this story and in a new writer, and Andrea Hurst for understanding my writing so completely—I enjoyed every bit of our editing process.

And to my Stanford Novel Writing cohort: Thank you for reading rough excerpts, for your generous encouragement and sincere feedback.

To all the women authors who have inspired me. My desire to write stories started with your stories—the solace there, the kinship. Your books made me want to write a book that could give others a tenth of what yours gave me.

My deepest gratitude to Dr. Burns C. Blaxall for talking me through the finer points of Huntington's disease and offering your expertise, energy, and feedback. I will always be grateful to all those who research this disease and who advocate for the patients and families it impacts.

To my incredibly supportive husband: I often think of all the times I asked you if I should slow down, pause, reconsider . . . given everything else happening in our lives. Nick, through every hurdle, you have always been a champion of my dreams.

To our son, Finn, who will one day look at pictures of me writing this novel next to your very little body . . . you are my world, my darling. I would trade a thousand books for you.

And maybe most importantly and definitely most accurately: To everyone who has loved me in the truest sense, and to those I've lost along the way—I am grateful for all of you. You each taught me the same lesson in different languages. Together, you birthed this book.

About the Author

Photo © 2025 Molly Haley

Caitlin Forbes is a health care strategist, dog lover, and ski-racing adrenaline seeker who grew up in the mountains of western Maine. She received her bachelor's degree from Saint Anselm College in New Hampshire and her master's degree in English literature from the University of Connecticut. Forbes lives in Saco, Maine, with her husband, son, and one-hundred-pound Shiloh shepherd.